ALSO BY LILY ANDERSON

THE ONLY THING WORSE THAN ME IS YOU

LILY ANDERSON

WEDNESDAY BOOKS
NEW YORK

NOT NOW, NOT EVER. Copyright © 2017 by Lily Anderson. All rights reserved. Printed in the United States of America. For information, address St. Martin's Press, 175 Fifth Avenue, New York, N.Y. 10010.

www.stmartins.com

Designed by Anna Gorovoy

The Library of Congress Cataloging-in-Publication Data is available upon request.

ISBN 978-1-250-14210-8 (hardcover)
ISBN 978-1-250-14817-9 (ebook)

Our books may be purchased in bulk for promotional, educational, or business use. Please contact your local bookseller or the Macmillan Corporate and Premium Sales Department at 1-800-221-7945, extension 5442, or by email at MacmillanSpecialMarkets@macmillan.com.

First Edition: November 2017

10 9 8 7 6 5 4 3 2 1

For Dad and Nil

The truth is rarely pure and never simple.

—Oscar Wilde, *The Importance of Being Earnest*

Be yourself; everyone else is already taken.

—not actually Oscar Wilde

1

There was no empirical evidence that the Lieutenant wasn't a robot.

And, really, if the government was going to pick a family to test run a cybernetic human, why wouldn't they pick the Lawrences? Career air force going back to the Tuskegee pilots, all officers—except for our second cousin Terry, but no one ever talked about him. Strong bone structure with God and country stamped into the marrow. No genetic predisposition for diabetes or flat feet or nostalgia.

Then again, maybe living with my father and my stepmom, Beth, had made me soft.

There was nothing soft about the Lieutenant. My cousin was leaner than anyone else in the family, with ropy arms made for one-hand push-ups and cheekbones that tipped up the corners of her eyes. Her spine was a compass pointing her forever northward. She kept her hair at a regulation two inches high and her bare nails clipped short and her mouth set into a neutral line.

She didn't bob her head as the restaurant's speakers started thumping a Prince song. She didn't put ketchup on her French fries.

Her gaze flickered to her brother decimating a burger beside her, and then back to my face.

A slow blink. Another plain fry slipped between her teeth.

If the government was going to program the perfect airman, would they have thought to make them crave French fries to let them blend in with the rest of us? She could run on veggie oil like a converted diesel car.

Lieutenant Sidney Lawrence: now energy efficient! Fly, fight, win!

At least if she were a cyborg, she would have Asimov's laws of robotics written into her code. Forcing a late-night dinner at the Davis In-N-Out burger in the name of familial bonding definitely counted as harmful. Sid alone I would have been able to deal with. Sure, she was intense in a black Terminator sort of way, but she was my oldest cousin and sometimes she had nuggets of wisdom to pass down.

Having to sit directly across from Isaiah, however, was an exercise in torture. He was the baby of the family, a year and some change younger than me. And, in a perfect world, we would only see each other on federal holidays and the occasional milestone birthday.

But tonight Sid had paid for my burger and agreed to drive me to the train station without question, so I wasn't in a position to complain. At least, not out loud. It had been way too valuable to have my dad and stepmom see her drive me away from our house. It added real, tangible credit to my story.

"So, Ellie," she said in between nibbles. "Your family won't let you attend the summer program in Colorado Springs?"

Your family. No Venn diagram would force the Lawrences to acknowledge the other half of my genes. Even Grandmother Lawrence only referred to the Gabaroches as "those Creoles." Like knowing that there were French people somewhere in the higher boughs of my dad's family tree made them all suspect.

It'd been at least a century since any of the Gabaroches could even speak French. I'd been taking Spanish since middle school.

Plus, I couldn't wear a beret without pressing my hair. No, thanks.

"Dad doesn't want me to fly," I said. I heard the squeak of my sneakers rubbing together and tucked my feet around the legs of my chair. The cold metal helped settle the twitch that had started up in my calves.

"That's dumb," Sid said. "You're seventeen. We'd never let you in the air."

I thought of the Air Force Academy pamphlet torn to shreds and buried under the junk mail in the blue recycle bin. Sid didn't mean *never* the same way my father did. She was thinking of a temporary pause—a stop sign. But cadets turned into airmen. Not after the high school summer seminar, but eventually.

My father didn't like eventualities.

"Don't you miss In-N-Out burgers when you're deployed?" Isaiah asked his sister.

He'd grown since Christmas. Sitting down, he was almost a full head taller than Sid. It could have been true for a while. The three of us hadn't been in the same room at the same time since—when? Grandmother Lawrence's sixty-fifth birthday? Back when the whole family was crowing about Isaiah skipping the eighth grade. *He's so gifted, they let him move right on into high school. Looks like he and Ellie are going to graduate in the same year. The academy better watch out.*

Like anyone learned anything in the eighth grade.

"There's decent food everywhere," Sid said. "Especially burgers."

"But no spread," Isaiah said. His long Predator dreadlocks slithered around his shoulders as he squeezed more pink ooze onto his burger out of the red and white plastic tube. He'd always had a thing about sauces. He drenched his food until everything he ate could be considered a soup. I couldn't sit next to him at holiday dinners anymore. Watching him drown his plate in equal parts gravy and cranberry sauce made me heave.

Gwendolen is devoted to bread and butter, my brain hummed. I tried to shoo the thought away. Not now, Oscar Wilde.

"It's Thousand Island dressing," Sid said. "So, yes, we could have that anywhere."

"It's not just Thousand Island," Isaiah pouted, slurping a blob of Thousand Island off his dark brown hand. "It's *spread*. Does Thousand Island have pickles cut up in it?"

"By definition, yes," I said.

"Well, it tastes better when you can squeeze it onto burgers," Isaiah said, continuing to coat his burger in chunky goop. He shook his head and hiccupped a laugh. "Who would put ketchup and pickles on a salad? That'd be like putting mayonnaise on pizza."

"What do you think makes ranch dressing white?" I asked.

His upper lip curled. "Milk."

"Isaiah, I told you to stop buying salad dressing. It's empty calories," the Lieutenant said. Then, as though sensing the scoff building up in the back of my throat, she snapped her head toward me again. "Elliot, when am I supposed to drop you at the train station?"

"By ten," I said.

"I didn't even know the train went all the way to So Cal," Isaiah said.

"The railroads go everywhere. It's even in a 'Schoolhouse Rock' song," I said. "I guess they must have covered the Industrial Revolution in the back half of middle school."

"Must have," Isaiah said, not registering the dig. He idly licked a drop of spread off one of his dreads.

I pushed my fries away.

"I didn't know that Senior was so much of a tightwad," Sid said. "He must have the money for a plane ticket. Who the hell makes their kid take the train across the state?"

Since my father remarried, neither of my cousins felt the need to refer to him as "Uncle Elliot" anymore. I wished they would. I wasn't technically a junior. Not only because I'm a girl, but also because Mom had replaced Dad's middle name on my birth certificate with her even more masculine last name. Regardless, calling him Senior was a constant reminder that my name was barely mine.

Except, once I set foot on the train, it would be.

I scratched at my scalp with my prickling fingertips. It was slick with melting coconut oil. The air conditioner wasn't up high enough to permeate through more than the top layer of my hair. Even with the streetlamps burning outside the windows, I knew it would still be almost ninety degrees outside. I took a long sip of my lemonade.

Sid's biceps gave an unconscious flex. "They couldn't have picked something useful for you to do with your vacation?"

"No," I said. The truth came out cool and clean against my lips. "They really couldn't have."

When we perfect commercial time travel, everyone in the past is going to be pissed at us. It's not only that their quiet, sepia-toned lives will be inundated with loud-mouthed giants. And it's not even the issue that language is a living organism, so all communication will be way more problematic than anyone ever thinks about.

It's jet packs.

At some point, someone is going to ask about jet packs, and no amount of bragging about clean water and vaccines and free Wi-Fi will be able to distract them. Even if you went back before the Industrial Revolution, someone is going to want to know if we've all made ourselves pairs of Icarus wings.

Defrost Walt Disney and he'll ask to be put back in the fridge until Tomorrowland is real. Go back to the eighties and everyone's going to want to know about hoverboards.

Hell, go back to yesterday, find your own best friend, and they'd still ask, "Tomorrow's the day we get flying cars, right?"

People want miracles. They want magic. They want to freaking fly.

Unrelated: Did you know that crossing state lines on a train is pretty much the most boring and uncomfortable thing ever?

Despite sounding vaguely poetic, the midnight train to Oregon wasn't much for scenery. Unfortunately, running away tends to work best in the middle of the night, especially when one's cousins have a curfew to make and can't wait on the platform with you.

Twelve hours, two protein bars, and one sunrise later, the view was rolling brown fields that turned into dilapidated houses with collapsing fences and sun-bleached Fisher Price play sets. Apparently, the whole "wrong side of the tracks" thing wasn't a myth. Everything the train passed was a real bummer.

One should always have something sensational to read on the train, whispered Oscar Wilde, sounding remarkably like my stepmom.

With my headphones drowning out the screech of the tracks, I reached into my backpack, pushing past the heavy stack of books and ziplock bags of half-eaten snacks, to the bottom. Tucked between the yellowed pages of my battered copy of *Starship Troopers* was a folded square of white printer paper. I tried to smooth it over my leg, but it snapped back into its heavy creases.

Dear Ever,

On behalf of Rayevich College and our sister school, the Messina Academy for the Gifted, it is my great pleasure to offer you a place at Camp Onward. At Onward, you will spend three weeks learning alongside forty-seven other accomplished high school students from all over the West Coast as you prepare for the annual Tarrasch Melee. The winners of the Melee will be granted a four-year, full-tuition scholarship to Rayevich College . . .

The page was starting to wear thin in the corners from my fingers digging into it whenever it stopped feeling real enough. The packing list that had once been stapled to it was even worse off, highlighted and checkmarked and underlined. I'd had to put that one inside of an N. K. Jemisin hardcover so that the extra weight could smash it flat.

I ran my thumb over the salutation again. *Dear Ever.*

I shivered, remembering how my hands had trembled as I'd read those words for the first time, stamped to the front of an envelope with the Rayevich seal in the corner. It meant that everything had worked. It meant that freedom was as simple as a checked box on an Internet application.

The train lurched to a stop. I shoved the note back inside of *Starship Troopers* and popped out my headphones just in time to hear the conductor's garbled voice say, "Eugene station."

I staggered down to the platform, my laptop case and my backpack weighing me down like uneven scales. I sucked in fresh air, not even caring that it tasted like cement and train exhaust. It was cooler here than it was back home. California asphalt held in heat and let it off in dry, tar-scented bursts.

Oregon had a breeze. And pine trees. Towering evergreens that could have bullied a Christmas tree into giving up its lunch money. We didn't get evergreens like that at home. My neighborhood was lined in decorative suburban foliage. By the time I got back, our oak tree would be starting to think about shedding its sticky leaves on the windshield of my car.

As a new wave of passengers stomped onto the train, I retrieved the massive rolling suitcase that Beth had ordered off of the Internet for me. It was big enough to hold a small person, as my brother had discovered when he'd decided to use it to sled down the stairs.

I'd miss that little bug.

There were clusters of people scattered across the platform, some shouting to each other over the dull roar of the engine. I watched an old woman press two small children into her bosom and a hipster couple start groping each other's cardigans.

In the shade of the ticket building, a light-skinned black guy had his head bowed over his cell phone. His hair was shorn down to his scalp, leaving a dappling of curl seedlings perfectly edged around his warm brown temples. He was older than I was, definitely college age. He had that finished look, like he'd grown into his shoulders and gotten cozy with them. A yellow lanyard was swinging across the big green *D* emblazoned on his T-shirt.

"Hey," I called to him, rolling my suitcase behind me. My laptop case swayed across my stomach in tandem with my backpack scraping over my spine, making it hard not to waddle. "Are you from Rayevich?"

The guy looked up, startled, and shoved his phone into the pocket of his jeans. He swept forward, remembering to smile a minute too late. All of his white teeth gleamed in the sunshine.

"Are you Ever?" His smile didn't waver, but I could feel him processing my appearance. Big, natural hair, baggy Warriors T-shirt, cutoff shorts, clean Jordans. Taller than him by at least two inches.

"Yeah," I said. And then, to take some of the pressure off, "You were looking for a white girl, right?"

His smile went dimply in the corners, too sincere to be pervy. "I'm happy to be wrong."

"Ever Lawrence," I said, hoping that I'd practiced it enough that it didn't clunk out of my mouth. It was strange having so few syllables to get through. Elliot Gabaroche was always a lot to dump on another human being.

"Cornell Aaron," the college boy said, sticking his hand out. He had fingers like my father's, tapered, with clean, round nails. I spent the firm two-pump handshake wondering if he also got no-polish manicures. "I'll be one of your counselors at Onward. It's a quick drive from here."

He took the handle of my suitcase without preamble and led the way toward the parking lot. I followed, my pulse leaping in the same two syllables that had wriggled between the folds of my brain and stamped out of my shoes and pumped through my veins for months.

Bunbury.

It was a stupid thing to drive you crazy, but here I was: running away from home in the name of Oscar Wilde.

2

Officially, my stepmother, Beth, sold real estate. That's how she met my father. She'd needed a lawyer to help her with a contract dispute. Dad had lost her case but succeeded in knocking her up with my brother Ethan.

Real classy backstory here. I know.

To be fair, my mom and dad had been divorced for a while by the time Beth came into the picture. Mom had taken a job in Colorado, training cadets, and I'd ended up stuck in Sacramento to "maintain normalcy."

Anyway, Beth sold real estate. But her true passion was theater. She spent summers working at Shakespeare in the Park and winters hosting soirees for the other middle-aged people who worked regular day jobs and spent their nights doing scene work.

It wasn't all bad. She'd been in some good shows over the years. And some terrible shows that had fun results. Like when she'd been in a version of *A Midsummer Night's Dream* where all of the fairies were supposed to be extraterrestrial and she willingly sat through all four *Alien* movies with me for research. Or when the Shakespeare company's fight coordinator had cut me a deal on Muay Thai classes.

The trouble with my stepmother was *The Importance of Being Earnest.*

Somehow, she had ended up in the same play six times in ten years. Always in the same part. Sometimes in the same costume. There was something about her that made directors yearn to put her in an Empire waist dress and make her quip in a fake British accent. She called herself a career Gwendolen.

I thought, for sure, that after she turned forty, it'd stop happening. But a few weeks ago, as we'd all sat down to dinner at our favorite pizza place downtown, she'd proved me wrong.

"I have an announcement," she'd said, swirling her wineglass until she'd kicked up a tiny cabernet typhoon. "Woodland has asked me to return to *Earnest.*"

A chunk of tomato fell out of my father's mouth. Ethan slumped in his chair and groaned. I chugged iced tea until I thought I might puke. Honestly, I think that the entire Gabaroche family would have preferred she just have another kid.

Beth flicked a piece of faux-red hair out of her eyes with her index fingernail. "Well, at least I know all of the lines already."

Which meant that she'd already said yes. Balls.

"Isn't she getting a little long in the tooth for this shit?" my mom had asked, a few days later. She probably meant "theater" as a concept and not just *Earnest.* Mom had a hard time wrapping her mind around Beth. Real estate and theater and PTA fund-raisers all rang fictional to Lawrence ears.

I hadn't meant to bring up the influx of Wilde in the house to my mother, but Beth had already started humming lines to herself. While washing dishes: *The announcement will appear in the* Morning Post. Checking over Ethan's homework: *Ah! that is clearly a metaphysical speculation.* Nestled into the crook of Dad's neck as they watched TV: *Am I not, Mr. Worthing?*

And since we'd all seen the play a thousand times, most of the time someone knew the next line to keep her going. No one wanted to say it, but it was a compulsion. Like knowing the answer when the teacher isn't looking at you.

"It wouldn't be so bad if it weren't going to be all summer," I told Mom, pressing the phone hard against my ear. Mom refused to video chat. She said she didn't want to have to do her hair every time she checked up on me. I never pointed out that, with air force dress regulations, her hair was pretty much always done anyway. "But I won't even have homework to distract me. I'll end up getting dragged to every performance. They'll make me work the concessions stand again."

There were no tips in the concessions stand. All tips went back into the theater to keep the lights on. Community theater doesn't pay anyone but directors and technicians. Everyone else is supposed to be there for the love of the craft.

Love couldn't gas up my car.

"You can't choose your deployment, baby girl. You can tough out one more summer in Sacramento. It's your last one," Mom said. She liked to forget that I wouldn't be moving the second I left high school. Sometimes, I liked to live in that fantasy, too. "Soak up all those creature comforts while you've got them."

I took a deep breath, squared my shoulders, and spent another week quoting pieces of the play back to Beth as I skipped past her on my way to school and when I helped prep dinner.

And then the envelope arrived with "Elliot Lawrence Gabaroche" stamped to the front and the USAF wings printed in the top left corner.

Subtlety has never been one of my mom's accomplishments.

The pamphlet was for the summer program at the Air Force Academy in Colorado Springs, for high school kids who wanted all of the fun of cadet life minus the flying. And since Mom happened to work at the academy, it'd be only too easy to get me a last-minute placement.

Beth understood all of this in the instant that it took to take the envelope out of the mailbox. I could see it in the flinty way she looked at me over the dining room table.

Even after a decade of experience, I'd never learned how to translate Beth's eyes. They were blue and always seemed to be saying a lot in a language I didn't know. Dad's eyes were oaky brown like mine and Ethan's. Brown eyes said yes or no. Beth's eyes had subtext. She meant well, but the motives were churning around in all that blue. Translating her would require a degree in meteorology.

She had made it her mission to find me a summer distraction that wouldn't end in me joining the reserves. She and Dad liked to imply that the armed forces had stolen my mother from me. Which wasn't true. The air force didn't have rules about being married to shallow narcissists who got whiny about not being the breadwinner. She wasn't stolen. She just went. If she'd been a teacher or a pharmacist or something, maybe someone would have stopped and asked her why she didn't want to be my mom every day.

But Beth started talking about me volunteering at the theater and Dad started rumbling about some mock trial program down south—leaving the door wide open for me to choose his career over Mom's.

I didn't want to go into law like my dad. I didn't want to sell real estate. I didn't want to enlist the second I left high school.

I wanted the one thing that would unite all of my parents against me. I wanted to go to Rayevich College, the only school in the country with a science fiction literature program. I wanted four years of classes on Octavia Butler and Sheri S. Tepper and biomechanics and astrophysics.

I wanted what both sides of my family would call "an expensive waste of time."

Lawrences went directly into the air force. Gabaroches got degrees in something "useful," like law or business. Beth didn't get the military—in that way that a lot of people didn't get it. Maybe someone somewhere in the tangle of her ancestors there'd been a great-grandparent who had been drafted, but her dad—who insisted that Ethan and I call him "Poppy"—had been a conscientious objector to the Korean and Vietnam wars. They both talked about the military like everyone would be better off if it just disappeared. Beth's dream was for me to go to one of the local state schools.

"If you went to Davis, you could spend more time with your mother's family," she'd say, grinning with all of the ignorance of someone who had never had to watch Isaiah eat.

I'd given up hope of ever seeing Rayevich for myself, until the day that the Air Force Academy packet had shown up. I couldn't go to Colorado, but I could go somewhere. I could go see Bunbury.

See, in the first act of *The Importance of Being Earnest*, Algernon tells his family that he has to visit a sick friend named Bunbury, whenever he needs to peace out from their bullshit.

For some reason, that really spoke to me.

Getting admission to Camp Onward wasn't easy. I'd sat through a two-hour-long test while I was supposed to be at my last ACLU club meeting of the school year. I'd crafted an essay about why I was the perfect candidate for Rayevich College. I'd emptied my savings to pay for my train ticket. I'd changed all of my social media profiles to a picture of a sunset.

And then I'd spent weeks plotting out how to cover my ass. I'd learned from Algernon's mistakes. I wasn't looking for a comedy of errors to ensue. One fictional sick friend wasn't enough.

Dad and Beth thought I was going to stay with the Lieutenant on base in Washington. Mom thought she was paying for me to take a CrossFit boot camp class. My cousins thought Dad and Beth were shipping me down south to mock trial camp at UCLA.

Elliot Gabaroche was everywhere and nowhere.

Ever Lawrence, seventeen-year-old girl and newly certified genius, was going to summer camp.

From my vantage point in the parking lot, Rayevich College seemed like so much more than it had in the pamphlet stuffed under my mattress. In person, the low brick buildings were concealed behind clumps of giant trees. The cement pathways that cut swathes through the tidy lawns were unscuffed and snowy white. Everything smelled green. Not fakey pine spray green like those cans in your friends' bathrooms. Real fresh-and-alive green. The smell of things growing.

I leaned against the Prius and raked my hands over my hair. It didn't seem to be possible for it to be both summer and not face-meltingly hot.

Did everyone in California know about this "north" thing? Why did we keep suffering through months of triple-digit hell when there was all this livable space above us?

"They close up most of the residence halls for summer," Cornell-the-counselor said, popping the trunk and looping my laptop case over his shoulders before I could argue. He wheeled my suitcase over the sparkling cement. "So, it'll only be other Onward kids with you. It's better than it would be if class was in session. At least," he shuddered, "that's what I keep telling myself."

I swung my backpack over my shoulder as I skipped to keep up with him. He might have been a bit shorter than me, but he wasn't bothering to sightsee. "You're in the dorms, too?"

"Supposed to be. I'm a townie." The suitcase caught a crack in the cement and skidded onto one wheel. He shook it back into place without slowing down. "I mean, my parents live here. I technically live in New Hampshire now." He plucked at his dark green shirt. "I go to Dartmouth."

"Cornell," I said slowly. "At Dartmouth?"

"Trust me, I know. My mom was so disappointed when I wouldn't apply to my namesake. She thought it'd be cute. But my girlfriend and I agreed on Dartmouth, so that's where we went. She has bets against all of us who signed up to work this session." He said "girlfriend" with an apologetic weight. Like he was used to girls falling helplessly in love with him within seven minutes of shaking hands. Maybe Dart-mouth girls went bananas over him blaring NPR in his hybrid car. But he had "future fed" written all over him. He would have been right at home with the interns that swarmed around the Capitol Mall back home.

And he was wearing loafers. I couldn't get my swoon on for a guy who didn't wear socks.

He cleared his throat and picked up the pace toward the tallest of the buildings. It had giant greenish glass panels built into the bottom, windows and doors blending together. "Well, she's only betting against those of us who went to high school together. Half of the counselors actually go to Rayevich. But three weeks is a long time to go back to dorm life. Dining hall food and curfew and communal bathrooms—"

"Is this your version of a get-psyched speech?" I interrupted. "Because you kind of suck at it."

He grinned again. "Sorry. You'll be fine. You aren't used to having your own apartment like we are."

Brag.

We made it to the glass doors. I caught Cornell's eye in the reflection as I darted forward to grab the handle. He was hauling all of my stuff. I didn't need him proving what a gentleman he was. He frowned at me as he passed into the lobby and toward the elevator. He pushed a button and stood at attention in front of the closed metal doors.

"How much time do I have before the meet and greet?" I asked.

He swished my laptop out of the way of his pocket and checked his phone. He made a hissing sound of apology. "Two hours. Sorry, most of the out-of-towners are coming in from the airport shuttle."

"No, that's great," I said.

"It is?"

The elevator dinged and we stepped in, my suitcase standing between us like another person. Cornell pressed the Three button and I leaned against the wall, bracing as the floor pushed against my feet.

"I've been on a train for twelve hours," I said. "And now I have an entire campus to myself. I can get a run in before I have to get my Melee on." He cut his eyes at me. I frowned in response, gripping the strap of my backpack. "What? Is my newb showing?"

His lanyard jingled as he swung his head. It didn't quite seem to mean yes or no.

The doors swept open again. The wheels on the suitcase were muffled by the thin layer of taupe carpet on the floor here. There were half a dozen closed doors covered in black chalkboard paint. Cornell reached into his pocket again and produced a key from inside of a tiny manila envelope. He stuck it into the first door on the left and turned the knob.

It wasn't much to look at. Plain white cement walls. Two narrow beds on opposing sides of the room. Two desks with Camp Onward folders and plastic-wrapped T-shirts waiting on them. Two narrow pressboard wardrobes that were less Narnia, more IKEA.

I tossed my backpack onto the left bed. Cornell carefully disentangled himself from my laptop case and set it on the desk chair. He flopped a hand toward the folder.

"If you need anything, all of our phone numbers are in there," he said. "I'm down on second. It's the boys' floor. Or, it will be once everyone else gets here."

I sat down on the edge of the mattress. It was much smaller than I'd been picturing it.

"Don't be late to the meet and greet," Cornell said, edging toward the door. He reached into his back pocket, pulling out a chalk pen. He shook it before uncapping it with his teeth. "Your RA is kind of a hard-ass."

I tugged at the knots of my shoelaces. I was aching to set my feet to the pavement. I was going to make the most of this whole beautiful weather thing. "Yeah? What did your girlfriend bet against her sticking it out in the dorms?"

The pen cap fell out of his mouth as he laughed. It was a wheezy hiccupping sound that bounced off all of the bare walls and into the hallway. He bent down and scooped up the cap. "No one would bet against her. She's—well, you'll see."

He pressed the chalk pen to the door and wrote "Ever" in looping cursive.

I kicked off a shoe. "Can you work on being comforting, too? Or, like, less cryptic?"

He capped his pen and nodded to me. "I'll see what I can do."

3

Every building sprouted out of the ground like a Lego model of a university, all red brick and opaque glass with perfectly manicured trees set between. The schools back home were prison-like cement fortresses compared to this.

The campus was eerily empty as I cruised through it. The paths that curved between buildings were endless stretches of bare benches and clean trash cans and absolutely no signs of life.

I turned up the volume on my running playlist. Pop music never lets you feel alone. There are people and parties and someone turning up the bass until everyone's heart thumps in time with the 808.

My room key was warm in my pocket. I couldn't shake how bizarre it was to have my own place, hundreds of miles away from any of my parents. Blowing my allowance on sheets too small to fit my bed at home felt less ridiculous now that they had a place to go. My dorm. Well, my slice of my dorm. There was still the roommate thing to deal with.

And even that was exciting in a stomach churning sort of way. New people. New space. Not another month of Beth knocking on my door in the morning to ask me to drive Ethan somewhere. Or long-distance phone calls from my mom, where I kept from asking when she was coming out to visit next because I didn't want her to feel guilty. Or going to hunt for public air-conditioning with my friends and ending up sneaking into crappy movies or sipping expensive smoothies.

I'd broken out of the time loop of Elliot Gabaroche's life. I was Ripley waking up in *Aliens*, fifty-seven years in the future and away from the monotony of before.

Except without the PTSD and the being chased by Xenomorphs part.

Hopefully.

I turned a corner, following the path behind the dining hall, back to my building. Cornell's warning about not being late to the meet and greet poked at me. Now wasn't the time to meander, no matter how nice it was to be moving under the cloudless sky and not stuck in a metal tube. Somehow, getting lost at genius camp seemed worse than getting lost anywhere else.

Ahead, off of a fork in the road and tucked back behind some trees, was one of the closed residence halls. It was taller than mine, with dark windows. The buildings around it threw shadows onto the bricks. Tucked into a corner of the cement steps, there was a boy sitting alone. His black hair was a shaggy approximation of a Beatles bowl cut. It flopped into his eyes as he leaned over a typewriter.

A typewriter.

Pencil lead gray and perched on top of a small suitcase. Or a type-writer case, I guess. I'd never had to consider how people trans-ported typewriters. I honestly couldn't say that I'd ever seen one in person before. It was like a rotary phone or dial-up Internet. You heard stories, but they always followed the words *When I was your age* . . .

Typewriter Guy's fingers flew over the keys. The sunlight was bouncing off all of the shiny metal parts on his writing contraption, making him squint. The pad of his thumb went between his teeth for a second before he cranked up the paper, slid the top to the left, and resumed typing.

Hipster or ghost?

The only way to know for sure would be to take out my head-phones and try to hear the clicky-clack of the keys. I really didn't want to start off the summer by announcing to all of the campers that we had a wannabe Jack Kerouac specter haunting the closed dorms.

Sure, ghostbusting would be more interesting than the off-brand academic decathlon we were supposed to be here for. But it would raise all kinds of ethical issues. Which would open the door to de-bating the legal rights of the dead-but-not-gone. If we exorcised one ghost, we'd have to start an ectoplasmic genocide, finding all of the other ghosts on campus to eradicate them.

I veered into the quad and picked up my pace.

Peace out, Casper. Happy hauntings.

The residence hall had come to life while I was out. As I paused at a drinking fountain, voices hummed against the walls and I could hear faucets running in the communal bathroom. Every door had been decorated with acid-green chalk. *Trixie, RA. Perla and Kate. Avital and Yuri. Itzel and Kayla. Fallon and Meuy. Allison and Annie.* My door had "Ever" in Cornell's white cursive, but another name had been added under a flowery ampersand: Leigh.

The writing on the door to the left of mine was in a third hand, this one sloppier and sharper. It read "Her Imperial Majesty Mar-garet Royama, supreme overlord."

I jumped back as the door opened, revealing a tiny girl with short, dark hair. She had a cell phone pressed to her ear. Her hand slapped against the door with a *thwack*, right on the *M* of *Margaret*, which she set to erasing with the heel of her palm.

"You are setting a fucking terrible example," she said to the person on the other end of her call. Her voice was a cartoonish squeak. She pulled a chalk pen out of her jeans and scrawled "Meg" where the *Margaret* had been. "Of course it was you. Your handwriting is chicken scratch. Do not teach your campers that they're allowed on this floor. If I catch you up here, so help me, Benedict, I will destroy you. I've done it before . . ."

I reached for my doorknob and was relieved to find it unlocked. I slipped inside before the teensy, raging RA could notice me.

There was a skinny girl sitting on the bed across from mine, cross-legged on top of zebra print sheets. It took a second for me to see anything other than her hair. It was shaved down to a fine fuzz and bleached so unnaturally yellow that it looked like she'd painted it with highlighter ink. It matched the Onward folder that was open in her lap. She blinked up at me as the door clicked shut, her dark eyebrows bushy and stark against her rosy skin.

Brown-eyed roommate. Score.

"Ever?" she asked.

"Yeah," I said. "You must be Leigh."

We both twitched as the windows rattled with the force of a door being slammed in the hall. Leigh glanced at the wall and then back to me.

"Meg finally noticed that the other RAs rewrote her door?"

I collapsed onto the bare mattress on my side of the room. "If Meg is an Asian girl who wants to murder someone named Benedict, then yes."

"Yep. That's her," Leigh said. "Lucky us, we get to sleep next door to one of the weirdo RAs."

I stripped off my running shoes, quickly stuffing my old socks inside before they could funk up the room. "You've met her before?"

"No." She held up her folder and wiggled it at me. "But it said in here that she was a Messina alum. So you can just tell, you know?"

I grabbed the handle of my suitcase and dragged it toward the bed to search for fresh socks. "The counselor who picked me up from the train station told me that half of the RAs went to the same high school. Is that a bad thing?"

"Oh. You're not from here," she said. "From your shirt, I'd guess you're Californian? Unless you just hate Oregonian sports teams. It's always seemed to me that fan loyalties are more related to familial and societal influence than actual proximity. It's not like the players are actually from the states they represent."

I glanced down at my Warriors shirt, uncomfortable with how much it telegraphed about me. "I don't have anything against Oregon teams." I shook out a sock and tugged it on. "But, yeah, I'm from California. You're local?"

She addressed her sheets, tracing the stripes with her nails. "Not exactly. I'm from Florence. It's on the coast."

"No way," I blurted, the nerd quadrant of my brain clicking faster than the "don't geek out at strangers" portion. "That's where Frank Herbert got the idea for *Dune*! You guys have the moving sands."

"And the largest sea cave in the world." She smiled, revealing slightly elongated canines that twisted inward. "It's about an hour away, but . . ." She leaned forward and lowered her voice to a stage whisper. "We still hear stories. The Messina is this giant academy where they, like, play cricket and build nuclear reactors and stuff. You took the IQ test to get in here, right?"

I thought of the paper-and-pencil test I'd sat through back home. I'd been alone in a classroom at the community college for almost two hours while the proctor ignored me and graded papers. After I'd spent weeks drilling through AP guides, trying to commit all of the information to memory, the test had ended up being mostly patterns.

"That's only half of the test that the Messina kids have to take to get in," Leigh said. "They only take ubergeniuses. But their school helps Rayevich sponsor the camp, so a bunch of their grads come back to be counselors."

I hadn't given much thought to the other schools sponsoring the camp. The Onward website had made the Messina seem like any other bourgeois private school.

"Having an ubergenius for a counselor ups the odds on us winning, doesn't it?" I asked.

"I think everyone gets one, so, no, not technically. And since everyone here passed the test to get in, we all qualify as geniuses, too. The girl who checked me in said that every team has to have an equivalent median IQ, but we don't get to know what it is. It's a Messina policy."

I shrugged. I was cool staying in the dark on everyone's IQs. I didn't even know my own. After years of having Isaiah lord his Mensa membership over me, I was kind of shocked that I qualified as a genius, too.

I knew I was smart, but I'd only pulled a B minus in geometry.

"As long as they don't ask me to play cricket, I'm fine," I said. "All I know about it is that a sticky wicket is a bad thing."

I lifted the package of sheets out of my suitcase. It would be best to get settled sooner rather than later. As I wrenched open the plastic, Leigh leaped off her bed and bounded toward me in two skips. She wasn't much taller than Meg-Margaret the RA had been. The top of her electric hair barely made it to my shoulder. Up close, I could see that her face was covered in clusters of zits and a slathering of pinkish foundation.

"I have to be super blunt with you, Ever," she said, wringing her hands in the hem of her T-shirt. "I need to agree, right now, that we're going to be besties. I can't do a month of drawing a line down the center of the room and calling our friends back home to talk smack. At best, it's Nick at Nite hijinks, and, at worst, it's a Berlin Wall situation." She paused, rolling her eyes up at the low ceiling. "And I don't have, like, a ton of people in Florence to call. Very few. Basically none."

I realized with a pang that my phone was full of numbers I couldn't call. Anyone I talked to outside of camp would have to be fed some lie of corroboration. Ever Lawrence didn't have any friends. Just a backpack full of sci-fi novels, a couple of protein bars left over from the train ride, and hella cool hair.

An image of Beth popped into my head. Last week, she'd been wandering from room to room with her hands folded against her stomach and her neck lifted high. She passed through the kitchen, tilting her face toward the sliding glass door to catch her reflection.

Gwendolen doesn't walk like me, she'd said when she saw me and Ethan staring. *A good character starts in your bones.*

I adjusted my posture. Ever Lawrence had never had a grandmother who smacked her with a hairbrush for slouching. My shoulders hunched in freedom.

"We can totally be besties," I said to Leigh. "I've never been to camp before. You can help me not make a total fool out of myself."

Her mouth quirked to one side, and for a second I thought of my little brother rolling his eyes at me from across the dinner table. "Did you not hear all of the crap I spewed at you? All I can do is make you less awkward by association." She took the sheets out of my hands, shaking the packaging onto the floor. "And help you unpack. We need to get settled before we can win."

I let her help me make my bed. Ever Lawrence didn't care about having hospital corners on her sheets.

4

orty-eight people hadn't seemed like a lot when I'd been praying to get a spot on the camp roster, but having everyone jammed onto the lawn outside of the residence hall was overwhelming. I knew from the Onward enrollment packet that only rising seniors were allowed to compete and that there must have been an even number of boys and girls. But all of the faces jumbled together into one mass of new. Tall, short, thin, fat. Some in T-shirts like me and Leigh. Some in ties or dresses.

The counselors formed a single file line at the base of the wide stairs that led to the dining hall. All of them were wearing shirts representing their colleges. Cornell was whispering to a towering guy with a scruffy lumberjack beard and a UC Berkeley shirt. The two of them broke into giggles, and a dark-haired girl from Bryn Mawr shushed them.

There was a single speaker mounted to a tripod at the top of the stairs. It buzzed to life as a bald middle-aged man in a brown Rayevich T-shirt patted a live microphone.

"Welcome, students!" he said, baring a gap-toothed smile at the crowd. "My name is Wendell Cheeseman. I am a professor of

American history and an associate dean here at Rayevich College, and I am happy to be the director of this year's Camp Onward."

The counselors led a lukewarm applause break, giving Wendell a moment to wipe the sweat off his large forehead with the back of his arm. His pit stains were rapidly traveling toward his belt.

"For those of you who skipped the history portion of your welcome packet," he said into his microphone, pacing the top stair in long strides, "let me give you a brief lesson. It is, after all, what I do best." He paused, possibly hoping for a laugh, which didn't come. "In nineteen seventy-seven, a collection of professors from Rayevich and the University of Oregon decided to turn their attention to secondary education. They opened the Messina Academy for the Gifted, an institution that would go on to foster the brightest minds in Central Oregon."

I heard someone cough. Glancing around, I spotted the hipster ghost standing alone, his arms folded tightly over his chest. From the look he was giving Wendell Cheeseman, I guessed someone was going to get the crap haunted out of them later.

"Do you see that guy?" I whispered to Leigh. I stretched my neck to the side, using my hair as a pointer.

Leigh tipped her head, scratching her nose in the ghost's general direction before glancing back up at me. "The one who looks like John Cusack? Or John Lennon. There's something very John about him."

I'd never considered what made someone Johnish before. But it suited the hipster ghost. "Kevin" or "Bob" would have clashed with the sharp slant of his nose.

"I saw him using a typewriter outside of one of the closed residence halls," I said. "I've been trying to figure out if he's a nerd or if he's straight-up haunting the school."

"Either would make sense here," Leigh said, leaning around me again. She sucked in a breath. "He's gone!"

I turned fully around. The slice of grass where John the Hipster Ghost had been was empty except for a few slices of sunlight.

"Ooky spooky," Leigh said. She ran her palms over her arms with a shiver. "Unless he just went to the bathroom."

"It became clear to the founders that only a small number of students could benefit from the Messina," Wendell Cheeseman's voice boomed. I turned back to the stairs, pretending to look engaged. "There were other gifted children all over the West Coast who weren't able to receive the same quality of education. The founders returned home to Rayevich and created a summer seminar program that would bring together both schools' mission statements. Camp Onward would bring students such as yourselves the best of Rayevich and the Messina Academy." He wiped at his face again in two quick slaps. "An uncompromising commitment to quality education for the gifted in a small community of liberal arts scholars. This utopia of academia is represented not only by yourselves but by our collection of counselors. Every year, Camp Onward proudly hosts Messina graduates and current Rayevich students to lead our teams for the Tarrasch Melee. They will guide you through each area of study and be your coaches as you enter into the competition phase of our seminar. Each team will have a representative from both schools."

I looked down the line of bored counselors. One of the girls in Rayevich gear had the most beautiful box braids I'd ever seen. They were impractically long, swishing around her waist in clean, black ropes. I patted my own hair, reminding it that braids that nice meant unending scalp pain and having to sleep in a satin cap.

"Who do you think we'll get?" I asked Leigh.

"She's on our floor," she whispered, giving a low point toward a girl standing between Meg and Lumberjack Beard.

The girl was about a head taller than Meg. Her hair was unnaturally orangey red and cut into a severe bob. The Stanford logo stretched to breaking across her chest. She nudged Lumberjack Beard and I caught a glimpse of a tattoo on her inner elbow, a tiny blue box.

"Jesus," I giggled to Leigh. "It's like the Internet took a poll of the perfect nerd girl and wished her into existence. Busty redhead who goes to one of the top schools in the country?"

"Huh. Can we give her a TARDIS tattoo and a Care Bear nose?" Leigh said, tapping her chin in fake thought. "I bet she has a Harry Potter tramp stamp."

"And is adorkably clumsy."

"And she thinks that hair color makes her look like Black Widow."

We both smothered our laughs into our hands as Wendell Cheeseman started listing off our seminar topics. My stomach rumbled. I really hoped that this recitation of the welcome folder would wrap up soon.

"Each of you will receive your study packets after lunch at your first team meetings," Wendell said. "But remember, there is more to this experience than the Melee. You will also make new friends and expand your horizons. No matter who leaves with the scholarships, all of you will always be Mudders at heart." He spun on his heel, revealing the bold yellow writing on the back of his T-shirt as he shouted, "Hey, bud! Do you mud?!"

The counselors in Rayevich shirts raised their fists over their heads and shouted, "Muck yes!"

Wendell peeked over his shoulder, the microphone in his hand drooping slightly. "Now, everyone. Hey, bud! Do you mud?!"

Leigh arched an eyebrow at me and mouthed, "Muck yes?" as the rest of the campers called back in various degrees of enthusiasm.

"That's right!" Wendell called. He reached behind himself and yanked open the door of the dining hall. "And now, we feast!"

"Originally, Eugene was called Skinner's Mudhole," Leigh explained, as we helped ourselves to the buffet of sandwich ingredients. "Feast" had definitely been an overstatement. It was more like someone had robbed a Subway for its sweatiest meats and veggies. "So Rayevich's mascot is a mud monster. It looks kind of like a golem."

"That explains why they don't have any sports teams here," I said, heaping shredded chicken onto my plate. It was the only thing that looked like it might have been carved from a real animal. "It'd be hell of awkward to have to dress someone up in a mud monster mascot costume."

"'Hell of,'" Leigh hummed, as though savoring the taste of the words. She cocked her head at me. "A deconstructed form of the colloquial 'hella'?"

"I guess?" I frowned. "I've never really thought about it."

"You don't have to. I was just trying it on." She reached for a pair of tongs and threw a heap of sprouts onto her plate, mostly missing her slices of whole wheat. "Tell me if I end up using it wrong?"

"Will do."

The line slowed as we approached the condiments table and the people up ahead started going to town on a variety of spicy mustards. Nibbling on a piece of chicken, I took in the rest of the dining hall. It was somewhere between Hogwarts and a ski lodge. Instead of the folding tables that populated my school's cafeteria, Rayevich had long hardwood tables with low polished benches that matched the exposed beams in the ceiling. The counselors had all been granted dibs on lunch and sat at the farthest table in front of a giant picture window. Wendell Cheeseman seemed to be attempting conversation with the girl from Bryn Mawr, who was edging closer and closer to a guy in an MIT sweatshirt.

A cluster of girls vacated the condiments table and the line inched forward. The hipster ghost was hovering near the drinks table. There was no plate in his hands and he didn't appear to have any interest in helping himself to the bounty of bottled water and organic sodas beside him. Leigh followed my gaze and bounced on her toes.

"Oh," she breathed. "A ghost at the sandwich feast. How very Shakespearean."

John the Hipster Ghost watched a couple of guys grab water bottles next to him. At least, I thought he was watching them. It was hard to tell. His hair mostly hid his eyes from view.

"He isn't eating," I said.

Leigh's face scrunched in thought. "And no one else seems to be noticing him. The only logical test is to check for corporeality." She thrust her plate at me. "Hummus, if they have it, please. Otherwise, light mayo!"

"Wait, what?" I squawked at her back, staggering to keep hold of both of the plates as the line started moving again. "Light in calories or quantity?"

I didn't get a reply.

It was impossible to lose track of Leigh in the crowd. Her hair operated as her own personal follow spot, keeping the rest of her in focus as she wove between other campers. She squeezed between two people at the beverage table and palmed a can of soda, holding it low against her leg. Her wrist flicked almost imperceptibly as she skirted the table. Before I could think to shout to her, she was standing in front of the ghost and cracking the tab.

It was like watching a bomb go off. Everyone within range dove for cover. Heads turned all over the room as Leigh screamed. The cola splatter had covered her face and shirt. She thrust the can at John the Hipster Ghost as she swept liquid off her cheeks. The counselors were on their feet, rushing around the tables toward her. John was saying something to her. She pressed her hand to his chest, shaking her head and gibbering at him.

The Perfect Nerd Girl counselor reached them with a wad of napkins in her hand. John took one to dab his face. He had to comb his hair back to reach the drops caught in his thick eyebrows. As one of the girls from Rayevich swept Leigh toward the bathroom, the Perfect Nerd Girl patted the top of John's head. He jerked away from her, swatting her hand away. He shook his hair back into place and glanced across the room. His eyes accidentally caught mine and held. His lips curved into a sheepish smile.

Did Ever Lawrence smile back at strange hipsters? Elliot Gabaroche wouldn't have. If I'd been in the cafeteria at home, I would have looked away before one of my friends started catcalling to the guy making eyes at me. For some reason, they believed that humiliation was the gateway to romance.

But Ever Lawrence didn't have a crew of nosy loudmouths.

I smiled back at him.

The person behind me nudged my elbow and I stumbled to take the open space at the condiment table. I dressed my own sandwich in a daze and found hummus for Leigh. I decided against getting a drink, since the table was being sopped up by counselors. The Perfect Nerd Girl was leading John toward the grown-up table. Wendell Cheeseman forced a barking laugh as he encouraged everyone to go back to their lunches by shouting, "*Mangia, mangia!*"

I found an unpopulated corner of the room and sat down. The counselor with the box braids appeared with a WET FLOOR sign and started navigating people around the spill. Lumberjack Beard wheeled a yellow mop bucket out of the kitchen, his face contorted in disgust.

Leigh skipped out of the bathroom and collapsed across from me at the table. Drops of water clung to her hair. She beamed at me as she took a bite of her sandwich.

"That was hell of effective," she said. "It would have been better if they bought brand-name drinks. Coke is the most carbonated soda on the market." She scowled at her sandwich. "This hummus is way too salty to be brand name. Who buys generic hummus?"

"So," I said, taking in her dripping hair and stained clothes. "You're an insane person."

"Don't be ableist. I already told you, Ever, I'm awkward." She took another bite of her sandwich. "And awkward people can get away with anything. No one's going to think, *Oh, she shook up that soda.* They're going to say, *Oh, that poor weird girl had an accident.* And now they'll discount everything else I do all summer. Which will be useful to us when we enter the Melee. People want you to be one thing. If I'm weird, then people will forget that I'm also a genius who's here to win."

My brain grappled with this for a moment. We were here to

compete. Everyone was working with the same base level IQ. Distracting the rest of the teams from that was a solid tactic.

"And," Leigh said, "I learned two very important things from this experiment. One, John is not a ghost. He has a heartbeat and a distinct lack of ectoplasm. Two, his name is not John. It's *Brandon*." She stuck out her tongue, as though the name was sour in her mouth. "A total failure on the part of his parents. Have you ever seen someone who looks more like a John?"

You look as if your name was Ernest, said my brain. *You are the most earnest-looking person I ever saw in my life.*

Great. The Wilde was back. Why couldn't Beth have repeatedly done a useful show? People who could quote Shakespeare seemed cultured, not possessed.

Leigh's forehead scrunched into a single painful-looking wrinkle. "There's a guy coming over here." She leaned to the side to see around my shoulder. "Do you want me to get another soda to make sure he's alive?"

I opened my mouth to laugh, but it died in my throat, threw itself a funeral, and dug graves for every ounce of joy that I could ever feel again, the second a plate fell down next to mine. There was a heap of deli meats and cheeses hidden under a tidal wave of ranch dressing. The air congealed with the smell of mango dreadlock wax and an entire can of drugstore cologne.

Run, my brain screamed. *Abort mission. Punch everyone who gets between you and the door. Get on the train back home.*

"Hey, Ellie," Isaiah said.

5

In an instant, I was off the bench and lugging my cousin out of the dining hall. His feet staggered and tripped behind me as he attempted to go full deadweight.

"Elliot, Jesus, stop it. People are watching."

"Shut up, shut up, shut up," I hissed, digging my fingernails deep into his arm. My heart was slamming in my chest, pushing me forward, deeper into the nightmare.

When we were little, Isaiah and I would get dumped together a lot. We were close in age and only half an hour's drive away from each other, and our parents never noticed that we didn't actually like each other. For years, we had to go to each other's birthday parties and share babysitters. Once, before my dad and Beth got married, we were stuck together for an entire summer vacation. It was months of jelly sandwiches and tattling and generalized punching and pinching each other while Sid watched TV.

I hated spending time with Isaiah so much that I cried when I found out that I was going to have a little brother, because I thought that he might turn out to be as annoying as my cousin.

Which, of course, Ethan wasn't, because it was literally impossible for anyone to be as annoying as Isaiah.

Now that we were both too old to need a babysitter—although I wouldn't have been surprised if Aunt Bobbie still had one on call for her precious baby—Isaiah and I only had to suffer through each other's company for holidays and family reunions.

Except that he was here. At camp. Which was twenty-one days long.

I kicked open the door. I shoved him out first and he stumbled back toward the stairs before straightening to his full height, exactly at eye level with me. He was wearing ratty jean shorts with round white skate shoes.

Skate shoes? Come on. How in the hell were we biologically related?

I dragged the heels of my hands over my eyes. The inside of my head felt muggy and punch-drunk.

"What are you doing here?" I asked. I looked out at the empty quad, waiting for an ambush to come dropping down from the skinny trees. "Where's Sid?"

"At home." He rubbed at the four crescent-shaped imprints on his arm; his lower lip stuck out. "Aren't you in L.A.?"

I gestured around wildly. "Keep up, idiot. Obviously, I'm not in L.A. I'm right here. Why are you here?"

Remembering that his pouting had zero effect on me, he switched into Lawrence defense mode: folded arms over a puffed chest and words clipped down into confetti. "I entered the Melee. Between my Stanford–Binet score and my PSATs, I was an obvious choice for the admissions board."

I refused to give him the satisfaction of asking what a Stanford–Binet was, but I made a mental note to Google it once I was back in my dorm.

"You decided to try to win free admission to Rayevich?" I asked. "Rather than tell your sister that you don't want to go to the academy next year?"

"And you're here to what? Learn to fly?" He cocked his head, sending his dreads sliding across his neck. "You lied."

I folded my arms back at him. He could use the Lawrence voice on me all he wanted. Only one of us had learned to argue from an attorney. My father wasn't a great lawyer, but he was the king of talking in circles until he found a chink in the armor.

"Sid and Aunt Bobbie know where you are?" I asked.

"I wouldn't lie to my mom," he said.

"Yeah, like when you told her about breaking her favorite snow globe? Remember how loud it popped? You got glitter water all over our church shoes. Oh wait. You swore that I did it and Grandma put me in time-out for all of Christmas."

He shook his head. "I'm grown, Elliot. I'm not six anymore."

"Tell that to your bottom lip. It's shaking again." The offending lip tucked back into a scowl. "And stop calling me that. I'm not Elliot here. I'm Ever Lawrence."

His eyebrows went up. "You stole my last name?"

"It's one of my last names, too. It's on my driver's license and everything. Not that you'd know what a driver's license looks like, since your mommy won't let you take the test until you turn eighteen."

He wasn't listening. He scuffed the toe of his offensive shoe against the cement until the rubber bent. "What kind of name is Ever? Like Everett? Did you really pick another dude name? Couldn't you live with a girl name for once? You could be an Ashley or a Lauren or something normal."

Embarrassment ratcheted up my spine as I thought about scrolling endlessly through baby names online. Ever had struck me as effortlessly feminine, a breezy giggle of a name. It was the sort of nickname that begged an adorable backstory: *My parents used to say, "I love you forever," and I thought Forever was my name!*

Or something less stupid. Whatever.

"Where do Sid and Bobbie think you are?" I asked Isaiah again. "You aren't even allowed to compete at out-of-state academic decathlon meets." Family gossip rattled around in my brain, vague information from phone calls with Mom and Grandmother Lawrence that had never been useful before. "Didn't you miss the finals last year because your mom didn't want you to go all the way to Nevada alone? She'd never let you leave home without a chaperone."

"She would for the leadership camp!"

He looked like he wanted to stuff the sentence back into his mouth, but it was too late. Triumph welled in my stomach as he squirmed.

"The air force leadership adventure camp?" I asked, shoving him hard in the shoulder. "The one in Washington? How are you this stupid? You know that they'll be able to track whether or not you're there, right? One phone call from your mom or my mom or Sid and you'll get caught. And that means I'll get caught!"

"No one is getting caught doing anything," he said. "Sid's ex is running the camp. He said that he'd keep my name on the roster for all three seminars. He's even going to mail a T-shirt here so I can wear it on the flight home. Did you make plans for a mock trial T-shirt?"

I goggled at him. "What? No. That plan sucks. Sid's ex could slip up. Sid could go back to base early and decide to come visit you and no amount of free T-shirts is going to save you. You need to go home. Now."

"Okay." He shrugged. "Let me take a selfie of us real quick—"

He started to reach into his pocket and I kicked him, hard, in the shins. I could hear my Muay Thai instructor crying foul. You were never supposed to hit someone who wasn't padded. But the rules needed to be broken for blackmailing douche-canoes.

"Ow!" he whined, taking two steps away from me before I could smash his nose into his brain. "It's mutually assured destruction, El—Ever. If anyone finds out that I'm here, then you have to go home, too. And then we'll both end up at the academy. I need this scholarship. My dad isn't going to pay for me to disappoint him." His mouth twisted into a mocking smile. "Not that you'd know anything about that."

Fear flashed through my system, raising the hairs on my arms. How disappointed would my parents be if I won the Melee? Would

I have to leave for college on the same midnight train, with no one to hug me good-bye?

I swallowed, struggling to hold on to my rage as I glared at my cousin. "You're running away."

"Duh. So are you."

"Did you just 'duh' me? Who says 'duh'? How did you even qualify for a place here?"

The door to the dining hall swung open. Cornell-the-counselor's head popped out. He was already smiling. It was possible that he never stopped smiling. It was obnoxious.

"Hey, Ever," he crowed, like we hadn't seen each other in years. "Everything okay?"

"Great, good, thanks," I grunted.

He took a step out, aiming his goodwill and two-pump handshake at Isaiah. "Cornell Aaron. I'm one of the counselors here."

"Isaiah Lawrence," Isaiah said, his voice dropping down to match Cornell's postpubescent bass. "Sorry, I got here late. My flight was late. I guess my sister had the right idea, taking the train."

It took a second for me to catch up with that statement. Before I could open my mouth to point out that we were cousins, Cornell was bobbing his head and saying, "No sweat, man. Good to meet you. I think you're on my Melee team."

"Cool." Isaiah bobbed his head back. "I didn't think I'd see any other brothers up here. You hear things about Oregon, you know?"

I tilted my head back and cringed at the cloudless sky. Even the darkest recesses of my brain wouldn't have been able to conjure up a moment more horrifying to me than this.

"The camp's very diverse," Cornell said, regaining his bearings. "You guys should head back inside. Wendell's going to announce the teams soon." He waggled a finger at us. "No collusion. I don't care if you're twins."

My jaw flopped open as he disappeared inside again.

"Twins?" I spluttered at Isaiah. "Twins? We don't look anything alike."

"We've both got Grandpa's eyes. Everyone says so."

"Everyone" being Grandmother Lawrence.

Really, Isaiah and I both had buggy eyes—round, with a lot of eyelid. And we weren't exactly the same shade of brown, but we were both dark. Darker than the Lieutenant. Darker than Cornell-the-counselor.

After that, all comparisons ground to a halt. Isaiah's head was almost perfectly square. Mine was round. My legs took zero pit stops from the ground to my shoulders, whereas Isaiah was built like a satyr, with stubby little bowlegs. I'd always be taller than him by at least an inch.

"We're the same age," he said with an irritating calm. "We'd have to be twins."

"I'm a year older than you!"

"We're both seniors. And everyone at camp has to be at least seventeen. Like enlisting."

"But you aren't seventeen."

His face split into a maniacal grin. "I am now, Sis. Mutually assured destruction."

"This is some racist bullshit," I said. "I am not going to spend all summer pretending to be your sister. I don't even like being your cousin. I'm not upgrading our genes because of one color-struck counselor."

"Hey, you're the one who stole my last name. It's an understandable mistake."

"It's my name, too, you—"

"You heard the man," he interrupted, with an infuriating chuckle. "We need to head back. I haven't eaten since I left for the airport. Who was that girl you were sitting with? I saw her bust a soda on some skinny kid when I got here. She better not have touched my sandwich."

I followed him back inside, feeling like most of my more vital organs had been replaced with steel wool. There was no argument to make him leave. If I tattled, I was screwed. We'd both end up at home, grounded until we left for the academy together next year.

On the same plane.

In the same cadet training.

If one of us didn't win the scholarship at the end of the Melee, we'd be shackled together for the next five years.

Mom was right. I couldn't choose my deployment. I'd ended up in my first combat zone—a liberal arts college in the second-largest city in Oregon, crawling with geniuses and kamikaze roommates. And my entire future rested on the hope that Isaiah didn't take both of us down in a rain of friendly fire.

"You're going to have to be nicer to me, now that we're twins," he said as we walked back toward Leigh.

What nonsense, said Oscar Wilde. *I haven't got a brother.*

6

This is a competition, not a bacchanalia," Bryn Mawr shouted at the eight campers sitting in a circle around her, as she stabbed the makeshift flag into the ground. The hot pink poster board attached to the top of the wooden dowel read "Team Six" in silver glitter. "I go to an all-girls' school. If I can keep it in my pants for twenty-one days, so can you."

"Whoa, whoa, Mary-Anne," the Rayevich counselor next to her said. "I really don't think that we need to—"

Leigh pulled me away from their group. "Are you sad that you and Isaiah aren't on the same team?"

Wendell Cheeseman had announced all of the Melee teams before we'd been excused from the dining hall. Every team had eight campers—four boys from the same floor, four girls from the floor above them. Isaiah was one floor below mine, but too far to the side to end up on my team. Thank God.

"No," I said. "We don't really get along."

No matter what ideas Isaiah had about us playing nice for the summer, there was no way that this was going to build into some movie moment. There would be no tearful confessions or hugs of understanding.

First of all, Lawrences didn't hug.

Second, if I got too close to Isaiah, I'd never be able to wash off the stink of his cologne.

Thankfully, Leigh had taken Isaiah's appearance in stride. They'd bonded over a shared love of academic decathlon. They'd spent the rest of lunch trading war stories about the worst books they'd been required to read for competition.

It was boring, but harmless.

"For the next three weeks, you will refer to me only as 'Captain,'" the Perfect Nerd Girl from Stanford was saying to her team as she tossed binders at them. "And if we lose a single competition to Team Four, I will have all of you wishing that I had an airlock to throw you out of. Do I make myself clear, nuggets?"

"This is what I was telling you about," Leigh hissed, keeping her head down. "Messina people are freaking strange."

I started to point out that the Perfect Nerd Girl was referring to *Battlestar Galactica*, but the speaker set up in front of the dining hall thrummed to life.

"Victor Onobanjo," growled Lumberjack Beard. His mouth was way too close to the microphone, garbling his voice. "Please report to Team Four. Victor Onobanjo."

I yanked Leigh back as a scrawny, dark-skinned kid in a soccer jersey raced past us, waving his arms over his head.

"Seriously," Leigh said, wrenching the hem of her cola-stained shirt down around her shorts. "With this many smart kids in one place, you'd think they could follow basic signage. This is the problem with trusting an IQ test for admission. It doesn't factor in common sense."

"Says the girl who attacks ghosts with soda."

"You're going to have to let that go, Ever." She sighed. "It's very twenty minutes ago."

In the shade of a wide oak tree, the green poster board Team One flag was planted. A circle of mismatched blankets was set out. Meg was sitting cross-legged next to our Rayevich counselor, who was thin with owlish brown glasses balanced on his long, light brown nose. A stack of thick plastic-wrapped binders sat between them. Most of the team was already seated—two girls that I vaguely recognized from the lobby of the residence hall were sharing a My Little Pony blanket, and two boys were beside them, staring vacantly at their cell phones.

"Oh, honey," Meg said as Leigh and I approached. "I told you that you could go back to your room to change."

"I'm fine," Leigh said, folding her arms over the worst of the stains on her shirt. "I don't want to slow us down."

"I love that you're already a team player," Meg said. She sounded as though she really meant it, but that could have just been because everything she said sounded vaguely like it was licensed by Disney. She twisted to the side and her face lit up with a megawatt smile as Brandon-Who-Was-Not-Named-John and a boy in a sweater vest approached. Each of them was carrying an armload of the water bottles from the beverage table.

"Oh, B, you sweetums," Meg said as the boys set the water bottles next to the flagpole. "Thank you both."

"Tosh," said the boy in the sweater vest, collapsing down next to Meg.

Brandon looked around, as though hoping for another blanket to appear, before he sat down next to me. He folded his elbows and knees close to himself, making sure not to brush a single thread of my blanket.

Uh. Did we not share a moment back in the dining hall? I totally fought my resting bitch face for that not-John.

That's it, Ever, I thought. *Take a page out of the Elliot Gabaroche handbook. No more smiling back.*

He leaned forward, his shirt riding up in the back, revealing a stretch of snowy skin that had never seen the sun before. He snagged two water bottles from the pile and sat back, holding them out to me.

"Do you want one?" he asked. His voice was surprisingly husky. Not smoker raspy, but softly scratchy. Like a wool sweater.

"Oh," I said. "Yeah. Thanks."

I took the bottle by the top, carefully avoiding his fingers wrapped around the bottom. He held the second bottle out farther, as though hoping to create a small wrinkle in the universe to pass it through. When that didn't work, he said, "Leigh?"

"Yes, please," Leigh chirped, not moving.

"Sorry," he mumbled at the toe of my shoe. "I don't want to reach. It'd be rude—"

"It's fine," I said.

He started to reach past me as I put my hand out to take the bottle. He sat back, and I dropped my hand.

"I'll pass it," I said.

The bottle thumped into my palm and I thrust it at Leigh.

"Much safer than soda," she said, grinning at Brandon.

"Much," he said. He glanced up at me for a second, widening his eyes as if to say, *I'm never letting her near soda again.*

I smiled back at him. Screw the rules.

"Now that we're all here," said the Rayevich counselor, adjusting his glasses, "we can go ahead and get started."

Meg clapped her hands together. For the first time, I noticed that her shirt had the UCLA logo on it. Was the pleasant weather here making her more chipper or had she successfully murdered the person who'd written on her door?

"I'll start," she said. "I'm Meg Royama. I'm a Messina Academy graduate and I am currently double majoring at UCLA in gender studies and psychology. I'm so happy to be at Camp Onward. My parents never wanted to pay the tuition to let me go here when I was eligible for the Melee. I am the cocaptain of Team One, and I will also be your social science tutor."

"And I am Hari Bhardwaj," said the Rayevich counselor, inclining his head to Meg. "I am your other cocaptain, and I will be your literature tutor. I just finished my junior year here at Rayevich."

"Hunter Price," said the guy next to Hari, slipping his cell phone under his leg. He was sitcom pretty, with expertly mussed blond hair and laser-cut cheekbones. He was giving the Perfect Nerd Girl a run for her money on who could wear the tightest T-shirt. His sleeves were in danger of popping their seams. "I'm seventeen and from Seattle. I'm homeschooled, but I row crew and play soccer."

"And what will you do if you win the guaranteed admission to Rayevich?" Meg asked.

He gave her a smile so lopsided and disarming that it had to have been rehearsed. "Major in environmental science, with an emphasis in urban farming."

"Wonderful," Meg said. "And do you know when and where Greenpeace was founded?"

A ripple of tension went around the circle. I heard Brandon sigh. Meg kept her placid smile aimed at Hunter, whose fingertips inched toward his phone.

"It was founded in Vancouver," he said. He reached up and scratched at his temple. I'd never seen someone scratch their head in thought before. "But I don't know when."

"Nineteen seventy-one," Hari answered flatly. "Next."

"Galen Emiliano-Mendez," said the boy next to Hunter. He was heavyset, with sharply parted hair. He was sitting on his hands. "I'm from Medford. If I win, I want to study anthropology."

"And where were the oldest known human footprints found?" Hari asked.

Galen gulped. "Africa."

Meg's eyes narrowed, but her smile didn't falter. "Can you name the country?"

"K-Kenya?" Even Galen couldn't seem to tell if he was asking or telling. He relaxed as Hari nodded and turned to the next person.

Had we all listed our future majors, or were Meg and Hari flexing their ubergenius prowess? I tried to remember what I'd put on my application, but my brain was too busy racing through trivia. Isaac Asimov's middle name was Yudovich. Octavia Butler died in February 2006. John Scalzi named his main character in *Old Man's War* after two of the members of Journey.

Or was that a Wikipedia lie?

"My name is Perla Loya," said the first girl on the My Little Pony blanket. She tucked her glossy dark hair behind her ears. "I'm from Santa Monica, California. When I get into Rayevich, I will major in literature."

"What year was *The Canterbury Tales* published?" Hari asked.

Perla stiffened. "American literature."

"Same question," Meg said sweetly.

Perla looked at her roommate and then back at the counselors. Her voice came out in shreds. "I don't know."

"Okay," Meg said. It sounded like a check mark on a clipboard. "Next?"

We could be asked questions about subjects tangentially related to our interests? Balls.

Okay, time to dust off the mnemonic devices. My Very Educated Mother Just Showed Us Nine Planets. Mercury, Venus, Earth . . . No, wait. There was no way Meg and Hari would softball me with elementary school science.

Why couldn't I remember why Pluto had been demoted to a dwarf planet? Something about sharing space with things other than moons. What else was in its neighborhood? Comets? Asteroids?

"Kate Brant," said Perla's roommate, smoothing her skirt over her knees. "I'm from North Bend, Oregon. I want to study psychology."

"A girl after my own heart," simpered Meg. "Which region of the human brain is the last to mature?"

"Jesus," Brandon muttered.

"No cheating, B," Meg snapped, without looking away from Kate's narrow, bloodless face.

"Are all of the teams doing this?" asked the boy on the other side of Brandon. All of the blood in his face seemed to have been rerouted to his large ears. It was a good question, but one that we weren't going to get an answer on. I hoped that Isaiah was also being grilled.

But, really, Cornell was probably going to shake everyone's hand until it was time for dinner.

"The last region of the brain to mature is the prefrontal cortex," Kate said. She frowned at Meg. "You published a paper on it three years ago in the *Journal of Adolescent Developmental Behavior.*"

Meg gave a delicate shrug. "With some help. It was high school, after all."

My throat tightened. Leigh hadn't been exaggerating. If this was what the Messina Academy was churning out, there was a good reason that they only served Central Oregon. If they ever franchised, there would be terrifying evil masterminds all over the country.

"I'm Leigh Faber," Leigh said, not waiting for anyone to acknowledge her. "When I start at Rayevich, I will double in computer science and art studio."

"That's quite a double major," Hari said. He glanced at Meg. "Do you want computer science or art studio?"

"Art," she said. "Leigh, darling, what is the chemical compound of Egyptian blue?"

"Oh, goody. I get twice the fun," Leigh said without a hint of sarcasm. "Egyptian blue was made of calcium copper silicate." She cracked her knuckles and shook out her shoulders. "Hit me, Hari."

"What year was Hewlett-Packard founded?"

"Nineteen thirty-nine, in Palo Alto, California, which is now known as the hub of Silicon Valley." Her lips pursed. "Is that all?"

Hari adjusted his glasses. "For now."

I heard a crackle. Looking down, I saw that I'd smashed in the sides of my water bottle. I shoved it aside.

"My name is Ever Lawrence," I said, saying each letter carefully to keep from spewing out my real name. "I'm from Sacramento. I want to major in science fiction literature."

Hari's gaze zeroed in on me. "And who were the Hugo Awards named for?"

I pictured the Hugo seal—a silver rocket on a round sticker that was plastered to the front of so many of the books I owned. I knew that the award began in the early 1950s, but the exact date seemed to have dropped out of my head. The early winners were all the golden age writers, magazine short stories that turned into cheap paperbacks.

The first Christmas after my parents divorced, I got a box of old science fiction magazines from Santa. I didn't know that they were literally priceless. Inside of the pages of Tales of Wonder *and* Amazing Stories, *I found worlds to disappear into.*

I remembered the words set against the burning white screen of my laptop. I'd whispered them aloud before I clicked Send on my entrance essay, barely making the midnight deadline.

"The Hugos are named after Hugo Gernsback," I said, "the editor of *Amazing Stories* magazine."

Hari and Meg turned to Brandon. Leigh gave me a congratulatory bump with her knee.

"I'm Brandon Calistero," Brandon said. He wound one of his shoelaces around his index finger. His black and white Converse Chuck Taylors were battered to the breaking point. "I haven't decided on a major yet."

I saw the first glint of ice in Meg's face. It froze her lips into a single line and sent her eyebrows into stiff arches. She didn't like having her game derailed.

"That's fine," Hari said. "In a game of poker, how many combinations of a full house are possible?"

Brandon dropped his shoelace and frowned at Hari. "Three thousand seven hundred and forty-four ways. Providing that the cards haven't been dealt yet. Probability drops down to—"

"Correct," Meg interrupted. "Next?"

The boy with the big ears raised his hand in a nervous wave. His hair was shaved down to a light brown fuzz. It was oddly military, paired with his gray sweater vest and the Windsor knot of his tie. "Hi. I'm James Hobart, but everyone calls me Jams. I'm from Kent, Washington. I'm planning on majoring in theater arts. Well, dramaturgy, but it's under the umbrella of—"

"And what was Julie Taymor's first professional production?" Meg asked.

"*Oedipus Rex*? In Japan." Jams swallowed as Meg and Hari kept staring at him. "It was an opera."

"The purpose of this exercise . . ." Hari said, addressing the circle at large. Jams closed his eyes in relief. "Other than getting to know each other, is to instill in you the importance of being able to back up your work. Peripheral knowledge won't get you through the Melee. Always be prepared to show your work. If you're faking, you will be found out."

The hair on the back of my neck stood up. I resisted the urge to take another sip of water. Fidgeting was for the guilty.

"That said," Meg said with a titter, "these are the people you're going to spend your summer with. So let's play a quick name game before we crack open our binders. We are here to have fun, right?"

No one returned her smile but Leigh.

7

The binders didn't appear to have ever been touched by human hands. The edges were sharp yellow plastic. Inside, slabs of immaculate white paper were sectioned off with eight printed tabs: literature, art history, social sciences, history, music, science, philosophy, and essay.

The weight of what we had all signed on for had gone from figurative to literal, quick.

"Can anyone tell me the significance of the Tarrasch Melee's title?" Meg asked.

Kate's hand went up. "The Tarrasch rule is a finishing move in chess. The rook is placed behind passed pawns to protect its advance toward the opposing king."

"Right," Meg said. "The Melee works the same way. In order to make it to the final four, you have to be willing to use your teammates' abilities to move you forward."

Hunter gave a low whistle through his teeth. "Harsh."

"Only if you get cocky," Hari said sharply. "Right now, you know that the seven people sitting with you are going to go into the first skirmish with you. After that, all bets are off. If we make it to the final round—"

Meg raised a finger. "*When* we make it to the final round."

Hari huffed, but accepted the correction. "When we make it to the final round, the team will split in half. Just because you're entering in with your roommate doesn't mean that you get to win with them."

Meg folded her legs and clasped her hands around her flip-flops. Her cheerfully pink toenails wiggled under her fingers. "Statistically, yes, you have a one in four chance of making it to the championship once you get past the last skirmish. But it's impossible to truly calculate the odds. You'd have to pull in too many unknown factors—randomized test questions and percent-correct averages and the base IQ of the team. Until the final four are announced, you won't know if you're a pawn or a rook."

"Right now, all of you have an equal shot. Everyone at camp will be receiving the same study materials and the same prepared lectures from the counselors," Hari said. "You will eat the same meals and," his voice dipped down to a mutinous growl, "go to sleep at the same time on identical tiny beds."

"Which brings us to the last bit of business," Meg said. "Because I have to be able to tell the camp directors that I told you: overnight guests of any kind are verboten in your dorm. And the floors of the residence halls are not coed. That includes the meeting rooms and bathrooms. Remember that this is a competition. If someone sees you sneaking around and reports you, they are down one competitor. That's not exclusive to campers. Counselors of the opposite sex are also forbidden from your floor." She shot a dark look around the circle, but it lingered on Brandon. "Even if they're your bros."

Brandon's shoulders crept up toward his neck like he was trying to disappear inside of his own rib cage. It didn't seem likely that he had many bros scattered around the campus. But what did I know? There could be a bunch of typewriter guys around, trading tips on how to keep their keys greased.

"If you aren't comfortable reporting to me or Meg," Hari said placidly, "you also have Wendell Cheeseman's number in your welcome folder."

Somehow, I didn't think anyone was going to rush to chat with Wendell. He'd run off the second lunch was over, probably to change into a dry shirt. It was already clear that the counselors were the law here.

Around the quad, the rest of the teams started packing up their binders. The sun was starting to dip behind the dining hall. I couldn't believe that I was thinking about a sweater. I hoped that Beth had snuck one into my suitcase. She could usually be counted on for that sort of thing.

Hari checked his watch. "You will have all two hours to get acquainted with your study binders before reconvening for arts and crafts in your floor lounge."

"Arts and crafts?" Perla echoed. "For real?"

"Of course," Meg said. "This is camp. And I don't know about you, but I can't live in a plain cement box for three weeks. We're going to have a decorating party!"

"How avant-garde," Leigh observed, craning her neck to admire the splatter of glue and foil shards stuck to my poster board.

I held up my glimmering and gloopy hands. "I don't know what you mean. These are lens flares, obviously."

She giggled and handed me a wad of paper towels. Some things were true no matter what school you were at. Scratchy brown paper towels followed you from kindergarten to college. It was kind of comforting.

I scraped the glitter off of my hands before trying to salvage the mess that had been a sweet Firefly-class spaceship when Leigh had freehanded it, using a picture on my phone for reference.

The lounge's ergonomic stools and modular couches had been shoved against the lemon-yellow walls. The carpet was covered in a patchwork of brightly colored plastic tablecloths and dollar store art supplies. A phone speaker was pumping out twangy acoustic guitar that no one was paying any attention to.

Meg was at the front of the room, taping pieces of poster board together into a long banner. The Perfect Nerd Girl was beside her, looking up from her phone only when someone dared to ask her for another piece of paper.

Kate and Perla had set up next to Leigh and me out of team obligation. Already, everyone was sticking to their own packs. The other eight girls in the room were nameless crafters, making quiet conversation with their own teams as they shook glitter and passed around puff paint.

"You were serious about your space thing," Perla said, throwing side-eye at my paper.

"Science fiction," Leigh corrected for me, blithely running a paintbrush over her plain white paper. A trail of thorny vines trailed in the brush's wake.

"Science fiction isn't space?" Kate asked, not looking up from writing her own name in puff paint curlicues.

I reached for a Sharpie. Markers seemed safe. It was hard to spill a marker. I pushed the glitter pot farther away from me. "Space, robots, nuclear holocaust. Throw in ray guns or swords and I'm in."

Perla reached for a pair of child-safety scissors and snipped a piece of red construction paper into a large heart. "I've never heard someone list 'nuclear holocaust' as one of their interests."

"I don't want to live through one or anything," I said, concentrating on making the planets around the glittery ship-blob as round as possible. "I've always liked space. Other planets, other people. It's exciting."

Leigh switched paintbrushes and twisted blotches of yellow paint into blossoms. "What about your brother?"

I thought of Ethan and his endless collection of superhero T-shirts and his deep and abiding love of Cam Jansen mysteries. He could hang with lighter sci-fi movies—*Galaxy Quest, Star Wars*, anything that was animated—but he was nine and mostly freaked out by aliens and robots. And he'd fallen asleep during the last two of my Fourth of July showings of *Independence Day*, a sin I couldn't quite forgive.

I was starting to lose hope that he'd ever be ready for the grand *Terminator* marathon that I'd been saving to initiate him into the true sci-fi canon.

"Does he have a major picked?" Leigh asked.

"A major?" I asked, Ethan's round, light-skinned face still hovering in my mind. He was going into fourth grade. The last time I checked, he was still set on wanting to become a roofer because he liked ladders.

The marker went slack in my hand as I remembered that Ethan was Elliot Gabaroche's brother. I hadn't considered that I'd have to erase my real little brother from Ever's biography. Guilt sucker punched my heart as I forced myself to think about Isaiah instead.

"I'm not sure," I said. That was something that I should know. Sid definitely would, but she'd know something was up if I randomly texted her to ask. I'd spent Isaiah's entire life purposefully not memorizing facts about him. Since I couldn't admit this, I turned back to my paper. "He likes a lot of stuff."

It wasn't a lie. Isaiah had plenty of interests. But even Rayevich wouldn't let him major in whining, tattling, or disgusting food combinations.

"Ever's a twin," Leigh explained to Kate and Perla. "Her brother is on Team Three."

"You both got in?" Kate asked. She studied my face with a sudden curiosity. "Dizygotic twins only share fifty percent of their genes. What's the discrepancy between your IQs?"

I shrank back from her intense stare. I didn't like knowing that she was picturing my brain. "I don't know. It's not like we got the results back from the admissions test."

Perla tossed her scissors aside with a clatter that made Leigh and Kate jump. "Well, this is great. If Ever takes it easy on her twin, we'll never make it to the final round."

"We aren't those kind of twins." I didn't know much about being a twin, but I knew that there was no way I would ever take a dive for Isaiah.

"Oh yeah?" she sneered. "What are you going to do if only one of you gets the scholarship?"

Throw a parade from here all the way back to Sacramento? Buy his plane ticket to the academy?

"I'll go to school here and he won't," I said.

"Entering the Melee is a shortcut," Leigh said. "It's not the only way to get in. Isaiah could always apply in the fall."

"Not if I have anything to say about it," I muttered.

"Is that a Firefly?" asked a voice above me.

I tilted my head back and saw the Perfect Nerd Girl staring down at my poster. Her eyes were pale to the point of being nearly reflective. Combined with her supremely fake red hair, the overall effect verged on terrifying.

"'Love keeps her in the air,'" I said, unable to stop the quote from tumbling out. I didn't know if I wanted her to like me or if I just wanted to stop her before she started gatekeeping. A lot of old-school Joss Whedon fans thought that anyone who couldn't talk about the vampire shows didn't deserve to be a fan of the rest of the Whedonverse. Like just enjoying something wasn't enough to be considered a fan.

Besides, I might not have known anything about *Buffy* or whatever, but I could talk about *Titan A.E.* or *Alien Resurrection* for hours.

The Perfect Nerd Girl smiled. Not enough to show teeth, but it took some of the edge off of her face as she said, "And the glitter makes her *gorram* fancy." She nodded to the other girls. "I'm here to take your water cup. We need to pack up before dinner. And Meg is . . ." She glanced over her shoulder at Meg, who was deep into making her banner. "Otherwise occupied."

Kate looked up, the puff paint tube poised between her thumb and forefinger. "You went to the Messina, right?"

The Perfect Nerd Girl twitched a shrug. "All four years."

"What's the incentive for you to come back to be counselors?" Kate asked.

"Yeah," Perla jumped in. "Don't you guys have jobs and apartments and lives?"

The Perfect Nerd Girl pressed her lips together, locking back whatever had first leaped to the tip of her tongue. She tried again, measuring the words. "We get class credits and free housing. Not paying rent for two months is a definite bonus. And we get to see each other again. We all spread out for college." She tucked her hair behind her ears. "But mostly we all owed a favor that got called in. The proverbial 'offer you can't refuse.'"

"Then why didn't Cornell's girlfriend come, too?" I asked.

Her eyes locked in on my face. I had to force myself not to flinch away. "Because she's much, much smarter than the rest of us."

She bent down and took the water cup before moving on to the next group.

"Do you think the Messina teaches all of their students how to be that vague?" I asked no one in particular.

"Okay, everybody," Meg crowed, bouncing to her feet at the front of the room. "It's time to decorate. But the rule is, no one can decorate their own room or the room of anyone on their team! Go introduce yourself to a new Onward lady and get her room key!"

"No," Perla said, mashing her valentine heart to her poster. "I think they're all dicks."

8

While lights-out was set, unshakably, for ten thirty, there wasn't a real "lights-on." The sun threw a wrench into the idea of controlling when people could and couldn't be awake. As I stretched on the cement outside of the residence hall, I considered that, if I'd bothered asking one of the RAs, there were probably rules about when we were officially allowed to wander campus.

But that was why I hadn't asked.

After hours of falling in and out of consciousness on my new tiny mattress and scratchy sheets, it was bliss to be out under the bruise-purple sky. The air was so cold that it felt solid as it scraped through my sinuses and pressed against my cheeks.

I'd left my headphones in the dorm. The only music I wanted this morning was the patter of my own feet on the concrete.

Hours away from breakfast, I stopped worrying about getting lost. Losing myself on campus was the first step to knowing where everything was. I passed the library and made a sharp turn, heading straight toward a cluster of buildings and the arboretum that spread across the back of the campus.

As I approached a squat brick building with a sign that read

"LeRoy Hall," there was a clomping sound in the grass behind me, and a wheeze, before, "El, wait up!"

I closed my eyes but didn't slow down. Not my name. Not my problem.

"You're the worst twin in the world, you know," Isaiah gasped. From the sound of his footfalls, he was stumbling behind me. He must have been trying to run in skate shoes. Too slippery.

"I believe it," I said, refusing to look behind me. "Considering I was born to an entirely different woman from an entirely separate egg over a year before you."

In my peripheral vision I could see a hint of dreadlocks. I turned my head a fraction and saw my cousin gasping for air beside me. I was moderately surprised to see that he didn't sweat ranch dressing.

"I can see why you're trying to get out of the academy," I said. "You're in terrible shape. BMT would kill you."

"I have asthma," he panted. "And I had to catch up with you."

Against my better judgment, I slowed—just a little. "Had to?"

"I figured you wouldn't want to talk about our, you know, *secrets* in front of your team."

"Don't get all winky-nudgy with me. The secret that we aren't really twins is entirely your doing, remember? I really don't care what people think."

"You don't care if people find out that your name is Elliot Gabaroche and you ran away from home to win a scholarship to a school your parents would never let you attend?"

"Is this the part where you start legitimately blackmailing me?"

He snorted. "You don't have anything I want."

"How did you know that I would be up this early?"

"I saw you stretching outside of the dorms and followed you out."

"Oh, good. I was afraid the answer was going to be something creepy."

"It's not creepy. I thought we should clarify our story."

I lengthened my stride again. "You can clarify as long as you can keep up."

His face tightened into pained concentration as his arms flapped wildly. "I assume you've been telling people that you're from Sacramento?"

"You mean because that's where I live?"

He rolled his eyes grandly, lids quivering and tongue lolling. If I also looked like a demented ventriloquist dummy when I did that, I'd have to stop immediately.

"Are you going to answer every question with a question?" he asked. "Because eventually my lungs will start to spasm. I can already feel my mucus thickening . . ."

"Don't talk to me about your mucus," I begged. While the dining hall's food wasn't going to win any awards, I did have to eat it at some point after the sun was fully risen. "Yes, I have told people that I'm from Sacramento."

"That's fine," he said, apparently no longer in danger of having a full asthma attack. "So, we live in Sacramento and go to your high school—"

"And you never skipped a grade because apparently you're my age now."

"Huh." He frowned at a cement bench as we passed it. "I hadn't thought about that. That sucks. It's really rare for people to skip a grade."

"Uh-huh. Now how will the rest of genius camp know how smart you are?"

He wasn't listening. He swatted one of his bouncing dreads away from his face. "I guess we can keep your parents. Does your stepmom have to be white?"

I curled my lip at him. "What do you mean? She *is* white."

"It raises a lot of questions."

"No. It raises literally zero questions."

"Okay, fine. So, we have a white stepmom—"

"You could also call her Beth. That's her name."

"—and a half brother."

I clenched my teeth together. I hated the term *half brother*. I hadn't found out about it until after Ethan was already in preschool. No one ever explained to me that there was a difference, that I was supposed to have some kind of lesser relationship with him because we had separate moms.

"What's his name?" Isaiah continued in a huff. "Evan?"

"Ethan," I snapped. The day he was born, I'd climbed up on Beth's hospital bed and petted his conical bald head. I'd apologized that I got to share Dad's name and he didn't. "And keep his name out of your mouth."

"Don't bite my head off. I've never met him. How old is he?"

"He's nine. Just . . . forget about it. We don't have to have a little brother." I didn't like the idea of sharing Ethan, even a fictional version of him. Isaiah would probably tell everyone that he was Ethan's favorite twin, or make him into a Tiny Tim character to get sympathy from his team.

The sidewalk curved left into a man-made forest. I wondered if talking to Isaiah had distracted me from the sign or if the university assumed that everyone on campus would be smart enough to figure out that they were in the arboretum by the lack of buildings and increase of arbor. The path wound between trees and bright bursts of flowers as colorful as the sunrise we could no longer see through the thick branches that twisted together into a twiggy ceiling.

If Isaiah was moved by the beauty of our surroundings, he buried it in a sniff. "How did you hear about the Melee?"

"In real life or in your fantasy world where we're twins?"

"In real life," he said, unperturbed.

"I got an admissions packet so that I could look through the brochure not on my computer. There was a flyer included about the Melee. I didn't give it a lot of thought, but . . . I don't know. I started thinking about it more and more." Whenever my mom pointed out that I didn't have much longer left at home. Or when my dad made a snide comment about the air force over dinner. When my future started to feel too much like the final event in the Mom versus Dad championship fight, like my choice of career would decide who got to be the good parent.

"And then I was signing up to take the admissions test," I finished. I hazarded a look at Isaiah. "What about you?"

"There was an article about it in *Young Mensan Magazine*."

I tried to be shocked that (a) there was a *Young Mensan Magazine* and that (b) Isaiah was a subscriber, but it checked out as his brand of uncool and elitist. Aunt Bobbie had always padded out Isaiah's ego with useless accessories, as though his IQ wouldn't count unless it was tangibly better than other people's. Like when we were kids and he got all of the Smithsonian science experiment kits. Or when Bobbie had decided to move off the air force base so that Isaiah could be closer to his chichi charter school.

I'd never asked how Sid had felt about her family moving off base while she was at the academy. Or how Uncle Marcus felt, coming back from deployment to a new home. Not that he came back very often. Lawrences weren't great at being tied to anything but the military.

Up ahead, the path forked. At the point of divergence, there was a tall wooden fingerpost with multiple arrows pointing in all directions—like the signage in the 100 Aker Wood, but instead of guiding toward Eeyore's house or Pooh Corner, there was Fort Farm, Community Garden, Mud Trail, and South Parking Lot.

"Fort Farm," Isaiah read. "What's with all the alliteration here?"

I shoved the sweat from my forehead back into my hair and took the right branch of the road. Isaiah made a gurgling sound before his frictionless shoe soles started scraping behind me again.

"What if we jog instead of running full out?" he asked. "It's hard to talk and run."

"Aren't we done talking? Because I feel done."

"A couple more things," he said. There was a rustle of paper. I turned in time to see him pulling a piece of lined paper out of his back pocket. He narrowed his eyes at me before I could say anything. "It'd be suspicious if our stories didn't line up. I don't want to get caught and be sent home, do you?"

I resisted the urge to groan.

It turned out that the paper was full of questions, most of them inane. Did we share a bedroom? *No.* Whose bedroom was bigger? *Neither. Beth used her real estate prowess to find us a house with bedrooms with exactly the same square footage.* Was I allergic to any foods? *Kiwis.* What was our high school mascot? *Warriors.* Could I pretend not to know how to drive, since it'd be weird if I knew and he didn't? *No problem. Left my license at home anyway.*

"What the hell is that?" Isaiah blurted as we hit the edge of the arboretum. The trees abruptly stopped and the world ahead of us was flat and green, except for a dozen small wooden structures sprouting out of the ground.

"Fort Farm," I said. "They meant it literally."

Each building was built out of five wooden pallets—the kind usually seen on forklifts at Costco. With sharply pointed roofs and only two walls, they looked like house skeletons. Except for one that had been draped in navy blue sheets. A literal blanket fort in the middle of a field.

The sheets rustled. Isaiah took a jump backwards, as though expecting a wild animal to come charging out. Instead, there was red bedhead, an unfolding of limbs, and then the Perfect Nerd Girl standing in an R2-D2 nightshirt that skimmed the top of her knees. On brand, even at sunrise.

She squinted her reflective eyes at us and yawned. "Ever, right? From Meg's team?"

I nodded. "Yeah. Uh, hi." Isaiah coughed and I jerked my head at him. "This is my brother. We were out for a jog."

"Mm," the Perfect Nerd Girl grunted, her mouth set into a deep frown. "Jog elsewhere."

"Sure thing," Isaiah said. He spun on his heel and put on speed for the first time, tearing back the way we came.

I thought I heard voices behind me as I followed him, but when I glanced over my shoulder the counselor was gone and the sheets were still.

"God," Isaiah whispered as we passed the directional sign again. "Can you imagine how much shit we'd be in if that RA had heard us talking about not being related? We almost outed ourselves."

"Yeah, we really lucked out there. I guess we'll have to stop talking about it forever."

I wondered if anyone else knew that one of our resident advisers had forsaken her post on our floor. And—if no one else knew—what would it mean that I did?

9

The first day of classes loomed like an electrical storm over the cafeteria. Every table seemed to be filled with equal parts excitement and terror. And supreme disappointment in the breakfast options.

I should have remembered, said Oscar Wilde, *that when one is going to lead an entirely new life, one requires regular and wholesome meals.*

"What's our first lecture today?" I asked, looking up from the oil slick that was my plate. The sausages were cold in the middle. I dipped one in lukewarm maple syrup, hoping that the temperature would balance out.

It didn't.

"Literature with Hari," Leigh said. "Then philosophy, lunch, art history, and essay prep."

Galen snorted. "How can we have an entire class on essays? Didn't we all prove we could write one when we got in?"

"It'll be fine," Brandon said, balancing his tray under his nose as he settled onto the bench between Galen and Hunter. "Ben's our essay tutor. It'll probably be a study hall."

I had hoped it was the whole mistaken-for-a-ghost thing that had made Brandon so interesting yesterday, but there was something about him that immediately made my skin feel too tight. I couldn't stop myself from examining him—his hair wet around his ears and neck, his voice extra woolly from sleepiness. It made me feel hot and gangly and like maybe Oregon didn't have enough oxygen.

"Who's Ben?" Kate asked.

"Third-floor resident adviser," Leigh said. "Messina graduate, currently attending the University of California at Berkeley, majoring in political science." She winced around at seven blank stares. "What? I'm the only person who read through the binder?"

"You can just say UC Berkeley," I said.

"Noted," she chirped. And I was positive that she actually had made a mental note. While I'd dressed for the day, she'd started memorizing the brands and properties of the hair products I used. She claimed it kept her brain limber.

"I am dying," Perla wailed, digging her fingertips into her temples and smooshing the skin forward. "Who do I have to blow for a cup of coffee?"

"That would also be Ben," Brandon said. "He's in charge of the kitchen." Perla glared at him, and he shrank back on the bench as though he could hide behind Jams's right ear. "Sorry. Didn't mean to be heteronormative. There's a female counselor on kitchen duty, too. I think her name's Simone?"

"Simone Freeman, Rayevich rising junior," Leigh said. She propped herself up on her elbows and leaned toward Perla. "Regardless of your sexual preferences, I would suggest appealing to Simone for coffee. She's a philosophy major with an emphasis in ethics. You could present a case for the social mores of daily caffeine intake versus the subjugation you feel juice presents to your lifestyle. And I thought I heard her talking about doing a Starbucks run for the counselors."

"Oh hell no," Perla snarled, launching herself off the bench.

"When did you overhear the counselors talking?" I asked Leigh under my breath, as we watched Perla stomp across the dining hall toward the counselors' table. "We stood in line at the breakfast bar together."

"Hm?" She blinked at me as she took a bite of squelchy pancake. She shook her head as she chewed. "Oh, that was a statistical gamble. Adults eighteen to twenty-four make up forty percent of Starbucks' annual sales. With twelve counselors that fit that demographic currently fighting off sleep deprivation and looking forward to their first day of teaching, someone's going to share Perla's need for coffee." She batted her eyelashes at the rest of the table. "I could call her back over?"

We all turned to watch Perla wedge herself between two counselors at the table in front of the window. Her hands immediately starting pointing and flapping as her rant built up steam again.

"No," Galen said firmly. "Let her get her fix. Maybe she'll be nicer."

"Caffeine causes your cerebral neurons to increase fire," Brandon said, stirring his cereal. "Your pituitary gland shoots out adrenaline, in case you're being attacked. Most people aren't nicer when they enter fight or flight."

Kate sighed. "We've established that she's neither an afternoon nor a night person. Our last hope was a spike in cheerfulness before noon."

Hunter put his head in his hands. His shoulders quivered against today's too-tight T-shirt. It took a second before the sound of his giggles slipped between his fingers.

"Sorry," he wheezed, wiping his eyes with his knuckles. "It's just—I don't know. When you think about going to genius camp, you don't think, *I'm going to be surrounded by geniuses.*"

"Because it's implied in the name?" Jams asked.

"Technically, it's not 'genius camp,'" Kate said, wiggling a dozen air quotes next to her long face. "It's a camp for the gifted."

Galen laughed. "Tell that to your IQ test."

"I get what you mean, Hunter," I said. "Back home, my friends would have just called Perla a downer and moved on."

Jams snorted. "'Downer' would be a decent start."

Kate rolled her eyes. "Borderline personality might get us closer to the heart of the problem."

"But that's what's great about being here," Leigh said. "There's no dumbing anything down. Everyone can keep up. Can you imagine what life would be like if you always got to hang out with people as smart as you?"

"More problematic than you'd imagine," Brandon said to his cereal. He caught my eye and added, "Probably."

I felt like I'd eaten a crate of kiwis and had surrendered myself to anaphylactic shock.

Not that it mattered. Boys were the gateway to full-on *Importance of Being Earnest*-y farce. First it was one cute boy making eyes at you over breakfast, and then it was all Wildean misunderstandings and double entendres.

No, thank you.

"At least we get to see the library today," Kate said.

My thoughts evaporated into a record scratch as I whipped to look at her. "Wait, what?"

"The library," she repeated. Slower this time and with more tongue flapping. "Where else would we study literature?"

"Ever, seriously," Leigh scoffed. "Open your binder."

10

The Maurice T. Lauritz Memorial Library was cold and quiet inside. Brass placards gleamed on the edge of each bookcase. The floors were covered in deep crimson carpet that muffled even Leigh's skipping steps. Every study table had a small lamp with a pleated yellow lampshade.

No matter how much Hari insisted that every self-respecting Mudder called it "the Mo-Lo," I refused to besmirch the Lauritz's majesty with skanky abbreviations.

This building, this palace of literature, was the entire reason I'd run away from home. Somewhere below me, past the spiral staircase, deep in the jungle of polished redwood bookcases, was The Science Fiction Section. All capital letters.

Rayevich didn't have the standard Asimov to Zahn catalog that you could browse at the county library. There were no gaps in the Rayevich collection. If there was an English translation, it was here. If it'd been out of print for fifty years, Rayevich had found a copy and bound it in plastic to keep the dust off. And they kept the fantasy books elsewhere. No cross-pollination to distract.

I had read an article about the collection on a blog my freshman year. I'd ordered my first Rayevich admissions packet the next day.

And now I was here. I was so close. I could almost taste the hundreds of books that—if I won the Melee—I would spend four years consuming. And by the time I got here, the collection would be even bigger.

Hari burst my bubble with the slam of a yellow binder. It rattled the mason jar full of pencils and highlighters on the coffee table in front of him. "For the literature portion of the Melee, each of you will be required to analyze the short stories in your study materials. There are five stories, covering multiple categories of English literature. Wilde, Hammett, Jackson, Lahiri, and Murakami."

The air-conditioning sank deep into my skin and froze my bones. I hugged my binder closer to my chest. "Oscar Wilde?"

"Oscar Fingal O'Flahertie Wills Wilde," Jams said, eagerly squishing himself deeper into the armchair he'd claimed. "Born in 1854 to—"

"There will be no questions on the author," Hari interrupted sharply. He took a deep pull from the Starbucks cup in his hand. Leigh's gamble had paid off, although it didn't seem to be enough to erase the purple bags magnified under Hari's glasses.

I flipped past the pages describing proper literary analysis techniques and found the list of our short stories. There it was, the very first title, printed in bold: "The Nightingale and the Rose" by Oscar Wilde.

More Wilde quotes to clutter my brain. Balls.

"The library will be at your disposal for the hour you're with me and during your study periods," Hari said, smothering a yawn that twisted his lips into a Picasso slant. "But because you are guests here, none of the books can leave the Mo-Lo. The book sensors at the front door are armed. Once you finish with a book, place it on the return cart and a counselor will come through to reshelve at the end of the day." He gestured to the mason jar on the table. "Help yourselves to a pencil and a highlighter. Both will need to be returned at the end of the hour."

Galen wet his lips and shot a look around at the rest of us. "That's it?"

Hari took another long drink. "Have any of you read all five of the stories and made notes on the authorial intention and literary allusions contained within?"

I felt Leigh's hand start to raise. I kicked her foot and she stilled.

"Off you go," Hari said, losing the fight against his yawn. It muddied his words, but his hand waved us away. Apparently, we'd worn out our welcome in the lounge.

I stood up, tucking my binder under my arm as I grabbed a pencil and a highlighter. The rest of the team followed me down the stairs.

"Ten bucks says he's going to nap up there," Hunter muttered.

"He's drinking green tea," Perla said, her voice weighted with disgust. "With soy milk."

"That's just wrong," Leigh shuddered.

"Green tea only has a third of the caffeine that coffee does," Kate said, pulling up the rear. "So, no, Hunter, I don't think anyone will be taking your bet."

We all gathered at the base of the stairs, eight yellow binders displaying the camp logo held close.

"I guess we'll split up?" I said, jerking my head toward the tables laid out between aisles.

"What else would we do?" Perla asked. "Do it elementary style and play popcorn?"

"I was always more of a Heads Up, Seven Up kind of guy," Brandon said.

"Oh, man," Hunter laughed. "I ruled at Heads Up, Seven Up."

"You peeked, didn't you?" I asked.

His lips lifted into that practiced smile. "Of course. How else do you win?"

"Sensing the auras of your classmates," Kate sniffed.

"Not cheating," Brandon said.

"Elementary school was the tits," Jams said. "When was the last time you got to have a Capri-Sun?"

"Everyone track down a dictionary and look up *facetious*," Perla said, swishing toward the nearest table.

"Tomorrow," Leigh said, "I will not help her get coffee."

"Tomorrow," Galen said, his eyes disappearing under the apples of his cheeks, "we should totally play Heads Up, Seven Up."

As the rest of the team claimed tables and study cubicles, I wandered deeper into the stacks. I'd come too far not to glimpse the sci-fi section.

Luckily, there were signs leading the way. After weaving through M–O literature, a hard left at philosophy, and passing a dark information desk, I was standing at the rounded arch that had been the background on my laptop for three years. Another brass plaque was built into the side of the arch. I pressed my fingers into the engraved letters.

SCIENCE FICTION SPECIAL COLLECTION, EST. JANUARY 1, 2001.

Underneath, the message repeated in binary.

I honestly didn't know if I'd ever been happier.

Other than the gallery wall of screen-printed posters advertising different fictional planets, the room wasn't much different from the rest of the library. The study tables had the same small lamps and there were a few of the armchairs that had been up in the lounge. But they were set apart from the collection.

I settled on my stomach between two of the tall redwood bookcases. When I won the Melee, this room would be my reward. These books were the only incentive I needed.

Not ready to start committing more Wilde to memory, I started with the last story in the packet, switching between highlighting and making small annotations in the margins—*monkey, magical realism, secret name.*

After I wrote my first note on the second story—*What kind of name is Twinkle?*—I popped my knuckles and stretched. My eyes slid right. On the bottom shelf, there was a myth wrapped in an ivory jacket and printed with bold yellow font.

I have to keep studying, I thought. *I can't fall behind.*

But the forbidden book was already in my hand.

Octavia Butler's books took up an entire shelf on my bookcase at home. When I was up late and too restless to sleep, Butler's stories kept me company. Considering she wrote terrifying books, this was probably not normal. But I'd been addicted to her prose since sixth grade, when my mom had sent me a copy of *Kindred.*

Survivor was the only book of hers that I'd never been able to get my hands on. Butler had hated it so much that she'd refused to let it stay in print. It could have been three hundred pages of stick figures for all I cared. It was the missing link in the Patternist series.

All three of my parents had laughed every time I'd asked for a copy. Even used, it was worth hundreds of dollars.

But it was here. It was in my hands. Ignoring it would be the height of sacrilege. Like spitting on the pope or telling Katee Sackhoff that you preferred Dirk Benedict's Lieutenant Starbuck.

Ugh. I offended myself just thinking about that.

It wasn't like I was going to go to sleep at lights-out anyway. I could catch up on the rest of the short stories before the next time we met with Hari.

I opened the book. The pages were musty sweet.

"Ever?" Leigh's voice dragged me away from the Kohns' planet and thrust me—bleary-eyed and wobbly—back into the present. I took a breath as the seconds since I'd started reading righted themselves into long minutes. Balls. Were we late for our next lecture?

"I'm here," I said hoarsely. I tore off a strip of paper from my binder and stuffed it into *Survivor.* I forced myself to put it back in the empty space on the shelf. Looking down, I realized I'd cut off the first paragraph of "This Blessed House." Balls again.

Leigh appeared at the end of the aisle. "Oh, good. I knew this is where I'd find you. Kate went to check the bathrooms. Not that you couldn't have to pee, but—Are you okay?"

I closed my binder, hiding the evidence of my academic infidelity.

I was sure that Leigh wouldn't understand getting sidetracked on the first day of classes. She'd probably read through all five stories with time to spare and moved on to finding research books for the next section. That morning, she had talked about wanting to find the text our art history guides were pulled from.

I got to my feet, making a show of patting down the pockets of my shorts.

"I lost track of time," I said. "I don't know where I left my phone."

"It's on your desk, between your face wash and your lotion," she said, the worrying draining out of her face. "Come on. Hari's counting the pencils and highlighters before he lets us leave the building. And I'd like to, you know, learn something today."

11

We learned nothing.

Okay, it wasn't exactly nothing. The study packets were full of new ideas, dates, and philosophical questions. My retinas burned with words emblazoned with highlighter strokes. My hand cramped from making notes.

It was the counselors' silence that was starting to wear on everyone's nerves. In all of our classes, our collegiate advisers hadn't said more than "Open your binders." Some of them hadn't even introduced themselves. I still didn't know the Perfect Nerd Girl's real name.

All of the vim and vigor of the first day had disappeared like fog burning off in the sunlight. Each morning, we fought for shower stalls in the communal bathroom. The teams sat together for breakfast, lunch, and dinner. We trudged from building to building, sitting in silence except for the rustling of binder paper. Even our first music class had consisted of us reading our notes while we "imagined a symphony," and our counselor, Faulkner, put on a pair of headphones.

"It has to be a test. Like hazing," I said, as the team sat down to yet another lackluster lunch on Friday afternoon. We'd been released from Cornell's class without so much as a handshake.

"I think they're all completely incompetent," Perla said. "It's not like they're that much older than us. They aren't certified to teach us anything."

"You're just mad that they got your coffee order wrong this morning," Kate huffed.

"Well," Perla said, stabbing her fork into her iceberg lettuce salad, "if they can't tell the difference between white chocolate and caramel, then I don't want them trying to explain something that would actually require a spare neuron."

Galen dragged his hands over his face, his fingers leaving trails on his cheeks. "I've got a massive study hangover. It's all I've done for three days. I miss TV."

"There's a movie in the quad tonight," Leigh said.

"They're playing *The Breakfast Club*," Jams growled. "Again."

I tugged at my hair. "That's every night this week."

"They could switch it up next week and give us a night of *Pretty in Pink*," Brandon chuckled.

"I hate Molly Ringwald's face," Perla said.

"You hate everyone's face," Kate said under her breath.

One of Perla's eyebrows arched. "Mostly yours. You're looking particularly moisturized today."

"I didn't take your stupid face lotion!" Kate groaned. "Why would I?"

"Yeah, someone else came into our room and took my moisturizer," Perla said stiffly. "I'm sure Cheeseman needed my Kiehl's for his gross, sweaty head."

Galen threw up his hands. "What happened to Cheeseman? Shouldn't he be supervising something?"

"He was at dinner last night for about a minute," I said. I'd caught a glimpse of Cheeseman's bald head bobbing around the counselors' table, but he'd disappeared before we'd been excused to stack our plates.

"We are two weeks away from the first round of the Melee," Hunter said. "We're totally screwed."

"We'll mutiny!" Jams said, punching his fist into the air. "It can't be only our team who isn't learning anything. There's forty-eight of us and only twelve counselors. If we rally, they can't hold us down."

"Truth," said Galen.

Kate crouched low, her chin almost landing in her sandwich as she used the rest of us as cover. She lowered her voice to a hiss as her bright blue eyes slid from person to person. "Do you really want to unionize with our competitors?"

Jams mockingly mirrored her hunched back and loud whisper. "No. I really want to tie down all of our fake professors until they're forced to actually bloody teach something, but I don't think that will work."

"James—Jams—whatever you're calling yourself," Perla said, "you are an American. You are from Oregon. You do not have an accent, pip pip. So stop being so bleeding, bloody, bollocksing barmy."

Jams's ears lit up neon pink as he thrust a shaking finger at her. "My mum—"

"'Mom,'" Perla corrected loudly. "You're putting a *U* where an *O* goes, you Anglophile arsehole."

"I am not an Anglophile!" he shot back.

"Yesterday, you wore Union Jack socks," Leigh noted, running a hand over her scalp.

"Leave him alone," Hunter said. "He has dual nationality."

"Ch-cheers, Hunter," Jams said, his tongue tripping with indignation. "Not that I have to prove anything to you all, but, yes, I am a citizen of both the United States and the United Kingdom."

"Fifty bucks says he's never been outside of Oregon," Perla said in a cruel singsong.

Jams's mouth pinched tight into whatever the opposite of a poker face was.

I couldn't stomach the idea of Perla winning this argument. None of us would benefit from her having a feather in her cap. "We can't mutiny and we can't force anyone to teach us anything. We'll just keep studying."

"And watching *The Breakfast Club*," grumbled Kate.

"Screw that," Hunter said. "I'll study, but I refuse to watch the same movie every night. I tried watching it on Monday. And guess what? *The Breakfast Club* sucks."

I gave him a small salute, remembering at the last minute to let my wrist limp to keep it from being too regulation. "'So say we all.'"

"Mail call!"

All of our heads turned toward the source of the trill. Meg was prancing toward us, flapping an envelope around her face like a fan.

"Mail?" Galen repeated, his mouth slack.

"For one B. Calistero, care of Camp Onward," Meg said, handing the envelope to Brandon.

Jams craned his neck, trying to see the return address. "I thought you were local, Bran?"

"I am," Brandon said, tucking the letter into his binder. "I have friends."

"Friends who don't know your email address?" Galen asked.

"Or what century this is?" Perla added.

"Be nice," Meg said, smiling daggers. "There's something to be said for epistolary discourse. If you want the handwriting analyzed, B, you know that Mary-Anne is—"

"Thanks, Meg," Brandon interrupted, squirming under the team's attention. "I think I'll be all right without."

She planted her hands on her hips, swaying cheerfully. "And how is my favorite team doing? I didn't see any of you at movie night yesterday. We have a machine on loan that makes the most delicious kettle corn you've ever eaten. Seriously, I thought about it the whole flight here. And there's always regular popcorn and candy." She ticked off her fingers. "Skittles, sour straws, licorice—both red and black—and all the fun-sized chocolate you could ever hope for. Unless you were hoping for peanut butter cups. I think Peter ate all of those already."

She shook herself and clasped her hands to her chest like she was bracing to burst into song. "It would really mean a lot to me if you guys could come tonight for some Team One bonding time. I know you have a ton of studying to do, but I feel like I haven't seen you since classes started. And we're showing a great movie . . ."

"Bollocks," muttered Jams.

I couldn't have agreed more.

12

I grant you that it was a different time," Leigh whispered, a fistful of kettle corn clutched in her fist. "But are we really supposed to believe that a parent would buy their son a whole carton of cigarettes for Christmas?"

"Cigarette packs have had the surgeon general's warning on them since nineteen sixty-six," Kate whispered back. "I looked it up after I watched this last night."

I bit a licorice whip in half. "If he said, 'I've never had a Christmas present in my life,' I'd feel worse for him. Now, it seems like his dad was trying to get him something he'd want. He probably is a smoker, right?"

Kate scrunched her face in thought. "I think the implication is that Bender's dad wants him to die."

The movie flickered against a sheet hung between two trees in the center of the quad. With the blankets spread out in the grass and the kettle corn machine churning out sweet and salty gold in the lobby of the residence hall, movie night had a sort of drive-in feeling to it.

Day five of the *Breakfast Club* marathon had chased off most of the other teams and their counselors, leaving us with room to sprawl in the grass. Bryn Mawr was writing in a small notebook next to Meg, who was contentedly stuffing her face with kettle corn. Hari was sitting behind the projector cart, unabashedly reading a hardcover book that was missing its dust jacket.

"That blond kid is the smallest wrestler I've ever seen. What's his weight class? Ninety pounds?" Hunter asked from behind us, twitching as a mosquito flew too close to his head. Meg's homemade bug spray succeeded in making us smell like Vicks VapoRub but didn't do much when it came to repelling insects.

"Does anyone else think he and the nerd kid look too much alike?" Jams asked, hugging his knees to his chest.

"That's the point," Perla said. "The movie is trying—heavy-handedly—to point out that, despite their archetypes, they're not that different after all. It's total horseshit. Five white kids from the same rich imaginary suburb would be basically interchangeable."

"You had me and then you lost me," Galen said. "With the racism."

"You can't be racist against white people," Leigh hummed. "FYI."

"For real," I agreed.

"Five Caucasian cisgender heterosexuals from homes with a median income that would allow for all of them to go to school in Shermer do not represent range," Perla drawled. "Popular versus not popular is not diversity of circumstance. It's caring too much about what other people think."

"Oh," said Galen. "That makes more sense."

"Of course it does," she snapped. "I'm a fucking genius."

Brandon's black and white Chucks crunched through the grass toward us. He held a brown paper bag of popcorn close to his chest—his third. Not that I was keeping count.

"What'd I miss?" he asked as he collapsed next to Jams.

"Perla said something insightful and then ruined it by continuing to talk," Jams said, scooping up a handful of fresh popcorn and stuffing it in his mouth. A fun-size Snickers flew through the air and bounced off his shoulder.

Brandon picked up the Snickers and unwrapped it. "Pretty standard."

"Whatever," Perla said. "I didn't come here to make friends."

Hunter giggled. "Even you have to know that makes you sound like a reality show villain."

Perla sneered at him as she unwrapped a fun-size candy bar and dropped the foil on her blanket. "I've been going to college summer sessions since I was nine. Princeton, Berkeley, Yale. I've tried them all on, stuck on teams with people like you." She popped the candy into her mouth and chewed as she continued, "I pack to a science. I study alone. If there's a talent night, guess what? I'm gonna skip it because it's extraneous bullshit."

"What does a nine-year-old do at Yale?" I asked, unable to contain my curiosity. I tried to picture my little brother at an Ivy League school for the summer, but it wouldn't compute. He would be so tiny next to all of those ivory towers.

"Algebra and creative writing, mostly," Perla said, nostrils flaring. "So, sorry, but I used up all my camp BFF energy like five summer institutes ago. I'm here to get my scholarship and go home where it's actually summer. And I literally could give a fuck about how that makes you feel about me."

"Then why come to movie night?" Galen asked.

She let out a short sigh and threw a glare over her shoulder at the counselors. "Meg wouldn't let me bring the kettle corn up to my dorm."

The pocket of my hoodie buzzed. I reached in and pulled out my cell phone. Beth's picture stared back at me, her button nose scrunched in response to the camera being aimed at her.

"Who's that?" Leigh asked. The bright light of the phone's screen threw bluish shadows on her face as she peered over my shoulder.

"My stepmom," I said. I hopped to my feet. "I'll be right back."

"Bring more kettle corn!" Kate called after me.

"And some sour straws!" Hunter added.

I gave them a thumbs-up as I jogged to the edge of the field.

Behind me, I could hear Jams's voice saying, "Hey, Perla. I've been meaning to ask you: Who is John Galt?" Holding in a snicker, I pressed the phone to my ear.

"Hello?"

"Hi, sweetheart," Beth's voice echoed. She didn't believe in holding phones near her face. She said the screen made her skin greasy. She was perpetually on speakerphone. "I'm not interrupting anything, am I? I'm on my way home from rehearsal. I wanted to say hi. We miss you."

I slipped inside the heavy glass door of the lobby. The warm sugar smell of the kettle corn machine filled my lungs like airborne cotton candy. "I miss you, too. I haven't had a decent breakfast in days."

"Poor darling. We had Snoopy waffles this morning. They didn't taste the same without you. Also, I forgot to put the cinnamon in."

I smiled into the phone as something cold ricocheted around my ribs. "I found the sweatshirt you packed for me. I'm wearing it now."

"Well, I'm glad you're warm, if hungry. It's about ninety-two here right now. I'm running the air conditioner for all it's worth. You know how the theater swelters in the summer. And tonight was my first time wearing my wig."

"They're wigging you?" I asked, walking up to the small concessions table that the counselors had put together. I shook out a sandwich bag and started filling it with candy. "But your hair is basically the same length it was the last time you did *Earnest*."

"Oh, the director has very firm ideas about the duality of Gwendolen and Cecily. We'll have identical wigs in different colors. Big Gibson girl buns. It's exactly like wearing a fur hat stabbed into your head with bobby pins. They're a little much, if you ask me. But no one did."

The fact that I wouldn't see Beth on stage this summer hadn't sunk in before. I'd known it logically. Thinking about *Earnest* was what had inspired me to leave home to begin with. But Beth had never played Gwendolen without me in the audience. Would Woodland recycle her costume from the last time? Or would they do something kooky—like set the play in the Old West or feudal Japan or something else that would piss off the subscribers?

I wondered if she'd miss me quoting lines with her. The show would go on, because it had to. The saying said so. But still, it made me sad to know that I wouldn't be there.

"Costumers," I said faintly.

"Costumers," she agreed with a laugh. "But everything is the same here. Your father is deep into this new case and Ethan continues to hate baseball camp until it's time to come home."

"Has he hit a ball yet?"

"I don't think so. But he stopped getting hit by them, so that's a start." I could hear the whir of the car engine as she accelerated. I pictured the on-ramp out of Woodland, the fast-food restaurants disappearing in the rearview mirror as the car hurtled onto the tiny two-lane freeway toward home. "Don't let me keep you. I just wanted to hear your voice. I know that this is practice for next year, when you're off at college."

College, not the academy.

I doubted whether my mother or father would ever truly understand why I'd lied and come to camp. To them, it would always be a betrayal of trust. The very idea of Rayevich was familial treason. But it was possible that Beth would understand, someday, that this was practice for both of us. I had to try on the idea of being something beyond a Gabaroche or a Lawrence. I had to try on this choice before I made it.

"It's only three weeks," I murmured.

"I'm already planning your homecoming dinner," she said. "How does pork belly from Thai Canteen and white mint chip gelato from Hot Italian sound?"

I thought of the congealed mac and cheese I'd had for dinner an hour ago. "Amazing."

"I thought so," she said. "I'll let you go. I love you, sweetheart."

"Love you," I whispered, holding the phone too tight. "Love to Dad and Ethan."

"Kisses!" There was the faraway *mwah, mwah, mwah* sound of air kisses and then the road noise disappeared.

I dug my thumb into the Power button, watching as the screen blinked into blackness. My reflection stared back—lips pulled down in the corners, eyes too glossy, a pucker above my nose.

I could imagine how nice it would feel to cry. To set down the team's candy and go back up to the dorm and curl up on my too-small bed. To think about how the carpet made the residence hall smell and to try to remember what my sheets at home felt like. To feel the weight of all of my stupid hopes and dreams and all of the trust that I'd sold out the second I'd climbed onto that train.

I took in a breath so deep that it burned the back of my throat, killing a sob before it could start. I could taste the eucalyptus baked into my sweater.

No more phone calls, I swore to myself.

I had to leave California where it was. It'd wait for me. If I didn't want this summer to be a wash, I had to focus. On Ever. On the Melee. On two more weeks of work.

Even if that work was currently bad-mouthing *The Breakfast Club.*

13

I burrowed deeper into my sheets, pulling them up over my forehead. The creases from the packaging scratched against my arms. On the other side of the room, Leigh's nose whistled. She'd crashed the second Meg had called lights-out. I wasn't even sure she'd brushed the popcorn kernels out of her teeth first.

I had never been good at falling asleep. The family psychologist my dad had dragged me to after Mom left had sworn that it was a by-product of the divorce. *Keep her on a regular bedtime schedule and she'll acclimate. Once she feels safe in this new normal, her body will accept the change.*

Total bull. It's not like I was staying up late, pining for my mother. Especially now, when I'd lived longer without her nearby than with. When I laid down, my brain just clicked on like it'd been waiting all day to run through scenarios and idle questions.

In the dark, it was impossible to stay in character. Telling myself that Ever didn't have mild insomnia couldn't change my brain chemistry.

Besides, was there an Ever Lawrence if there was no one to perceive her as someone separate from Elliot Gabaroche?

If I was setting up Buddhist riddles for myself, there was no way I was going to fall asleep.

Lights flashed through my blankets as sirens split through the night. I almost jumped out of my skin. I heard Leigh slap into the wall, and something crashed downstairs. I flung the sheets off my head. The red fire alarm box built into the ceiling over my wardrobe was blaring and blinking.

I lurched over the side of my bed, stuffing my feet into my Jordans. Leigh struggled against her zebra sheets, kicking wildly.

"Come on," I shouted to her over the wail of the alarm. "We need to get downstairs!"

Fists pounded on doors up and down the floor, accompanied by a squeaking voice—Meg, telling us to get out and take nothing.

I yanked Leigh to her feet. She scooped up her shoes as we flew out of the room into the glare of the hallway. There must have been dozens of alarms hidden in the ceiling. The lights burned white in strobing intervals and the noise was a constant screech, drowning out the sound of doors opening and yawned questions.

"Take the stairs!" the Perfect Nerd Girl yelled from the end of the hall.

Leigh hopped into her shoes as I kicked open the stairwell door. A crush of pajamas cascaded down the stairs. I couldn't smell smoke, and the cement walls were cold as my arms brushed them. But there were shouts from counselors, pushing us forward, pushing us out. I kept Leigh in front of me, using her yellow hair as a guide through the crowd.

Lumberjack Beard was at the base of the stairs, holding open the door. "Get away from the building! This is not a drill!" A kid stumbled into him. Lumberjack Beard scooped him up by the armpits and tossed him out into the lobby. "Come on, Onobanjo. I'm not gonna lose you. Not tonight."

The sirens echoed through the quad. Hari was already outside, directing traffic away from the residence halls with two flashlights.

"Everybody go toward the library!" he called. "Go quick!"

The path toward the library was dark. The trees grew thicker in between the buildings, blocking out the streetlamps. The alarms persisted in a constant scream. I imagined the residence hall smoldering behind us, flames licking through laptops and twin XL mattresses and the novels I'd unpacked on my desk. I tried to catch a glimpse of Isaiah, but there were too many strangers shoving by me.

Don't burn alive, you moron, I thought. *I cannot handle Grandmother Lawrence making a martyr out of you.*

The people ahead of us skittered to a stop and took a sharp left turn into a copse of trees. The path to the library had been sectioned off with caution tape. One of the RAs was shooing everyone away.

"There's a clearing through the trees!" she said. "Go through and find your teammates! We need to get a head count as soon as possible!"

Leigh shot me a nervous glance before we stepped off the path and into pitch darkness. The ground was squishy under my sneakers. Twigs snapped and people cursed that they'd run out without their shoes. The sound of the alarms started to fade behind us as we snaked through the trees.

"Team Four!" someone shouted.

"Team Six!"

"Team Three!"

Leigh and I entered a clearing where half a dozen flashlights were waving. The starry sky stretched above us, illuminating the sparse grass and trees hung with garbage. No, not garbage exactly. Dream catchers. Silverware on ribbons. Birdhouses. Christmas ornaments.

"Ever! Leigh!"

A light hit my face. I threw my hands up and squinted between my fingers. Jams came into focus, first as a big-eared shadow and then as a pale wisp. A body next to him raised a hand in greeting—Brandon.

"Hey!" Jams said, waving wildly at us. "I recognized your hair!"

I looked down at Leigh and found her staring up at me. It dawned on me that, while no one had hair brighter than my roommate, I was also the only girl at camp rocking a full 'fro. I was the pot judging the kettle's coif. Oops.

"Where did you get the flashlight?" Leigh asked Jams.

"Hari shoved it at me before he went out to direct traffic."

"So," I said to Brandon. He, I noticed, had managed to put his Chuck Taylors on. "This is more exciting than *The Breakfast Club*, huh?"

He tucked his hands into the pockets of his pajama pants and blew out a shaky breath. "Yep."

More flashlights broke through the trees. We broke into a chorus of "Team One!" to guide Galen and Hunter toward us. Or a fully dressed Galen and Hunter's very bare chest. Leigh's nails dug into my arm. I hadn't considered that not everyone would go to sleep in sweats and an undershirt, like me. Hunter was unabashedly standing only in his boxers and a pair of flip-flops.

"Praise to the Flying Spaghetti Monster," Leigh whispered. "My eyes just adjusted to the darkness."

"Mine too," Jams said. He and Leigh shared a giggle.

Kate and Perla stumbled through the trees next. Perla had braided her hair into two long pigtails. A fork was dangling from the end of one. She ripped it out and threw it on the ground.

"Where's Meg?" Kate panted.

"Where are any of the counselors?" I asked, scanning the crowd. Every flashlight seemed to be held by a camper.

"Maybe we should go back and make sure they got out of the building okay," Hunter said.

"There she is!" Galen said, pointing at the trees.

Meg trotted out, a flashlight in her hand. She broke into a smile as she saw all of us together.

"You all made it!" she said. "Good job!"

"What's going on?" Hunter asked.

She ignored him, unclipping a walkie-talkie from the waistband of her yoga pants. She pressed it against her mouth. "Team One checking in."

The walkie-talkie coughed static as the other counselors checked in. Team Two, Team Three—that meant Isaiah was safe—Team Four, Team Five, Team Six.

"We don't have Hari!" Kate said, panicked.

"Oh, he's around here somewhere," Meg said. "He'll find us."

"We are a go," crackled the walkie-talkie.

The trees erupted in Christmas lights that refracted off every piece of trash strung up in the branches. The distant sirens cut off mid-yowl. There was a loud crack as a butcher paper sign unrolled from the low branches of the largest tree in the clearing. It read "Aut Vincere Aut Mori."

"Victory or death?" Brandon hissed at Meg.

"You know she likes to make an entrance," Meg murmured back.

Perla glanced at Brandon. "You speak Latin?"

He blinked, seemingly surprised to find that he wasn't invisible. He opened his mouth to say something, but Meg shushed him.

"Welcome to Mudders Meadow!" the counselor from Bryn Mawr called from under the banner. "I am Mary-Anne France, your activities counselor. And this—" She lifted a trophy high over her head and struck a pose. "Is the Cheeseman trophy. Four of you will win the Melee. One of you will win the Cheeseman. Or, as the camp directors call it, the counselors' endowment. The twelve of us can grant a full ride to one of you based on your achievements in this tournament. Each counselor will choose a Cheeseman event. The person who wins the most events gets the endowment."

The meadow drowned in gasps and shouts. The idea of a fifth scholarship plucked the breath out of my lungs and carried it off into the garbage trees. Leigh huddled closer to me, trembling in barely contained delight as she squealed, "Plot twist!"

"Still talking," Bryn Mawr snapped. She shook the trophy in annoyance. It glittered in the Christmas lights. "You can't prepare for the events. You won't know when they're coming or what they will entail. Participation isn't mandatory, but attendance is. Clearly." She planted the trophy in the dirt and crossed her arms over her chest as she barked, "Faulkner?"

Faulkner, the blond counselor in charge of our music class, broke apart from her team. Her long, spray-tanned legs stuck out from under pajama shorts printed with kitten faces as she skipped into the center of the field.

"Tonight's event is a Mudders Meadow tradition," she said. She flung her arms out wide, as if to embrace the trash trees as her throat ululated, "Amoeba tag!"

Every dream catcher, fork, and Christmas ornament trembled as a dubstep beat dropped.

"What. The. Hell," I breathed.

"Hidden speakers," Leigh called over the music, bursting into applause. "Very impressive. There must be a generator somewhere! Or possibly solar paneling!"

"They pulled us out of bed to play tag?" Galen asked.

Perla tore at her hair and screamed "Dicks!" at the clear night sky.

14

You're in or you're out," Faulkner said, bringing everyone back to the matter at hand. "If you're in, step forward. If you're out, take a seat."

Hunter, Kate, Leigh, and I stepped forward. Brandon stumbled, as if shoved, and thrust his hands into his armpits. I glanced back, but the rest of our team was helping Meg get a blanket she'd stashed in the nearest tree. Perla was sulking in the dirt, her knees pulled up to her chest.

"The rules are simple," Faulkner said over the persistent beat of the music. "Two people are it. If you get tagged, you join the amoeba and become responsible for absorbing the next person. The chain may split off into two or more players and reabsorb itself at will. The last person not attached to the chain wins."

With a ballerina's grace, she swept an arm out. Bryn Mawr's co-captain walked into the center of the clearing and gripped Faulkner's wrist.

"Maxwell and I are it," she said, lifting their tethered hands into the air. "The game starts in three, two—"

A whistle sounded, high and shrill over the music. I didn't have a chance to check to see where it had come from. Faulkner and Maxwell were already speeding through the field, scooping up two campers who hadn't moved fast enough.

"And that's two down right after the whistle."

Who had given Lumberjack Beard a bullhorn? I could see him sitting in the tree above Bryn Mawr, his spindly legs dangling over the Latinate sign.

I broke away from my teammates and ran, pell-mell, out of the way of the amoeba's wobbling path. Shouts rose up from the edges of the meadow. Team numbers. People's names. Cheers and boos. Complaints that we could all be asleep right now.

"We have our first split," Lumberjack Beard boomed.

I spun and saw three groups of pajama wearers, linked together at the wrist. Hungry hands extended in all directions. I leaped back out of the way and skidded sideways on a lost flip-flop.

I thought of the week when Ethan had become obsessed with somersaults. Beth had dragged us to the theater and we'd ended up learning parkour rolls with the cast of *Julius Caesar*. Ethan had made me practice with him in the backyard for hours. It'd never been a particularly useful skill.

Use the momentum, my brain screamed.

I threw myself forward, tucking my head to the side. My shoulder landed in a patch of dead grass and my legs flew over. I propelled forward and jumped back to my feet, grateful to find myself momentarily out of harm's way.

It'd be hell of embarrassing to get tagged while showing off my rusty stage combat skills.

The amoeba had connected again into a long chain. Leigh and Brandon had been absorbed. But they moved slower with so many people connected together. The line of people billowed out in the center, where Faulkner and Maxwell were struggling to regain control.

"Only ten players left on the field," Lumberjack Beard announced. "Finish them, Faulkner!"

"Split!" Faulkner screamed.

One chain became six. I could see the girl who'd been assigned to hang my Firefly poster careening toward me, her face flushed under her cat-eye glasses. I kicked off my shoes, leaving them as land mines behind me. There were screams in my wake as the small chain fell. Twigs bit into the soles of my feet as I feinted between another cluster.

In the distance—underneath the butcher paper sign and Lumberjack Beard's feet—a glimpse of dreadlocks.

Isaiah had always been a hopeless cheater. He stashed Monopoly money in his sleeves and moved battleships and double dribbled so much they'd kicked him off his fifth-grade basketball team.

There was no way I was going to let him hide until he was the last person standing.

I pivoted on my heel, throwing myself toward the amoeba. Faulkner took the bait. I could hear the feet pounding behind me. I darted between clusters of other runners and heard Lumberjack Beard announce another three people being absorbed. I didn't know how many of us were left.

I careened between the observers, ignoring as Lumberjack Beard cried foul above me. Isaiah's back was to me as I swept around him. I could see his shoulders hiccup as he breathed—incorrectly—from his chest. I reached out, grabbed a fistful of dreadlocks, and pulled him backwards.

"Are you still in play?" I shouted into his ear.

"Are you insane?" he screeched back.

I tightened my grip on his hair and chopped up my words. "Are you still playing?"

"Yes! Jesus!"

I dropped his hair. Before he could protest, I gripped his wrist and tugged him onto the field. Hunter was hopping near the rest of our team, stuck to his remaining flip-flop. Leigh scooped up his hand, cackling over the music. A girl in striped pajama pants was joining hands with Faulkner, who was rallying her troops together again. The chain was nearly long enough to span the entire meadow.

Isaiah tugged on my arm. I wouldn't be able to hold him for much longer. I had one chance to make this work.

"Victor Onobanjo has been absorbed," Lumberjack Beard called. "Would that I had a trumpet for you, Onobanjo. Three players left."

I scanned the field for the third person. A girl with a long ponytail was bouncing from side to side, debating the safest route.

I bolted for her, forcing Isaiah to follow. Her eyes went wide as she scampered, thinking that she was being targeted by a small chain. Together, Isaiah and I chased her toward the last person on the end of the real chain, the scrawny kid who'd stumbled in the lobby. His hand shot out, his fingertips grazing the girl's elbow.

I dug my heel into the dirt and spun, following the line of the chain in the opposite direction. Isaiah was pulling so hard that my shoulder was threatening to pop its socket. My hands were sweating, loosening my grip on him in clammy increments. Lumberjack Beard was talking, but I couldn't break my focus long enough to listen. I watched as the line of the amoeba started to break apart. They were going to swarm us.

I flung myself hard to the side, stretching my arm as far as it would go while still holding on to Isaiah's wrist. I ran as fast as I could, making a full circle in the dirt while Isaiah frantically tried to shake me off.

My lungs burned. I could taste dust and salt on my lips. My ears were clogged with dubstep and screams and the static from the bullhorn.

I let go.

Isaiah and I careened away from each other, both momentarily airborne. I collapsed to the ground, my palms slicing against dead blades of grass. Isaiah landed on his feet and staggered. He pressed his hands to his chest like he was taking inventory of his organs. He seemed satisfied that everything was in place.

And then Faulkner appeared behind him and set one hand on his shoulder.

He looked at me and swore.

Sorry, bro, I mouthed back.

The whistle sounded again. Game over.

"I've just been informed that our first winner of the Cheeseman trials," Lumberjack Beard boomed from the treetop, "is Ever Lawrence from Team One!"

My body went limp. My hands and feet stung in dubstep throbs, but I could feel myself smiling.

Brandon appeared above me, his hair mussed, his dark eyebrows drawn together above his nose. His cheeks were flushed and shining.

"So," he panted, extending an arm to help me up. "You know parkour."

"Not, like, a lot," I wheezed, carefully taking his hand while my palms screamed. My legs resisted straightening, but Brandon was stronger than he looked. I swayed into a standing position and took my hand back, blowing a cool breath over the broken skin. "Why do you speak Latin?"

He coughed, stuffing his hands back into his pockets. "I took two years of it. It was that or Mandarin." He glanced up at my face and sensed more questions coming. "Messina Academy. It's pretty much as weird as people say it is. Weirder, really."

"You go to—" I tried to take a step and hissed. Brandon gripped my elbow to keep me from tipping over. "Balls. I need to find my shoes."

"Leigh's getting them," he said. His head popped up. "Cornell's coming this way with your ribbon."

I craned my neck to see past him. Cornell and Bryn Mawr were striding across the field. The audience had given up on participating. There were already scads of people marching back through the trees.

"Brandon," I breathed, turning my head discreetly toward his shoulder. "I need you to promise me something, right here, right now."

His Adam's apple rose and fell with a gulp. "Okay?"

"You are prepared to do this terrible thing?" Shit. Accidental Wilde. I barreled ahead, trying not to let my mortification show. "Do not, under any circumstance, let Cornell shake my hand right now. Or at any point until I have taken a bath in Neosporin."

His laugh was an abrupt rising sound, like footsteps running up stairs. "I can do that."

15

Even with Meg pushing our wake-up call forward to our new weekend schedule, I could barely drag myself out of bed the morning after amoeba tag. My palms were scabbed and the soles of my feet burned as I set them against the carpet.

By the time I made it to the communal bathroom with my towel and ziplock bag of toiletries, Bath and Body Works steam was pouring out of all four beige shower stalls. The smell was aggressively fruity, like being punched with candied apples and vanilla frosting while pretending worse smells weren't hanging out around the corner.

I had come to expect having to get ready out of order. For all of Rayevich's state-of-the-art facilities elsewhere on campus, the bathrooms were plain and barely functional. I had a hard time believing that the same shower stalls that my fellow campers and I had to share would serve twice as many students in the fall. How could anyone ever be on time to anything?

Unless everyone was like Leigh and adjusted to waking up predawn to shower in peace.

Avoiding my ragged reflection in the water-speckled mirror,

I unloaded my supplies onto the nearest sink. I lathered my cheeks in face wash, tuning out the noise in the showers behind me. Every morning, there was a din of splashing and bottles clacking and razors dropping that drew way too much attention to how communal this whole situation was. I'd considered asking Meg how often the janitorial staff was cleaning the residence hall, since the school was technically closed for the summer, but had decided against when I realized that I'd never seen any sign of a janitor who wasn't Lumberjack Beard.

I didn't consider myself a clean freak, necessarily; it was just that the idea of our entire floor's filth being rinsed down the same drains made me uneasy. The other girls all seemed fine to run their bare feet over the tiles. I didn't believe that germs could be deterred by body wash alone, especially the super perfumed stuff that everyone seemed to favor. I'd heard one too many *drunk girls peeing—and worse—in the showers at boot camp* stories from Sid and the rest of the Lawrences to not wear flip-flops. They were hidden under my towel so that I could slip into them once I was safely behind the shower curtain.

The bathroom door crashed open. The girl with the cat-eye glasses from across the hall staggered in, her arm looped around her roommate's hunched shoulders. The roommate shimmied away, made a heaving sound, and rushed into the closest toilet stall.

No one ever went into the stalls without checking them first. That was public bathroom common sense.

"Fallon," the girl with the cat-eye glasses called, as the toilet stall slammed. "Are you going to be—"

Behind the metal door, there was a wet splash and the unmistakable gurgle of bile.

I loaded my toothbrush with toothpaste and popped it into my mouth, hoping to smother sympathy gags in minty freshness.

A shower curtain rustled as a damp head peeked out. It was one of the brunettes from Isaiah's team. "Meuy, who's puking?"

"It's Fallon," said Meuy, pushing up her glasses.

Fallon moaned inside of her stall, probably trying to ask her roommate not to blast her illness to the world.

"Did she realize how gross breakfast is gonna be?" asked a voice behind a closed shower curtain.

"Hey, Fallon." I recognized Perla's voice coming from the farthest shower stall. "You pregnant?"

"No," Fallon's wavered voice came out of the toilet stall.

"Leave her alone," Meuy snapped at the wall of closed shower curtains. "She's having a panic attack. Her binder is missing."

I spat a mouthful of toothpaste into the sink, wiping the remnants from my lips with the back of my hand. "Seriously?"

Meuy widened her eyes at me and nodded solemnly. "An entire week's worth of work—poof! Gone."

Fallon gave another bark of barf. I winced, resuming my toothbrushing with vigor.

"Someone probably stole it. Someone took my shampoo and my flip-flops," said the voice behind the farthest shower curtain.

"Are you sure she didn't try to take her binder with her when the fire alarm went off?" asked the girl in the shower next to her.

"Do not even talk to me about that fire drill," said another voice. "That was beyond cruel."

Meuy glanced back at me, possibly waiting for me to announce my presence to the other girls or to gloat over last night's win. When I did neither, she twisted her shoulders in a shrug and lowered her voice to a hush, "It's her own fault. She left her binder in the lounge. What did she think was going to happen? I'm sorry that she's got an anxiety disorder, but come on. We are in a competition, right?"

I spat another wad of foam and frowned. I wasn't comfortable blaming the puking girl for her own misfortune.

Meuy seemed to sense my weakness. She whirled away from me and strode from the door, calling over her shoulder, "Fallon, I'm gonna go get you a bottle of water." She left the bathroom without waiting for a response.

Perla yanked back her shower curtain, sticking her face out and craning her neck to see around the corner. Her hair was twisted on top of her head in a thick white lather.

"Seriously, Fallon," she said in that singsong that was starting to make me feel like peeling off my fingernails. "If you're pregnant, you'd better drop out of the Melee. You won't be able to use the scholarship."

The toilet flushed.

"Fuck off," gurgled Fallon.

Perla flicked her eyebrows at me. "I'm in her head now." She grinned before disappearing behind the curtain again.

I rinsed my mouth at the sink and couldn't help but think about how much I would truly relish watching Perla—of everyone—lose the Melee.

"It was like—bam! Total beast mode!" All of our plates jingled against the table as Hunter slapped his hand down. "I knew that the rest of us were in trouble the second you took off."

"You should have heard Meg," Galen said. He plunged his spoon deep into his bowl and brought up a heap of soggy cereal. "I thought she was going to scream herself hoarse."

Jams bobbed his head. "It was a proper show."

Perla frowned at him. "I don't know what's proper about Meg shouting 'Kill, kill' at everyone. If they pulled that shit at Princeton, I promise you there would be lawyers involved."

"Proper," Jams stressed, "as in 'good.'"

"Like jolly good," Leigh added.

Jams flicked a dismissive wrist. "Only tossers say 'jolly good.'"

"Pretty sure only 'tossers' say 'tossers,'" Perla said.

As Leigh had pointed out as we'd walked out of Mudders Meadow last night, no one at camp would be able to say that Isaiah and I were going to take it easy on each other in the Melee. Throwing him headlong into the amoeba had solidified my place as the camp's first cutthroat.

It was strange. I'd never been considered a cutthroat before. As Elliot Gabaroche, I mostly slid under the radar. If anything, I was known for wearing my hair big and having a dude's name, which led to a lot of horrifically transphobic questions from my less evolved classmates.

Otherwise, I'd never been truly noteworthy. I'd taken some AP classes, but not enough to be considered one of the smart kids. Thanks to overprotective parents who liked having me on call to babysit, I didn't play school sports. I had friends on teams, so I could sneak an invite to their more inclusive parties. But there was no corner of Hiram Johnson High that I'd stamped as my own.

And here I was, less than a week into being Ever Lawrence, and I'd already made a name for myself. Literally and figuratively.

It'd be nice if we could stop talking about it now, though.

Hunter pointed his fork at me. "You have to show me some of that kung fu."

"It's parkour," Brandon mumbled. "Or *parcours du combattant*. It was developed by the French military."

"And I don't really know much more than the rolls." I shrugged, staring down at my breakfast. "I could show you some Muay Thai techniques, if you want." I dipped a sausage in syrup and took a bite before I noticed the silence of my teammates' shock. If they'd been manga characters, there would have been a fog of question marks hovering over us like a quizzical storm. I swallowed with some effort and waved my fork. "I couldn't join my school's cross-country team. I needed an extracurricular. Didn't anyone else want to be a superhero when they were little?"

Hunter grinned and slapped the table again. "Beast. Mode."

I really hoped that wasn't a nickname that would stick. I was having a hard enough time answering to Ever.

"Oh shit," Galen murmured, craning his neck to look at the counselor's table. "What now?"

Rather than their usual huddle of Starbucks cups and whispered conversation, the counselors had cleared their long table. The single speaker that Wendell Cheeseman had used on our first day was being carried over to the picture window by the MIT counselor, who had a mild limp.

Bryn Mawr climbed on the bench seat, balancing neatly as she held her cell phone to a cordless microphone. The speaker played a tinny series of twanging guitar and mushy synthesizer chords.

"Balls," I said as I recognized it.

"Isn't this the song from *Pitch Perfect*?" said someone at a nearby table.

Bryn Mawr grinned into the crowd. She let the phone fall to her side, where it continued to distantly plead for all of us to remember it.

"Good morning, campers," she said. "I told you that you wouldn't know when these were coming at you. Saturday, March twenty-fourth, nineteen eighty-four. Shermer High School. Shermer, Illinois. Six zero zero six two." She gestured at the bare table in front of her. "I need a criminal, a princess, a brain, an athlete, and a basket case."

"A what?" Jams asked.

"It's the goddamn *Breakfast Club*," Hunter said.

"Every contestant will recite the lines of their assigned character," Bryn Mawr announced, as people started to line up on the sides of the counselors' table. "You can ask for assistance once. Forget a second line and you will be replaced. Anyone who looks at their phone will be disqualified, including those in line. The camper who can get the farthest into the movie, wins."

"Someone's a big *Ready Player One* fan," I muttered, my stomach sinking. So much for my head start on the fifth scholarship. There was no chance I'd retained enough of *The Breakfast Club* to make it through a single scene, much less to the end.

"A *what* fan?" Leigh asked, sticking her thumb in her mouth and biting at her nail with her crooked teeth.

"*Ready Player One*," I repeated, waving her off. "It's a book. At one point, they have to reenact a movie word for word—"

"The *War Games* simulation," Brandon interrupted, nodding vigorously. "At the first gate. I was thinking the same thing. I love that book. It's a shame about *Armada* . . ."

I swallowed thickly and gaped at this vision of nerd boy, who picked up my references as I set them down. With his fuzzy bedhead and tremulous smile.

"I know, right?" I said, forcing a laugh that ended up slightly maniacal. "Why do second books suck so much?"

"I'm going for it," Kate said, throwing herself to her feet. Her fists balled at her sides as she stared at the lengthening queue at the counselors' table. "I sat through the movie three times this week. I think I have a shot."

"It's two hours of people sniveling about their virginities," Perla said, also climbing off the bench. She brushed by her roommate, her elbow scuffing against Kate's. "How hard could it be?"

Kate's face went chalk white. She closed her eyes. Her nostrils flared. Her anger was almost a separate entity—a hissing, writhing snake winding itself around her extremities, holding her in place and pushing her to strike.

"Now you have to try," Hunter said to her. "Because you can't let Perla win."

"Amen," said Jams.

"Don't make us chant for you, Kate." Galen chuckled. "We'll do it."

Her eyelids flew open. "Don't you dare."

"Kate, Kate," Galen murmured. He threw a look around the table until the rest of us joined in, whispering, "Kate, Kate, Kate . . ."

The color came back to Kate's face in a rush as she skittered away from us, joining the line a few people behind Perla.

Leigh bit another of her fingernails. "I knew I should have paid more attention to that stupid movie."

"How could you have known that there'd be a quiz?" I asked. "None of us knew."

"This whole camp is a quiz," she huffed. "Apparently."

16

With the second Cheeseman trial ribbon awarded to one of the girls from Lumberjack Beard's team, and the rest of the morning open for studying, I laced up my running shoes and sprinted out of the residence hall. There were clusters of people spread out in the quad and on the steps of the closed buildings. Most had their faces deep inside their binders, prepping before we were due to report to our team meetings. Others napped in the shade of the trees or tossed Frisbees. A solitary white kid was flinging himself around the green, bouncing a hacky sack off of various parts of himself.

Because how would we know that we were on a college campus if there wasn't a loner with a hacky sack?

My feet burned with the aftermath of amoeba tag, but I needed a mental break. I'd been expecting the weekend to be easier than the constant shuffle of classes during the week, but with the addition of the Cheeseman events, the tension had ratcheted up instead. Kate had cried when Hari buzzed her out of *The Breakfast Club*. The second we'd been excused from the dining hall, Leigh had started quizzing herself aloud on every meal we'd eaten this week, in case it ended up being pertinent.

When the Melee was over, they'd recover. We would all go back to our normal lives in a few weeks and coast through senior year, fifty geniuses—five of whom would be coming back to Rayevich next fall.

But that was just it. College wasn't like high school. You couldn't drag yourself through the same halls every day, counting down to when you could leave. I'd realized that when I talked to Beth. I'd known for years that this school was where I wanted to be, but I'd never considered that homesickness could be a roadblock.

You had to leave home to make a home. You couldn't wait to leave to be yourself.

I couldn't let myself start to crumble under the pressure. If I couldn't hack it for the summer, how could I expect to spend four years here?

When I was in the fifth grade, Sid finished basic training. She'd always been intense, but her new short hair and official air force ranking doubled her aloofness. After all, I was ten years old and still wearing my hair up in two puff balls that Beth thought made me look like a cartoon mouse. Seeing Sid was like looking into my own future and seeing someone terrifying on the other side. She was everything my mom wanted me to grow up to be.

Still, as we both sat on the back porch of Grandmother Lawrence's house, I had been compelled to ask my cousin if boot camp was hard. I guess I had thought that it was harmless chitchat, the sort of obvious question that adults asked to keep you talking when they didn't have anything to say.

But Sid had run her tongue over the tip of her canines as she thought about it. Her eyes stared off a thousand yards and then some while her hands held on tight to a sweating bottle of water. When she finally spoke, her voice was low.

"It's the worst food and the hardest physical challenges and the shortest, coldest showers. It's people screaming at you more than you've ever been screamed at in your life. And through it all, do you know what you're wearing?" She had paused, staring me down until I shook my head.

"Granny panties," she said. I must have looked shocked, because she actually smiled as she went on. "Big, white, itchy-ass cotton panties. You can't wear anything with a logo on it, so good-bye Calvin Klein and Under Armour. You're running around and getting yelled at and thinking, *I'm gonna do this shit for the rest of my life?* And when you think that you can't handle it—you're going to truly fucking lose your mind—they let you put your own chonies back on. And it all makes sense. They turn up the heat so you can transform into something else. Hot sand doesn't turn into glass, Ellie. Molten sand does."

I hadn't understood it then. Then, my main takeaway was that I must have been getting older, because Sid had never sworn in front of me before. She never cursed in front of Isaiah. He would have told.

I understood it now. Now I was feeling the heat get cranked up and my sand was figuring out how to melt.

This was my trial run. At the end of my senior year, I was going to have to make a choice as to which parent I hurt. If I enlisted, my dad and Beth would be crushed—constantly scared, always half in the dark about what I was doing. If I stayed close to home and got a business degree, coming home on weekends to do my laundry and babysit my brother, my mother would be ashamed.

I wanted to try on my third option, the nuclear option—getting a degree that I wanted. Not close to home. Not with the military. The route that hurt everyone. I wanted to know if it was worth it.

And—bonus!—I got to keep my good underwear.

I slowed as the corner of the Lauritz library came into view. A familiar dark-haired figure was wedged into the corner of the stairs with a typewriter. I'd almost forgotten about the typewriter. Brandon made all of his notes in pencil, like the rest of us, during classes. It was strange to watch him mashing at the round keys and shoving aside the roller.

Now that I'd spotted him, it would have been rude not to say hello. We were teammates, after all. And, unlike Perla, Brandon wasn't a teammate that I fantasized about decimating in the Melee.

I took my headphones out and wound them around my wrist as I climbed the first stair.

"Hey," I said. My stomach immediately contracted as I waited for him to register my voice. This was already a mistake. This was why I had Leigh. She was supposed to help me not make an ass out of myself.

At least, once I humiliated myself, I could go inside and read more of the Octavia Butler book in the sci-fi section.

Hands still poised over the keys, Brandon's head popped up. He quickly pushed the hair out of his eyes, looking down at me intently. Like he was really trying to commit my visage to memory.

My sweaty, sweaty visage. I was sure my lucky Angry Robot shirt was sticking to me in big wet clumps. God, this was a dumb idea.

"Ever," he said. "Hey. Hi."

"Hello," I said, assuming this was the next greeting in the sequence. "Nice typewriter."

I wasn't sure if it was actually a nice typewriter. It could have been the worst typewriter ever made—*The Plan 9 from Outer Space* of typewriters. But it was shiny and not currently rusting in an antique store, so it seemed like the appropriate response. *What the hell is up with that ancient bucket of bolts?* didn't have the same ring.

"Thanks," he said, passing a possessive hand over the keys. "I don't have a laptop."

Mystery solved.

Well, no. Not really. I knew plenty of people who didn't have their own computers and none of them—literally zero percent—had opted for a typewriter. Generally, people used school computers or borrowed their parents' tech.

"It's not, uh, super practical," he said. He must have been used to questions about it. "Jams says that the noise is distracting, so I come here to transcribe my notes."

He gestured to his binder, laid flat on the step above him with a three-hole punch and a collection of pencils rolling toward freedom.

I shot a look toward the library's doors. "Why don't you go inside?"

"The general consensus is in favor of Jams," he said. He mimed typing in midair. "The clacking. It's not exactly white noise." His hands flopped into his lap. "But how are you? Leigh didn't kick you out of your room, did she?"

"No. I left of my own free will so she could have some space to do her yoga and study. She needs a lot of alone time. And she's kind of freaked out about not entering this morning's event." I winced a smile as I leaned against the warm metal railing. "All of this must be pretty standard for you. Compared to actually going to the Messina, a couple weeks of camp must be nothing."

"Oh. I guess. It's still a lot of work." He glanced around, as though expecting a crowd to gather, even though there wasn't anyone even remotely near us. "Look, I really don't want everyone to know that I go to the Mess. If you already told Leigh, that's fine. I should have been clearer about it when I mentioned it last night—"

"I haven't told Leigh," I interrupted. Curiosity fluttered around my insides. I tried to keep my face neutral. "Did you go to school with all of the Messina counselors?"

His long nose scrunched in the middle. "Yeah. Ben was my student government mentor when I was a freshman. I kind of fell in with their crowd. But only for a year. Then they all graduated. I can tell you that Trixie is a vegetarian and Cornell is a Magic cardsharp, but that won't help anyone win the Melee."

I searched my brain and came up with a blank. "And which one is Trixie?"

"Um." His cheeks went pink. "Red hair, blue-gray eyes. Not as tall as you, but tallish—"

"Oh. The Perfect Nerd Girl."

He sputtered a laugh. "Is that what you call her?"

"It seemed nicer than the busty white girl."

Not that I hadn't mentally referred to her as that also.

He started to say something but stopped himself with a twitch of his shoulders. "Since the Mess helps run the camp, if I told people I went there, they'd think I had some insight about what's coming at us. I don't. Being here is proof enough of that." Reading the continued confusion in my face, he added, "Most Mess kids already have their early admission locked. We have a class junior year that's just for perfecting admissions essays and picking out your safety schools. None of my classmates would ever consider going to summer camp to win placement." He brushed his hair back into his eyes, possibly to hide the lemon rind bitterness that had seeped into that last statement. "Ugh. That makes me sound like such an entitled, private school asshole. I don't think I'm too good to be here. I'm definitely not. Hey, is it rambling out here or is it just me?"

I laughed. "You don't sound like an asshole."

"Just batshit, then?"

"Stressed?"

"Everyone here is stressed. I'm . . . I don't know. Extra stressed."

"See, you wanting to be special is kind of entitled."

His mouth flinched into a smile. "Sorry. You were heading up to the library and I stopped you like a rambling troll. You've paid your listening toll for the day. Thanks for letting me rant."

"I wasn't going to the library," I said. "I was saying hi."

"Oh."

I wished that I could mine that single syllable for more meaning, but it was too quiet and his eyes were mostly obscured by his hair. The scuffed toes of his high-tops tapped against the brick.

"Do you want to study together?" he asked.

"Like, the two of us?" I asked.

Farce, farce, farce, said my brain.

A shadow passed over his face, a darkening of disappointment or hurt. This boy wanted to kick it with me and help me prep for this huge contest that we were in. Was I really going to turn him down because I was scared of a mostly dead form of theatrical comedy? He was cute and presumably very smart and, unlike so many other white dudes, he'd never told me how much hip-hop meant to him like my melanin made me a rap ambassador.

"I mean, three's a crowd," I said, my voice too loud, too jokey. God, I was already one foot into a bad community theater production of *Earnest.* "So you're gonna have to choose between me and the typewriter."

He sighed, but the corners of his lips quirked. "Everyone hates the typewriter."

17

I stood alone in the sci-fi section. The edges of my binder bit into my forearms as I hugged it to my stomach. Leigh hadn't been in the room when I had stopped in to grab my study supplies, so I had seized the opportunity to mop off my shiny forehead and reapply my deodorant, unquestioned. But I probably could have given my face another blot, now that the nervous sweats had fully set in. I was going to dampen my fresh shirt soon, and then how would everyone know how cool I was for owning a Tor Books shirt?

I couldn't choose between the armchairs and the study table. Sitting in the armchair might send the wrong message—like I was more into lounging than studying. But sitting at the tables could make me look like a joyless study-loving robot. And my normal spot—flat on my belly with Octavia Butler's books looming over me like a shrine—was clearly out for about a dozen reasons.

Hearing footsteps outside of the room's arched entryway, I threw myself down in the closest chair, which happened to be at one of the tables. I had enough time to set my binder down before Brandon shuffled into the room, unencumbered by his typewriter case. He smiled at me, almost surprised to find me sitting in front of him. His eyes slid up to the massive travel posters framed on the wall above us.

"Magrathea?" he read. "That sounds familiar."

"It's from *Hitchhiker's Guide*," I said.

"Right. Very cool." He gave an approving bob of his head. "Don't hate me, but I'm actually more of a sword and sorcery guy. Like Patrick Rothfuss and Robert Jordan?"

"Long books by middle-aged white guys?"

"Long books about worlds where no one cares what grade you got in calculus-level general physics."

"Was that a brag?"

"Not at all. Especially not if you knew what grade I actually got in calculus-level general physics." He took the seat across from me. He angled his chair to the side and stretched his legs out. "I've only been back here once. Wesley Chu did a book signing here last year. He gave a really good talk before it—did you read the *Time Salvager* series?"

Uh-oh. Was that my heart skipping a beat? I was literally wearing the shirt of the publisher that put him on the map.

"Now you're bragging," I said. "Wes Chu is freaking amazing. My jealousy is physically painful right now."

He cut his eyes at me and grinned. "If it makes you feel better, I missed it when N. K. Jemisin came to campus."

"That does make me feel better," I said. "Because if you told me that you'd met N. K. Jemisin, we couldn't study together because I would be stuck in a rage blackout for the rest of my life. She's one of my all-time favorite authors, hands down. No question. I literally brought the entire Inheritance Trilogy with me for the summer."

He snorted. "For all your downtime?"

"And the twelve-hour train ride from California."

He pulled a face. "Twelve hours? You should get the scholarship based on time commitment alone."

"If only it were that easy." I looked over at the rows and rows of redwood bookcases, each packed with literally every book I had ever wanted to read. "I really love it here. The campus, I mean. It's gorgeous. And the weather is so much better than at home, I can't even get over it."

"Have you found any of the tree houses yet?"

I turned back to him. "The what?"

"Tree houses," he repeated, pushing the hair out of his eyes as though maybe that was why I hadn't heard him. It was strange to glimpse his eyebrows. They slashed across his forehead, about as wide as my thumb. "The students build them during the school year. The administration has them taken down whenever they find them, because they're made of scraps and are structurally unsound. But there's usually a few around. It's not something they list in the brochure or anything, but you run a lot, so I figured you've seen more of campus than I have."

I felt a sting of shock that he knew that I was a runner, before realizing that I was literally wearing running shoes and running shorts—and that I was basically always wearing running shoes and running shorts. I hadn't even bothered to bring jeans with me, since back home it wouldn't be comfortable to wear long pants until at least October.

Get it together, Beast Mode.

"I haven't seen any," I said. "I guess I should look up more when I run. How do you know they exist if they aren't listed in the brochures?"

"I live here, remember?"

"Right. You have much Oregonian knowledge."

"Buckets of it. Did you know that Eugene was originally called—"

"Skinner's Mudhole?" I interrupted. "I've heard."

"Then I have nothing left to teach you."

"Well, shit," I said, snapping my fingers. "I was hoping you'd bring some of that genius school juice to this study session."

Juice? my brain screamed. *Please tell me you did not just ask this boy for his genius juice.*

He frowned at me. "You know that you have to be a genius, too? By virtue of being here."

"Yeah, but it's not the same. I go to public school," I said, grateful to be past the juicing part of this conversation. I resisted the urge to actually sigh with relief.

"There's nothing wrong with public school."

"I'm sorry," I laughed. "Say that again and then remember that we're in America."

"Okay. Fair enough. I get it. It's just—Really, the Mess isn't that great. We call it the Mess for a reason."

"People call this place the Mo-Lo," I said, gesturing around. "Which sounds like a hashtag or an epithet."

"Actually, the Mollos were a predecessor to the Incan people of South America . . ." He trailed off and tapped on the cover of his binder. "Oh. That's the juice you were talking about?"

"Yep."

He reached up, rubbing the back of his neck right above the collar of his shirt. In the last week, he'd rotated through a series of nearly identical shirts. Plain, solid-color T-shirts cut close to his narrow torso, with no decoration to betray any clues as to his interests. Today's shirt was heather gray and looked as flannel-soft as his voice. "You didn't study ancient Bolivia in sophomore year?"

"Uh, no."

"You have no context for the rise of the Incan empire?"

"Zero context. And I took AP world history."

"Huh." He flipped open his binder and yanked out a mechanical pencil. The lead clicked down as he chewed on the inside of his cheek. "There's a chance that my entire education has been useless and esoteric. I haven't taken classes on any of the history periods we're supposed to cover in the Melee."

"There's a chance that I've spent more time reading Octavia

Butler books than studying this week," I said, flopping open my binder and slapping aside pages until I reached the history section. I slid it across the table. "So you can help me with the esoteric and I'll help you with the obvious."

He smiled, pushing his binder to me. "That sounds good."

18

idn't she say that she didn't come here to make friends?" Galen asked, resting his chin on his hand and gazing over my shoulder.

"Apparently, she meant she didn't come here to make friends with *us*," Leigh said.

"Fine with me," Kate said, not looking up from the slice of pizza she was deconstructing. The tips of her fingers were coated in a fine slime of marinara. "One of them can trade me roommates for her. Her deviated septum has already stolen one week of sleep from me. And she won't shut up about the expensive lotion she lost."

Following the route of Galen's stare, I twisted around on the bench. Perla was seated across the dining hall with Bryn Mawr's team, planted firmly between a girl wearing a pale pink hijab and a girl with double lip piercings. All three of them were guzzling generic soda and laughing like they were in some cool, alt-girl commercial for Big K Cola.

"If it wasn't obvious we were spying on her before, it is now." Galen snorted. "Cool it, Ever. You're not invisible, you know."

I threw him a scowl. "What the hell does that mean?"

"You're an Amazon," Hunter said, snapping a carrot stick with his molars. "You could carry Meg and Leigh in your pockets."

"That's sizeist," Leigh said, wagging a finger at Hunter. "Even if it does sound like fun. I could get so much done if I wasn't responsible for walking myself places. Think of all the research I could do!"

"Joke's on you. I don't have pockets," I said with a faux-haughty sniff. "And I'm not that tall. I'm five ten. Maybe six foot if you include my hair."

"That's an ineffective spying height," Jams said.

I rolled my eyes. "Balls. There goes my career with the CIA."

"Because your degree in science fiction would be so useful as a secret agent," Galen snickered.

"Who are you going to turn to when our alien overlords take over the planet?" I asked. "Regular English majors? Good luck. They are way unprepared for the nuclear holocaust."

"You talk about nuclear holocausts so much," Kate said.

I looked around theatrically. "Whoa. Am I the new Perla? Did I start spouting Ayn Randian nonsense?"

"No," Jams said firmly. "We josh you because we like you."

"'Josh' isn't a Briticism, is it?" Kate asked.

"Why would it be?" Jams asked, blinking innocently. "I'm from Oregon, Kate. Haven't you heard?"

"Did you know that you only need a three-point-oh GPA in college to qualify to be a CIA special agent?" Brandon mused.

We all turned to him. His face pinched into an embarrassed scrunch. "That's not a normal thing to know, is it?"

The hour we had spent alone together in the sci-fi section had been mostly quiet, the two of us reading each other's notes. It was interesting to peek inside of his strange nerd-boy brain, to watch him decode passages of our study material while his hands fidgeted. His typewritten pages were, as expected, full of coded references to scraps of a very strange education—bits about the chemical makeup of emotional responses and allusions to texts I'd never heard of. But he had seemed equally ashamed to have to ask me to explain a comment about *The Red Badge of Courage* and a line of *Hamilton* lyrics I'd written in the margins of my history section.

We'd arrived at the dining hall separately, but he hadn't hesitated to take the seat next to me. Which felt like something.

Under the table, I swung my leg over into his and tapped the sides of our shoes together. "Esoteric to the max."

He gave me a split-second secret smile before turning back to his pizza.

On the other side of me, I could feel the intensity of Leigh's curiosity aimed at the side of my head. I really wished she were less observant.

"Did anyone else notice that they're completely out of water bottles today?" I asked, reaching for the small box of apple juice I'd had to settle for.

Jams took a deep pull from his soda. "Maybe our alien overlords want us chockablock with diabetes when they take us over."

"'Chockablock' is hella British," Kate said.

"'Hella' is hella Californian," Jams retorted.

"'Hella chockablock' is hell of redundant," Leigh giggled.

We were all laughing when Meg appeared and threw herself down on the bench next to Galen.

"Hello, happy people," she said, propping her elbows on the table.

Kate stiffened. "Hello, traitor."

Meg's face softened to a down fluff. She gave a curious cartoon kitten tip of her head. "Kate, I already told you that there was no way I could have warned you guys about the Cheeseman trials. We would all be disqualified if I cheated for you. That would mean no scholarship for any of you and no paycheck for me and Hari. It's not worth it. But it's okay!" She gave a shudder of excitement. "Since Miss Ever already placed in the Cheeseman, you guys are in the running to be the team that takes home five scholarships! With that in mind, I wanted to let you know that this afternoon we're going to do our first mock Melee. It's only amongst our team, just to get some practice in. You know, take the edge off a little bit." Her eyes scanned over

each of us, as though taking attendance. "Oh. No Perla? Well, someone make sure to let her know, okay? I need to track down Hari and
prep."

A look passed around the table, a nonverbal contract signed and
sealed in the span of two breaths. Kate's blue eyes flashed, a deto-
nation of glee.

"Don't worry, Meg. We'll make sure she knows."

Meep.

Meep.

Perla slammed her palms down on her knees. "Hari, if you buzz
that thing one more time, I will shove it down your throat."

Hari's thumb lovingly circled the buzzer's button, poised to
strike. "If you threaten the examiners, you will be disqualified."

"Are the examiners going to go apeshit on a Taboo buzzer?" Perla
snapped.

Meg daintily straightened the stacks of sample questions and re-
aligned her highlighters. "I know it lights up your limbic system,
but swearing is also an immediate disqualification."

Perla threw her hair behind her ears and stared at the door as
though imagining storming through it.

For privacy and comfortable seating, Meg and Hari had set us
up in the lounge on the uninhabited top floor of the residence hall.
I hadn't realized how acclimated I was to the noise of my floor until
we stepped off the elevator into silence. The blank-chalkboard doors
that lined the hallway had no voices or music pulsing behind them.
There were no muffled footsteps on the carpet. Even the communal
bathroom was locked. Meg said that it'd keep anyone from trying
to live up here.

The lounge was almost identical to the one on my floor, except
that the walls were burnt orange instead of yellow. It was like studying inside of a giant pumpkin.

Meg and Hari had seated themselves in two of the room's armless upholstered chairs, with a squat table set between them. My teammates and I sat across from them, cross-legged on the floor, with our binders piled out of reach against the wall.

Ten minutes into our mock Melee, I missed my binder.

Fifteen minutes in, I would have killed for it.

"Which language takes its roots from migratory farmers and Southwest Asian traders?" Hari asked Kate.

"Swahili."

Hari's thumb circled the buzzer again. "Name three of the languages from which Swahili takes its roots."

"Arabic. Portuguese." Kate rocked forward, the muscles in her shoulders roiling. Her narrow face started to purple. "French?"

Meep.

"The question passes to Galen," Hari said.

This was my least favorite rule of the Melee. Not only could the categories switch on a dime, but questions answered incorrectly could get thrown to another team member, so there was no time to relax. It was a randomized attack. Even the smallest distraction could tank your score.

"Arabic, Portuguese, and German," Galen said.

"Correct." Hari glanced over at Meg, who marked Galen's new score down in a notebook.

"Switch categories," Meg said. She and Hari leaned left in sync like they were controlling a mecha robot together. Meg planted her finger on the page they were looking for. "Art history. Hunter, please name three of the members of the Anonymous Society of Painters, Sculptors, and Printmakers credited with the creation of the impressionist movement."

Hunter raked his hands through his hair. "Are all of the questions going to ask for three examples?"

"Would you prefer that they ask for *all* of the examples?" Hari asked.

"Nope. Three is great," Hunter said quickly. "Impressionists: Monet, Degas, . . . Pissaro?"

Damn. I definitely hadn't known that one. I made a note on the single piece of plain paper that the counselors had allowed us to keep. Leigh had titled her page "Additional Study Needed."

I called mine "Crap You Don't Know."

"For full credit, you will need to know the first name of those artists as well," Meg said to Hunter, wagging a highlighter at him. "Can you list them now?"

He shook his head and leaned over his list of unknown crap. Out of the corner of my eye, I could see Jams bump their knees together.

"Ever," Hari said, pulling my attention forward. "For what painting was the impressionist movement named?"

"Claude Monet's *Impression, Sunrise*?" I swallowed. Even from however many hundreds of miles away, I was sure Grandmother Lawrence could feel me phrasing a statement as a question. Lawrences did not uptalk. It made one appear "flighty and uneducated."

"Follow-up question," Meg said. "Which French critic observed *Impression, Sunrise* to be more of a sketch than a finished painting?"

I tried to picture my binder and the notes I had jotted down while Cornell's cocounselor had ignored us in our art history "class." But nothing was there.

"I-I don't know." The words left my throat in a painful dribble, like water wrung from a towel. I closed my eyes against the sound of the *meep*.

"The question is passed to Leigh," Hari said.

Leigh swung her head, her eyes focused on the carpet. "I don't know the answer either."

One of Hari's eyebrows twitched as he checked Meg's notes to make sure that our scores were updated. "The question is discarded after two failed attempts. The correct answer was Louis Leroy."

Right. Like LeRoy Hall near the arboretum. I had made a particular note about that because I was almost positive that LeRoy Hall was one of the arts buildings. Balls.

"Switch categories," Meg chirped. "Philosophy."

She and Hari leaned in unison again, finding the proper quiz sheet in their stacks.

The mock Melee went on for another forty-five demoralizing minutes. Every ring of the buzzer set my teeth on edge. My Crap You Don't Know page was filled to bursting with notes that got smaller and more squished together until I was writing upside down in the margins.

Finally, Hari tucked the buzzer into the pocket of his jeans. "That's enough for today."

Kate flopped forward, throwing her arms out as she pressed her face into the carpet and groaned. Jams scrubbed his face with his hands. Perla let out a series of sighed curses.

Hari frowned down the line of us, making sure everyone got their turn to feel his radiating disappointment. "An actual Melee skirmish can last anywhere from an hour to three hours. Right now, none of you had a percent-correct high enough to carry this team to a second round. Keep that in mind when you're studying."

"Tomorrow is a free day," Meg said, as the team blearily went to retrieve our binders. "We'll have check-ins throughout the day so we don't lose anyone, but we won't have a team meeting and you're totally encouraged to take a full mental health day. There will be some field day games out, but it's your day and you're welcome to relax. You also have the rest of tonight free. It's taco night in the dining hall!"

"I hate when they play good cop, bad cop," Galen said, leading the way out of the room while Meg and Hari stayed to clean up the lounge. "It makes them feel like my parents."

"I think my brain is leaking out of my ears," Hunter said. "That's not great."

Leigh skipped forward, pressing the button on the elevator. "We've only been here for a week; of course we aren't ready for competition. None of the teams would be ready to compete yet." She stretched her arms over her head. "The dining hall can't screw up tacos, right?"

"Where have you been eating for the last week?" Perla asked.

I bounced on the balls of my feet, watching the sign above the elevator slowly light up each floor number. All of my wrong answers replayed in the back of my head, a dozen whispered failures. Could we really pull it together enough in a week to even qualify for a second round of the Melee?

"That was a special kind of awful," Brandon said quietly as he sidled up next to me. "Halfway through, I was sure I was having a nightmare."

"How did you convince yourself it was real?" I asked.

His mouth scrunched to the side. "I don't know if I have. If my sisters show up or if I get pantsed, I guess I'll know for sure that I'm asleep."

I smiled. "Or just having the worst day ever. How many sisters should I be keeping watch for?"

He shuddered. "Don't even joke about them showing up. If you talk about them too much, they appear. Like Bloody Mary. Or Beetlejuice." He held up his notepaper, which was so covered in notes that it was close to weeping blue ink. "I have to study tomorrow."

I showed him my page. "Me too."

"Sci-fi section?"

19

I know zilch about classical music," I said, pressing my head down on the table. After my morning run and the standard lukewarm breakfast with the team, Brandon and I had met under the Magrathea poster in the sci-fi section. We had swapped binders immediately, both flipping to the music section.

Except neither of us had made any useful notes in the music section.

Teal double knots looked up at me from the tops of my shoes. They bounced as I stretched my calves.

Brandon's black and white Chuck Taylors flexed. I was beginning to think that he had only packed one pair of shoes to wear for three weeks straight. "I can say 'zilch' in three languages and I don't know anything about classical music."

I peeked up at him, resting my cheek against the cold pages of the binder. "Three languages?"

He counted on his fingers, starting thumb first. "*Non*; that's French. *Nil*; Latin—obviously."

I snorted. "Obviously."

"And," he aimed three fingers at me smugly, his eyes flashbulb bright, "*sod all*."

"One week of living with Jams and you're already fluent in vaguely British slang. What would you do if you found out that his mom wasn't actually from England?"

He considered this. He must have been scrunching his forehead, because his hair slid all the way down to his eyelashes. His hair was hypnotically shiny and super thick. I kept thinking about running my fingers through it to test its depths, even though it was so hypocritical. There was literally nothing worse than strangers asking to touch my hair. It was so creepy and invasive.

But being this close to Brandon was starting to make me feel like a creep. So.

"I would take that secret to my grave," he said.

"Really? You wouldn't let it slip even in the split second before you died?"

He shook his head solemnly, letting the hair sway across his forehead. "No way. What if Perla heard me?"

"Oh, good point. The gloating would be unbearable."

"Besides, I think he might be telling the truth," he said, reaching for a pencil and twirling it between his fingers like a tiny baton. "This morning, I heard him say 'yaw-gert.'"

I pried my attention away from the whir of the spinning pencil. "What the hell is yaw-gert?"

"Yogurt."

"I don't think that's how British people say *yogurt*. I don't think that's how anyone pronounces anything."

"That's also possible." The pencil stilled, resting on top of his middle finger. "Okay. Classical music."

I patted the open binder in front of me and forced myself to sit up straight again.

"I blame Faulkner," I said.

"That's not fair. None of the counselors have actually taught anything."

"But I'm looking at this page," I stabbed my finger onto the offending sentence, "and it says that the baroque period was 'typified by its ornate sound and exaggerated dissonance.' Maybe if I'd actually heard a baroque symphony I would have an idea what that means. I can run back to my room and get my phone, I guess. We could stream a freaking symphony while we study—"

"No!" he blurted. The pencil dropped onto the table and rolled into the unlit lamp.

"No?" I prompted.

He shrank back, his mouth going wiggly. "Remember when you said you were hoping for some genius school juice?"

The most embarrassing thing I've ever said? I thought. *I wish I could forget about it so quickly.*

"I remember," I said.

"This is it. I think." He squinted at me as though bracing for impact. When I raised my eyebrows and waited for him to continue, he exhaled. "I think what the counselors were pointing out by not actually hosting classes last week was that it doesn't matter whether or not you've internalized the lessons. It's not about being the most well-versed person in the Melee. Actually, filling in too many of the gaps in the information that the binder provides would be a disadvantage. You can't live in the details. You'll drown." He knocked on the binder in front of him—my binder. "This is us drowning."

"Because we're in here and it's supposed to be our free day?"

He gave an emphatic nod that sent ripples through his hair. "Because everyone is studying on their free day. There were people with binders all over the place between the residence hall and here. And I bet some of them are thinking what you are—they should listen to symphonies. Or download the audiobooks. Or research in the library."

I could feel awareness starting to crest, a sunrise slowly filling the inside of my head in deep purples and streaky pinks. "But what the Melee is really measuring is how much we can take from the binders themselves. It's like our first lesson with Hari. Jams tried to add information about Oscar Wilde and he got shot down. They're overloading us to see if we can be overloaded."

Like boot camp, I thought. I could kick myself for not putting that together earlier. No one at boot camp would volunteer to get less sleep or to do an extra set of push-ups. You took what was given to you and proved that you could thrive in it.

"And to see who cracks under the pressure," he said. "If you want to know what the Mess is like, it's that. It's watching the smartest people you've ever met constantly melting down. Crying in the hallways. Getting notes from their psychiatrists that the workload is too much." He picked up the pencil again and wove it between his fingers. "But you get through it by sticking to the curriculum. You don't do them any good if you can't cope."

"And since they helped write the rules of the Melee, you think it has the same rhetoric?"

"Probably?" He swept a thumb over the edge of the binder's pages, making a heavy ruffling sound. "This is too much information for one person to memorize. The odds are against us going in. They start with overloading us with information, and then leave spaces where it would make sense to research. Filling in the gaps between dates. Listening to the music. Reading the books that include our short stories."

"Researching the Mollos before starting on the Incas?" I offered.

"Exactly," he said excitedly. "But can you think of a single question during the practice last night that didn't come from the binders?"

I replayed the night before on fast-forward, stealing a glimpse at my Crap You Don't Know sheet for reference. "Uh. None?"

"None."

"So we don't deviate from the binders at all. Even when there are gaping holes, like how ornate the sound of the baroque period was?"

"Even then."

I rubbed my lips together, feeling a snag of dead skin. I nipped at it. "Can I ask you something without you getting offended?"

He frowned. "That's ominous, but sure?"

"Did you really just think of this, or did one of your friends tell you?"

"You heard Meg tell Kate that cheating wasn't worth her losing her paycheck. Believe me. They all feel that way. If it were an internship, they wouldn't shut up. Now they won't shut up, but they aren't helpful." He hazarded an awkward smile. "I swear, the counselors won't tell me anything about the inner mechanics of the camp. And if they let anything slip, I will tell you." He held up two fingers. "Geek's honor."

"Getting into this school means everything to me," I said. "My family would never agree to let me go to a liberal arts school. They'd never pay for it. I have to win placement to go here."

His wide, hot chocolate eyes bore into mine. "I know you and your brother are here. I promise I wouldn't try to screw up your chances at this scholarship. I really believe that this is how they're testing us, Ever."

It was like he'd turned off the oxygen in the room. I struggled to take in a full breath, my pseudonym echoing in his quiet baritone. I had actually expected to hear him say "Elliot."

Your Christian names are still an insuperable barrier, quoted my brain.

Why couldn't things have worked out like they did in the movies? If my life were a romantic comedy, we would study *The Importance of Being Earnest* and I could dazzle everyone with my prodigious skill for quoting Oscar Wilde.

"I trust you," I said, forcing a smile. "Let's start memorizing this binder then. How do you feel about flash cards?"

"Noon," Brandon announced, checking the binary clock built into the wall above the archway. "We should go find a check-in."

In order to make sure that none of us strayed too far, we had been given a list of check-in spots at breakfast. Between each meal, we were expected to hit up a sign-in sheet manned by a counselor. I was sure it was a legal buffer that would not hold up in court.

"You know what would make these flash cards even better?" Brandon asked as we started clearing the Magrathea table.

"If they weren't scraps of binder paper?"

"Sure, if you're going to be picky about it. I was thinking they'd look nicer typed."

I closed his binder and slid it across the table to him. "Your typewriter obsession is so bizarre."

"Yeah. It's shocking that my genius school education didn't make me cooler," he said in a sarcastic monotone.

"Sure, blame the Messina." I laughed. "I'm sure you were super cool before high school."

"No one's cool before high school. It takes a while to figure out that popular and cool aren't synonymous."

I tucked my pencils back into the pocket of my binder. I certainly hadn't been cool before—or during—high school. Switching schools twice in elementary school had left me permanently on the fringes of high society. Hitting my growth spurts hard in middle school only made me noticeable in a *You look too old to be here* sort of way.

"Are the popular kids in genius school still the pretty people?" I asked as we walked out of the sci-fi section and into the dim of the library proper.

"Some of them," he said, hoisting his binder under his arm. "Or the rich kids. It's private school and it's not cheap, so there are plenty of rich kids to choose from. The basketball team is usually more popular than the cricket players . . ." He seemed to be waiting for me to flip out when he said "cricket." We slipped through the fiction section, side by side. "Mostly people stick to their extracurricular groups."

"And where do you fit in?" I asked.

He shrugged. "None of the above. I was on student council my freshman year because the administration picks the frosh cabinet. I got voted out my sophomore year. I've kept out of extracurriculars since. Keeping up with the workload seemed like enough. It wasn't. Apparently." He lowered his voice as we passed by a row of occupied tables with lamps lit and books stacked high with nonbinder study material. "What about you? Does your school have a club for parkour and Muay Thai enthusiasts?"

"Yes. But you have to be black and tall and nerdy to join," I whispered back. "Enrollment isn't great. But our one member does have excellent taste in books, and awesome hair."

"Damn," Brandon said as we reached the exit. "I have two out of the three requirements."

"Oh, did I not mention that members can't own typewriters?"

"Ha-ha," he said dryly.

The truth was, Dad and Beth let me take Muay Thai a couple of times a week because the schedule moved around enough that I could continue babysitting Ethan when needed. Neither of them had been thrilled when I announced that I wanted to learn a full-contact fight style, but they had shut up when I reminded them that they hadn't let me try out for track because Beth had been in her fifth production of *Earnest*.

The glare of summer sunlight and a whoosh of warm air hit us as we passed through the door and took the first step. I looked up just in time to keep from crashing into Leigh and Isaiah.

Together.

Binderless.

Did I mention that they were together?

"Hey, Ever," Isaiah said, stretching my camp name out a mile as he threw on a full shit-eating, teeth-baring grin that really made me want to pop him upside the head.

"This is my brother," I said to Brandon, and every word was like yanking out one of my own teeth. "Brandon, Isaiah. Isaiah, Brandon."

"Good to meet you," Brandon said.

Isaiah lifted an eyebrow at him. "Don't we share a bathroom?"

"Yeah," Brandon said slowly. "I'm across the hall from you."

Isaiah nodded. "Right. With the big-eared kid."

"Hi, Ever. Hi, Brandon," Leigh said, her shoulders inching closer and closer to her ears. "Isaiah was looking for his cell phone, so I volunteered to help him out. His team was totally useless."

"Do you guys need help?" Brandon asked.

"Nah," Isaiah said. "We've got this."

"If you're sure," I said stiffly. "I'd hate for you to miss any important calls from home. Let me know if you need help."

"Will do, Sis," Isaiah said, and I wondered if Leigh or Brandon noticed the hiss he threw in at the end.

"I'll catch you guys at lunch!" Leigh said with a small, sharp wave.

I watched the two of them skip into the library together. Isaiah's elbow bumped Leigh's. Her giggle floated to us on the breeze, riding on the back of Isaiah's astringent cologne.

20

"He was looking for you," Leigh said, stripping off her sheets and wadding them into a zebra print ball in her arms. "And his team really is useless. Fallon keeps locking herself in her dorm, and I don't think Cornell is running their mock Melees correctly. He's being way too nice."

"It's not a problem," I lied. Even after lunch, I hadn't been able to shake the uneasy feeling caused by seeing my roommate and my fake twin together. It was too farcical. Too *Earnest*. "I was surprised because you guys only met once."

"And then we met a second time, this morning, when he was searching for you in the quad." She kicked under her bed until her heel caught the handle of a voluminous blue IKEA bag that was big enough that she could have comfortably slept in it. She dropped her sheets into it. "Go ahead and toss in your socks."

"Thank you," I gasped. I unzipped my suitcase, rummaging to the bottom to find the dirty socks I'd tried to smell-proof in a zip-lock bag over the last week. "When is our next check-in?"

"Three o'clock in the lobby." She shook her head. "Not like they even need to bother. If anyone got seen breaking the rules, some-one would turn them in."

"It's a liability waiver," I said, shaking my dirty socks into the laundry bag. "If someone runs off campus or gets pregnant, the school can say that they have written proof of where everyone else was."

She giggled. "Okay, Miss Lawyer's Daughter."

My stomach dropped through the floor, landing somewhere in the lobby. I had never talked to her about my dad. "Isaiah mentioned that, huh?"

"In passing." She shook her pillow until the case slipped into her hands. She looked at me over her shoulder. "What's the deal with you and the ghost? Are you testing the corporeality of his mouth yet?"

"What? No. Of course not."

Her slanted front teeth peeked through her smile. "A few more protests, please."

"We're studying together," I said, slowly and pointedly. "Last night's Melee was a massacre. No one has time to think about anything other than these stupid binders. And when we do, it'll be time to go home. I needed a study partner, and my new bestie wasn't available."

Her smile vanished. "Oh. I'm sorry. I'm not used to my hermiting getting in other people's way. You probably don't have to deal with being completely invisible, but it kind of becomes second nature to blend in."

"You can go unnoticed while also being an Amazon." I folded my arms over my chest. "But you aren't invisible here. You don't have to blend in. That was our deal, remember? You can hermit when you want to, but I'm here to kick it whenever you need to be seen."

She wrung her hands in the hem of her shirt. "Have I told you recently how glad I am that I get to live with you this summer?"

I smiled. "No, but the feeling is mutual."

Underneath the wardrobe on Leigh's side of the room, there was a thump and a muffled roar. We both turned toward it.

"Um," she said. "If that's a possum, I am going to run."

Another set of thumps—this time under my bed. I got down on

the floor, gazing into the darkness under my bed frame. There weren't even dust bunnies under there. But with my ear against the carpet, I could just barely make out the next shout.

Eee! Mmfer!

I glanced back at Leigh. "Who lives under us?"

"Teams are divided up based on room number. Under us is the boys' floor. So it must be either Galen and Hunter or—"

The next thump landed right under my hand. I jolted back into a squat.

Leigh clapped her hands together and cackled. "G-g-g-ghost!"

"What do you think they want?" I asked, as two more knocks sounded under the wardrobe again. "We can't go in their room and find out. We'll all get disqualified. And I don't have either of their phone numbers."

"We don't have to go to their room," she said. She leaped into a pair of flip-flops and stashed her room key in her bra.

"Because you packed two cans and a piece of string?"

She bent down in front of her wardrobe and cupped her hands around her mouth. Lips dangerously close to the carpet, she yelled, "Hold on!"

"Wait," I called to the back of her head as she rushed toward the door. "What about our laundry?"

She was already disappearing into the hallway, the door hanging open in her wake. I scrambled to my feet and charged after her. Thanks to my much longer stride, it was easy to catch up with her. The two of us power walked down the hall. When we hit the elevator, Leigh made a hard left, throwing open the door to the stairs. I stumbled behind her, listening to the echo of her sandals slapping her feet as we trotted down.

I jumped the last step, landing in front of the first-floor entrance. Leigh's small, square fingers incrementally pushed in the touch bar handle until it gave a delicate *click*. The door inched open, revealing a long beige-carpeted hallway identical to our own, except for the handwriting on the chalkboard doors.

144 ★ LILY ANDERSON

"Give me your shoe," Leigh whispered. When I opened my mouth to argue, she tipped her head back to glare at me. "My flip-flop won't fly far enough. It's basic Newtonian physics."

"Effing Newton didn't pay a hundred bucks for Nikes," I muttered, hopping out of one of my shoes. I handed it over, shying back toward the stairs as Leigh held the door open with her hip and chucked the shoe as hard as she could at the first door on the left. The shoe bounced off the door and rolled pathetically on the floor.

Leigh looked over her shoulder at me, her forehead crinkled.

I cleared my throat and did my best impression of my father trying to scare the neighborhood cats out of our flower beds, stomping and letting out a deep, "Hey!"

There was a breath-holding, sweat-forming silence before Jams darted into the hallway, Brandon, Galen, and Hunter behind him. The four of them bum rushed the door.

"My shoe!" I pointed at the lone Nike on the floor. Hunter grabbed it without slowing and tossed it to me, underhand.

"Upstairs, upstairs," Jams puffed, rushing past us and swinging himself up onto the stairs by the railing. Leigh was at his heels, her sandals louder than ever.

I stuffed my foot back into my shoe and followed the stampede of my teammates.

"We have to keep an eye on the time," Hunter said, propelling himself off of the cement wall and onto the next flight. "If we miss check-in, we're screwed."

"I set the alarm on my phone," Galen said.

"Go get Kate and meet us on the top floor," Brandon called to Leigh.

"In the pumpkin lounge!" Jams added.

"I'm on it!" she said, running ahead and flinging herself back onto our floor.

I caught up to Jams and Brandon, the untied laces of my tossed shoe bouncing against my ankles. "What the shit is going on? Are we under attack? Are we being hunted?"

"Not yet," Jams wheezed.

"No one is going to hunt us," Brandon said quickly. "But we have to talk in private."

We all paused on the top landing. Jams pushed open the door, revealing pitch darkness. He, Hunter, and Galen dug into their pockets and pulled out their cell phones, holding them aloft like dim flashlights. Huddled together, we made our way toward the lounge.

I flipped on the lights as we entered the pumpkin. Jams dove for the switches, slapping them off again, leaving us with only the hazy light from the two skinny windows.

"We should stay away from the windows, too," Brandon said, pressing himself against one of the orange walls and crossing his arms. "They face into the quad."

Galen threw himself down on one of the armless lounge chairs. He tipped his face up at me. "You're going to want to sit down, Ever. This. Is. Big."

"Oh my God, can you guys stop talking like you're in a bad spy movie?" I asked. I felt my hands on my hips. I was one foot tap away from turning into Beth. Or one eye roll from turning into my mom. "For real. What's going on?"

Jams shook his head, making himself comfortable on the floor next to Hunter. "Not until we're all together."

With a growl, I threw myself onto one of the squat padded stools. It would have been too easy to kick all of them until they stopped playing games, but it wouldn't have been great for my social life. I tugged at my hair, snapping small snarls between my index and middle finger.

Finally, footsteps thundered down the hall again. All heads turned to see Leigh and Kate appear in the doorway.

"Great," Jams said. He lifted his butt to reach into his back pocket. He tossed a folded mass of goldenrod papers onto the center of the floor. "This changes everything."

"Don't mind them," I told Leigh and Kate, getting down onto the carpet to pick up the papers. "They've gone all *Bourne Identity* in the last ten minutes."

The wad unfolded into six pieces of paper. I smoothed them over my knee before holding them up to read in the dim light.

"You found the kitchen schedule?" Kate asked, reading over my shoulder. "I don't think being able to anticipate what the food could taste like will help. I'm happier when I don't know what they're trying to make."

Leigh shuddered. "Those tacos. So cold. So wet. Why were they so wet?"

"Past that," Jams said, motioning for me to look at the pages.

I dropped the first page and found more of the food schedule. Past that was a kitchen cleaning roster. And then a page that was handwritten. The writing was neat and rounded.

June 24: Amoeba tag—fire drill all call
June 25: The Breakfast Club reenactment—breakfast
June 26: Arboretum climb—afternoon check-in
June 29: Rubik's cube—timed in first period
July 01: Campus run—post lunch
July 02: Hula hoops—lunch clean up
July 03: Dagobah crawl and lightsabers—team meeting on Mud Trail
July 04: Patriotic talent show—after dinner
July 06: Extreme Hokey Pokey—before dinner
July 08: Playground day—after skirmishes
July 09: Treasure hunt—all day

"Where did you get this?" Leigh breathed.

"It was in one of the forts in Fort Farm," Jams said.

The page was starting to sweat between my fingers. All of the Cheeseman trial events, through to the last week of camp. It was overwhelming. I let it drift back to the carpet. Kate snatched it up and held it close to her face.

"What is extreme hokey pokey?" she asked.

"I've seen one of the counselors in Fort Farm," I said, remembering the Perfect Nerd Girl standing in her pajamas earlier in the week. "I think she might be sleeping out there. Were there any forts covered in sheets when you went there?"

Hunter shook his head. It could have been a trick of the light, but his face seemed pinker.

"What are the chances that this is a test too?" Kate asked, the list of events still hovering under her nose. "Like the movie night. What if we're supposed to turn this into Meg and Hari?"

"We're not giving this back," Jams said. "A gold bar dropped into our laps. You'd have to be off your freaking trolley to give it away. Do you guys know what we could do with this?"

The possibility that we had a list of the rest of the Cheeseman events buzzed around my brain like a swarm of overly hopeful bees. It was like finding a treasure map. If we could prepare for the Cheeseman as well as we prepared for the Melee, the chances of going home empty-handed went down to almost zero.

"We could win five scholarships," Galen said.

"Which is great, but there are seven of us," I said.

"Technically there are eight of us," Brandon said, kicking the carpet.

Leigh's fingers folded together, knuckles popping. "I know we didn't tell Perla about the mock Melee, but this is more serious, right? It'd be wrong not to tell her."

"And if she tells her friends on Team Six?" Hunter asked. "Or if she lets it slip to a counselor?"

Jams scoffed. "And also, do any of us want her to win?"

"Is that our place to decide?" I asked. I had no warm and fuzzy feelings for Perla, and I definitely thought she would spill our team secrets to anyone who would listen, but having her fate in my hands made me nervous. Sure, she was unpleasant and rude and generally awful to be around . . .

Wait, what was my point again?

"What do you think, Kate?" Leigh asked.

"Yeah," Galen said. "You have to live with her. If you don't want to keep this from her, we'll track her down and tell her what's going on."

Kate shook her head slowly back and forth. "I-I don't think she needs to know. Not because she's mean or because she took down my decorations or because her Starbucks order is pretentious. This is between us as friends. You guys are sharing this with us because we are your friends. And she's not our friend. She made it very clear that she did not want that."

"I'm on board with that," Hunter said.

"Pinky swears all around?" Leigh asked, holding up her hands.

I locked my pinky with hers and held my other hand out to Brandon, who only hesitated for a second before curving his pinky around mine. One by one, we formed a circle of connected pinkies around the kitchen roster, the lunch menus, and the list of Cheeseman events.

And Galen's cell phone alarm went off, announcing the next check-in.

21

C heck-in has been moved to the arboretum," Hunter reported, striding back across the lobby from the empty table where a counselor should have been waiting for us.

"Six twenty-nine, arboretum climb," Leigh recited, excitedly stretching the hem of her T-shirt. "The page foretold this moment."

"Does anyone know how to get to the arboretum?" Galen asked.

"I've run through it a couple of times," I said. "I can get us there."

The quad was empty as we left the residence hall behind. A lone soccer ball sat in the middle of the green, with the Team Five flag from the first day planted nearby, a remnant of the field day that the other teams had been enjoying.

"Keep your eyes out," I said to my lagging teammates. "Brandon swears that there are tree houses hidden around campus."

"You say that like they're fairy rings or something," Brandon said, slouching beside me. When the team was around, it was as though he was trying to hide his entire body in his bowl cut. "It's a real thing. It's on the Wikipedia page and everything."

"Oh, well, if it's on Wikipedia, it's no bullshit." I laughed, nudging him with my elbow. His smile crept out from under his hair.

"That could be what we're doing in the arboretum," Leigh said. "Building tree houses."

"The administration wouldn't allow that. It's not safe," Kate said.

"How much of the Cheeseman trials do you think the administration actually knows about?" Galen asked.

"They are named after one of their deans," Leigh said.

"But it's not a compliment," Hunter said. "His name is Cheeseman. It's a built-in joke."

Kate's face reddened. "That's not why they'd name it after him. It's just because he's in charge."

"Look," Galen said, pointing up ahead. "LeRoy Hall. Like Louis Leroy, who . . ."

"Was the critic credited with naming the impressionist movement," Kate answered automatically.

"It's our day of rest," Jams complained. "We're supposed to be resting our brains."

"You can rest your brain. I want to win," Leigh said, bouncing ahead and turning to face us like a tiny kangaroo drill sergeant. Skipping backwards, she barked, "The term *groupthink* was coined by which research psychologist? Ever!"

"Irving Janis," I said quickly. "From Yale."

Leigh punched the air. "What's the product of frequency and wavelength, Galen?"

"The speed the wave moves through space, ma'am!" Galen shouted.

Pogoing with more ease than should have been possible in flip-flops, Leigh kept lobbing questions at us until we came to the curve in the sidewalk that led under the tall trees that tangled together, blocking out the light.

"No one else is shocked that there's a random forest on campus?" Galen asked, craning his head to look at the ceiling of branches and leaves.

"We were out here earlier today," Jams said, nodding toward Hunter. "Fort Farm is on the other side."

"And there are pictures of it on the website," Kate said.

Galen hung his head. "I need to leave the dorm more."

The path tipped downhill, revealing the fork in the road. In front of the directions sign sat a check-in table identical to the one we had left in the residence hall. The counselor from MIT sat behind it, his gym rat bulk dwarfing the metal folding chair under him. He aimed a pen at us as we approached.

"Team number?"

"Team One," Leigh said. "All of us. We're missing Perla Loya, though."

MIT scratched the answer onto the check-in paper and waved us toward the right side of the fork. "Your counselors are waiting for you that way."

"Why?" Hunter asked.

MIT's eyebrows went up, highlighting how Cro-Magnon-like his forehead was. "Because we're in charge of you?"

"Peter," Brandon said, his hands in the pockets of his jeans, his shoulders rounded. "Is this another trial or what?"

MIT—*Peter*—narrowed his eyes to periwinkle slits. "You guys are like ten steps away. Just go before you get me in trouble."

"Got it," Brandon said, smothering a smile at the corner of his mouth.

We shuffled toward the right fork in the road, seven rigid spines and held breaths going deeper into the belly of the arboretum. Peter faded out of sight behind us as the voices of the rest of the campers rose out of the trees. Off the path, clusters of teams and counselors stood together around a single thick-trunked tree with a bushy canopy of pointed green leaves. Nestled on one of the pale branches was a pallet, the kind used to populate Fort Farm. With four posts built into the sides and a wrinkled blue tarp stretched over the top, it was more of a tree shanty than a tree house.

"Inside of the tree house is a bell," Bryn Mawr was saying to the congregated campers as we stepped through the tall grass. "Each competitor will scale the tree and ring the bell, one at a time. The camper who makes the best time wins this challenge."

"It's real," Kate whispered into her hands as she struggled to hold her face on her skull. "The list is real."

"See?" Brandon said to me, his face igniting into a grin as wide as a church door. "Tree house."

The line of competitors curved all the way back onto the paved trail. Our team had split up in the shuffle. Hunter and Jams were close to the front with Kate. Galen and Brandon had opted to sit on the sidelines. I noticed Perla standing in the grass not far away from them, her cool girls at her side, none of them looking impressed by another physical challenge.

The counselors stood closest to the tree trunk, phones out to keep time. Lumberjack Beard's bullhorn was back. The Perfect Nerd Girl seemed to be attempting to wrestle it away from him as he fussed with the volume over her head. I wished she tried this hard to keep him from serving us lukewarm slop for dinner.

"Ever!" I saw a brown hand waving high in the air, cutting through the crowd like a shark's fin. Isaiah's dreads were pulled back into a ponytail as big around as my fist, leaving his greasy forehead on full display. I had to stumble out of the way as he slid into line in front of me.

"Excuse you," I said.

"You're excused," he said, barely giving me a passing glance before leaning forward to invade Leigh's personal space. "Hey, Leigh."

"Hi, Zay," she said.

"Zay?" I echoed.

He turned back to me, his lips pressed together so tight they had a slope of zero. "Yes, Ev?"

Oh, wonderful. We had twin nicknames now.

"Did you find your phone yet?" I asked him.

"I'm working on it." He shrugged. "It probably fell out of my pocket when you tossed me around Mudders Meadow. Good thing they're only letting us up the tree one person at a time."

"Yes," I said. "Who would come get you if you got hurt? Dad is so busy."

Translation: *Your dad is deployed right now and if you break a bone up here the camp is going to have to call Aunt Bobbie to come get you. So don't mess with me right now because I will snap your arm in half.*

I hoped he got all of that from my tone.

"When was the last time you guys climbed a tree?" Leigh asked, stepping back so that she could get a full view of the tree house.

I thought about the rough bark on the oak tree in front of my house. Ethan often begged to sit on my shoulders so he could swing himself onto the lower boughs. It wasn't super comfortable up there in the company of territorial squirrels and falling acorns, but he liked the novelty of it. Dad had repeatedly and firmly denied his request for a tree house. A real one with walls and windows, not like the flimsy structure currently hanging over our heads.

"We have an oak tree in our front yard the perfect height for climbing," Isaiah said.

I planted my feet firmly in the grass to keep from jumping out of my shoes before I remembered that he and Sidney had picked me up from my house for our family dinner the night I'd run away. I wasn't used to Isaiah knowing anything about me other than the information relayed between our mothers.

To keep the trial from stretching on to lights out, everyone was given a three-minute time limit to reach the bell in the tree house. Most people didn't make it up the trunk by the time Lumberjack Beard called "Time!" into his bullhorn. Hunter was the first person to ring the bell, followed closely by Jams, who beat his time by fifteen seconds.

After Jams shimmied down to the ground again, Hunter greeted him at the edge of the field with a whoop. Panting but smiling, Jams threw his arms around Hunter's neck. They kissed like there was no greater celebration than mashing their faces together. And, really, there probably wasn't.

Isaiah opened his mouth—undoubtedly to say something shitty

that would leave me no choice but to start breaking his bones—but Leigh clasped her hands over her heart.

"Oh, I was hoping they'd get together," she said. "I was afraid their uneven levels of attractiveness would get in the way." She scrunched her face and looked up at me. "God, don't tell anyone I said that. I just mean that Jams is an awkward weirdo like me."

"You're not a weirdo," Isaiah said. "You're unique."

Leigh blinked at him, unaware that the line was moving again. "Oh. Um. Thank you?"

I held my tongue through the next few competitors. Once Leigh was stretching against the base of the tree trunk, I hissed at Isaiah, "What in the hell are you doing? Stop flirting with my roommate."

"What?" he squawked. It was easy to forget how young he was, until he started bugging out his eyes like a cornered animal. "I'm not flirting with her. You let her stand there and talk shit about herself. I was being nice. She's your friend, isn't she?"

"Yes," I said, shoving aside the hiccup of guilt in my throat. Why hadn't I defended Leigh to herself? She always seemed so comfortable announcing herself as awkward. It hadn't occurred to me that it might come from a negative place.

"And I'm your brother. Why wouldn't I be nice to your friends?"

"Why aren't you making friends of your own?"

"You don't know my life."

Just over his shoulder, I watched as Leigh kicked her flip-flops off, barely missing Simone, the Rayevich counselor with the box braids. Hugging the flat, ribbed bark, Leigh pressed her feet flat against the tree trunk, her butt stuck out in full squat before she jumped. Once, twice, three times, each jump propelling her impossibly upwards. When her arm was close enough, she reached up and swung herself in one fluid arc up into the tree house, landing with a resounding *ding* on the bell.

"Thirty-five seconds," Lumberjack Beard said, reading from the Perfect Nerd Girl's phone. He had forgotten the booming announcer voice he usually used into the bullhorn. He turned to face the line of us. "Does anyone think they can beat that?"

As Leigh descended Meg broke into wild applause, which the rest of us picked up. Leigh's cheeks went livid pink as her bare feet hit the ground.

"That was pretty cute, though," Isaiah said, clapping his hands loudly. "She's mixed, right?"

"Shut up, Zay."

"Never, Ever."

I couldn't stop my hand from flying up and slapping him upside the head. As he whined, I rushed out to the sidelines to watch Leigh receive her blue ribbon.

22

To: Elliot L. Gabaroche
From: Lieutenant Colonel Marissa Lawrence
Subject: Hey Stranger

Ellie,

I hope Cross Fit is going well. All that shit looks like too much jumping for my old bones. And in Sacramento summer? Whew. You're going to be a superhero by the end of all this.

I put a little extra money into your checking account. (Don't get too excited. It's not enough money for new shoes.) Do something other than sit around the theater and the gym, okay? Go get a smoothie or an ice cream cone. Oh, and return a phone call sometime. Your voicemail is tired of me.

Loving you,
Mom

My heart gave a painful squeeze as I closed the email. I wasn't ready to engage with my life outside of camp. I made a mental note to check my bank account and write a thank you text to my mom before bed. I closed the Internet browser, letting my unfinished essay take over the screen again.

"Ever, I need you to learn everyone's name," Leigh said, stretching her arms over her head and pointing her toes. She made tiny kicking motions like she was swimming through the grass in the quad.

I turned off my computer's Wi-Fi surreptitiously. Leigh was distraction enough. "We're only here for another two weeks. By the time I learn them, I'll be back in California."

"Don't say that." Her head popped up while her body remained planted against the ground. "I'm not ready to think about the end yet."

Since everyone at camp was hyperfocused on their binders and the Cheeseman events, the counselors had carved out an extra period for us to work on the essays that were also required for the Melee. We were allowed to use the essays we had submitted with our Onward applications, as long as we padded them out from two pages to ten.

Ten pages. Not including the required footnotes.

Rather than holing up inside while the sun was out, Leigh had agreed to sit with me in the quad. Her notebook and pencil sat forgotten beside her while she contorted her body into a variety of yoga poses that were supposed to get her inspiration flowing. It didn't appear to be working.

Lumberjack Beard—or *Ben*, as Leigh had just insisted I call him—had broken down the structure of our theses last week before letting us flounder in our own ideas. It should be a personal statement backed by historical facts and evidence, leading back into personal information. I'd gone through my essay on why I wanted to go to Rayevich and found all of the places where I could easily slip in information about the history of the science fiction I liked. It was harder finding the places where I could talk more about why I liked it.

Some things click into place so quietly that you can't even hear it, I typed, as Leigh tumbled backwards into a headstand. *I don't know the first time I understood what space was. It's always been there, waiting for me to return to it.*

Now how was I supposed to connect that with real, historical facts? It was like opening up my rib cage and stuffing memos inside. I remembered Galen scoffing at the idea of us needing help with our essays, on the first day of classes. I missed agreeing with him.

"Damn and crap and balls. I need to have a full draft of this ready to print by dinner so I can print it out in the library before we have class tomorrow." I closed the laptop screen and glanced at Leigh's rapidly reddening upside-down face. "You know, if you popped your head off right now, you would look exactly like the Cheshire cat."

"I hate *Alice in Wonderland,*" she mused. "And *Peter Pan.* We glorify so many books written by pedophiles." She bent her knees and slowly lowered herself into downward dog. "Are you studying again tonight?"

"Aren't we all studying literally all the time?" I asked the top of her head. The neon yellow was starting to fade, letting the hint of dark roots start to bleed through. Until Isaiah had mentioned her being mixed, I hadn't considered what her hair would look like grown out. I couldn't picture her with my springy-soft curls. Maybe her hair would be ringlety, like my brother's had been before Dad convinced Beth to let him start shaving it off.

It seemed rude to ask her, though.

"Are you studying with Brandon tonight?" she clarified, the question aimed at her own belly button.

"I don't know." And I didn't. Sure, we had studied together regularly for the last few nights, but every day was a new possibility that he wouldn't at some point look at me and say, "Sci-fi?," as though I wasn't already heading there or disappearing to the Magrathea table mentally throughout the day.

"Ever," she said. "Come on."

"What? You come on."

"No." She drew out the word into a trill. "You come on."

"We could do this for the rest of our lives and neither of us would get anywhere."

"Fine." She dropped into a push-up position and curved her body upward like a snake so she could look me in the eye. "If you tripped and fell into Brandon's mouth, would you immediately back away or would you—I don't know—make yourself at home?"

I glared at her. "I am not going to dignify that with a response."

"Okay. A nonconsensual hypothetical wasn't the best place to start. What if you had a written confession from him that he would be into you tripping and falling onto his face?"

"Why am I so clumsy in this fantasy?"

"There are trip wires everywhere. Or tree roots. Or you're so overwhelmed with ghostly lust that you forget how to use your feet."

I reopened my laptop. Working on my essay was way more useful than putting a magnifying glass up to how I felt about my study buddy.

God. Were we study buddies? That was the most sexless sanction you could give someone, outside of actually becoming related to them.

"How close are we to lunch?" Leigh asked, dropping back down onto her forearms so that her body went board straight. It was no wonder she'd been able to scurry up the ash tree in the arboretum. She had the abdominal strength of a steel beam.

I laughed. "You're kidding, right? We're fifteen minutes into this period."

She raised one arm off the ground and pointed toward the residence hall. Kate was marching down the steps, her binder hugged to her chest as tightly as possible. She took short, scuttling steps toward us.

"Sorry," she said, halting abruptly a couple of feet away. "It is so loud in the hall right now. I couldn't focus. It's like no one else is worried about their essays. You guys don't mind if I join you, do you?"

"Go right ahead," Leigh said.

Kate let out an audible sigh of relief and sat down next to Leigh's stretched legs, smoothing her binder over her knees. She plucked a pencil out from the rubber band holding back her ponytail and starting writing in a flurry.

Leigh caved to the peer pressure, finally lying down flat and drawing her notebook under her nose.

The three of us worked in relative silence for about ten minutes before I looked up to see Galen and Hunter coming out of the residence hall, both with laptops under their arms. They sat down with us in time to watch Brandon and Jams following their footsteps.

"In case you were wondering if we can hear what's happening on your floor," Jams said with a grimace as he sat down beside Hunter, "we can."

"I already knew that," I said. "You knocked on my floor yesterday."

"Well, we knocked on our ceiling," Brandon said. I was unsurprised to see that he'd left the typewriter behind. It really wasn't a practical piece of equipment.

"Is that girl still crying?" Kate asked Jams, who nodded.

"Who's crying?" Leigh asked.

"Someone on your floor," Hunter said. "There's been a lot of thumping and shouting and crying."

Jams nodded. "Sounds like a nasty row."

"He means 'fight,'" Brandon translated.

"That was an easy one," Hunter said, turning his beatific smile to Jams. "That one is in *Harry Potter.*"

"But who was it?" Leigh repeated, aiming the question at Kate again. "Did you check to see if she was okay?"

"It was one of Perla's friends," Kate said, her chin retreating into her neck. She was particularly horselike when she was affronted. "Meg is taking care of it. It is her job."

Leigh tapped her pencil against her teeth. "She must not be doing a great job if the noise drove you all out here."

"But now we get all this great quality time," I said.

Brandon brought his knees up to his chest. "I bet that was Meg's plan all along."

Galen's eyes widened. "I don't think so, guys . . ."

The doors to the residence hall opened and adults appeared. I was more surprised to see them than I should have been. The school couldn't be completely abandoned. Presumably there were people working in the admissions office, and custodians working in the shadows. But I hadn't seen a real, live, non-Cheeseman adult in a full week.

The single teen in the group was a girl with blunt bangs, blood-shot eyes, and two lip rings, who I recognized as one of Perla's cool cola-drinking friends. Now, her entire face was wet with tears and mucus and smeared mascara. She was flanked by Bryn Mawr, Meg, and three women I'd never seen before. Two of them—both young-ish and blondish—held suitcases and backpacks. The third was squat, with light brown skin, and spoke into a cell phone, with a slight Spanish accent.

"I understand your concerns, but this is an issue that comes up from time to time." She was smiling as she spoke, but she kept pushing the blondish girls forward, making them skip and stumble. "Students can become overwhelmed by the distance. Classic homesickness. My own daughter did the same thing her first semester at college. Of course, the course load is a factor. But I've got to tell you that there are forty-seven other students, as well as hundreds of Onward graduates, who have been extremely successful under our unique conditions . . ."

The girl with the two lip rings started to cry loudly again, her hands trembling against her mouth. Bryn Mawr cupped her elbow and steered her toward the parking lot; the rest of the assembled party marched behind.

"Jesus Christ," Hunter said softly. "It's not that bad here, is it?"

"Sometimes it is," Kate murmured.

"Feels like home," Brandon said under his breath. I thought about him saying that his school was full of people randomly sobbing in hallways. I hadn't considered how disturbing that would be in person.

"She will call you from the airport," the brunette woman shouted into the phone. She seemed to be attempting to be louder than the crying, which was impossible. Even as their huddle disappeared behind the dining hall, the girl's sobs left a bone-chilling echo.

"Let the record show that it was a Monday when the first camper fell," Galen said with an uneasy half smile.

"Is this where the summer takes a turn for the *Hunger Games*y?" Leigh asked.

Brandon shriveled under his hair again. "I've always preferred *Battle Royale*."

"What about *Lord of the Flies*?" asked Jams.

"Hell no," Galen said. "I am not going to be your Piggy."

"And I am not going out like Rue," I said.

"They never say for sure how Panem was formed," Kate said, her words gaining strength as she picked up steam. "It could take place inside of a nuclear holocaust and you'd never even know it."

"Oh, well, in that case sign me up for the freaking Quarter Quell," I laughed. It wasn't strong enough to soothe the feeling of the girl's cries burning in my ears.

Would she be relieved when she sat down on the plane or would she want to claw her way back? Was her family happy to have her coming home?

I turned back to my laptop, the essay fragments floating on the screen. I was going to keep clawing my way forward. I hoped it was the right choice.

That night, I stood in the upper level of the library, gnawing on my lower lip as I tried for a third time to get my laptop to hook into the

Wi-Fi. There had been a rush on the printers all day, but I had slipped out of dinner early to make sure that my essay would be printed, stapled, and set to be eviscerated before I went to sleep.

The library was sort of spooky when it was completely empty. There was no click of table lamps, no rustle of turning pages. Only the sound of my own laptop keyboard and the thrum of the massive old wireless printer that I was attempting to connect to. And the pounding of blood in my temples. A headache had taken root at the nape of my neck and had been sending tendrils of pain slithering around my skull since lunch.

The endless flicker in the fluorescent lights and the hard plastic chair I was sitting on weren't helping. Rayevich was all plush or ergonomic furniture until you needed to borrow one of their printers. Then it was the same aluminum-legged blue plastic chairs that we had in the computer lab at my school.

I checked the clock in the corner of my screen. Brandon was going to meet me in the sci-fi section after dinner. We had agreed to look over each other's essays and make flash cards for the social sciences section of the binders. It was the segment Meg was in charge of overseeing and I, for one, had not spent enough time studying it. Kate was the only person on our team who had any understanding of how the limbic system affected psychological development. That seemed to disappoint Meg on a personal level.

My computer finally registered the wireless at the same time that footsteps padded up the stairs. Someone else was ditching the end of dinner.

"Hey, Ellie."

My left eyelid twitched. I pressed my fingertips against it, hoping to settle it. It didn't work. "Why do you keep creeping up on me? If you're going to murder me, just get it over with."

Chair legs screeched against the floor and Isaiah threw himself down. "A girl on my team went home today," he said.

"The girl with the lip rings?"

He nodded, leaning over to pull a slim silver laptop out of the leather bag swinging from his shoulder. "Avital."

"I watched them take her off campus. What the hell happened to her?"

"Stress, I guess." He opened the laptop and plunked in a password, cutting his eyes at me as he did it. "That's what Cornell said."

"I've never seen stress do that to a person."

He gave a noncommittal grunt. "That's why folks at Lackland cry and puke."

The entire air force had been trained on the same base since the forties, so horror stories set at Lackland Air Force Base were as commonplace at Lawrence family holidays as Great Uncle Berry's watery cranberry sauce. "Like that guy in your dad's flight that kept shitting himself. What'd they call him? Double Deuce?"

Revulsion twisted his face. "Right. Not everyone can handle the stress."

"That's not fair." I turned away from my computer, hopping my chair to face him. "They're just handling it differently."

He scoffed a tiny, condescending laugh. "She went home, Elliot."

"That's her right."

"How is she going to handle college if she can't even do three weeks away?"

"Don't try to be cynical. It's perfectly easy to be cynical," I said, quoting *Earnest* without meaning to. "How often is college going to make her memorize three hundred pages of useless, unrelated facts and write a ten-page essay in MLA format in three weeks?"

His dreads gave an almost imperceptible tremble. He narrowed his eyes at his screen, scrolling and stabbing his fingers into his keyboard until the printer next to us whirred and chugged.

"Are you going to enlist after you get your degree?" I asked, as we watched crisp white pages slip out of the printer. "If you get in here, I mean."

"Of course—"

I held up a hand to cut him off. "Don't say 'of course.' That's what you're supposed to say. Not what you mean. If you could go to a four-year college and the entire family would swear to never give you shit about not joining the air force, would you still enlist?"

"Would you?"

I gritted my teeth and focused on my computer again. The pain in the back of my head doubled. I needed to print my essay and go downstairs, away from the stink of Isaiah's cologne. "I'm sorry. I thought I was talking to a grown person. I forgot that you're a child. God, are you even sixteen yet?"

"Next week." He sniffed. "Thanks for remembering."

"Not if we're twins, you're not. You're a Scorpio now." I dug the heel of my hand into my left eye as it twitched again. Isaiah was fifteen and at camp. If Aunt Bobbie ever found out, she would skin me like a cat. He was barely out of middle school. I hit Print and my essay started cresting out of the printer.

He puffed out his chest and folded his arm. It was possible he thought it made him look older. It didn't. "If no one would give me shit, I wouldn't go."

"But you will? Even if you don't want to?"

He lifted a shoulder in half a shrug. "Maybe. I don't know."

"And if you do what that girl—Avital—did, and wash out? What then?"

A loud whisper interrupted us. It was too far away to know for sure, but it sounded vaguely like "never."

"That's you," Isaiah said dryly.

I stood up and walked over to the railing that overlooked the first floor. Brandon was standing at the base of the stairs. With his head tilted back, his hair fell away from his face. His thick eyebrows were lifted high, two questioning black swooshes.

"Hey," he said in a carrying stage whisper. "Sorry. You weren't at Magrathea."

"I'll meet you down there in a second. Grab us a table," I whispered back.

He grinned. "But there are so many choices."

I felt my cheeks aching with the suppressed need to smile as I walked back to the printer. I extracted my essay pages from Isaiah's and scooped up my laptop. It was hot against my chest.

"Goodnight, bro," I said, giving Isaiah a quick salute before I turned my back on him again. I could barely keep myself from skipping away.

"Elliot."

I paused in my tracks and glanced back. "What?"

"Civilians don't say 'wash out.'"

23

After Lumberjack Beard read through the first drafts of our essays on Tuesday, attacking each with a tangle of red ink slashes and cursive, he retrieved a single Rubik's Cube from a battered army green messenger bag. The clack of the bag's buckle hitting the floor echoed throughout the dining hall, which Lumberjack Beard seemed to have sole dominion over. It was entirely possible that he was sleeping there. His hair was slicked back with what could have been the same grease that he'd cooked our breakfast in that morning. He certainly smelled of bacon and syrup, but I supposed it could have been a hipster cologne with a name like Brunch Bro or IHOP Fiend.

"If you decide to compete, you will be timed solving this Rubik's Cube. Every team is being tested during this period and the winner will be announced at lunch." He held the cube forward, letting it balance delicately on the tips of his fingers. Its sides were scrambled into a jumble of colors. "Any takers?"

I raised my hand, knowing that my teammates would do likewise. The list of Cheeseman events had become as important as our binders. Knowing that we were going to have to solve a Rubik's Cube meant that Leigh and I had spent the last two nights watching dozens of videos on my laptop and memorizing algorithms. Since we both had one blue ribbon displayed above our beds, we had a vested interest in racking up more wins.

"Why don't you give it a shot first, Brandon?" Lumberjack Beard said. He tossed the cube to Brandon, who caught it in the crook of his arm.

Lumberjack Beard kicked his feet up onto the table, displaying the muddy bottoms of his battered brown boots. Not exactly seasonally appropriate, but way better than the cracked sandals that Hari had been wearing for the last two days. Although it seemed, from the way Perla was audibly gagging, that she didn't agree.

"People have to eat here, you know," she said.

"I have to eat here. This is the big kids' table," Lumberjack Beard corrected, sweeping a hand over the table. He pointed both index fingers toward the door. "You have to eat over there somewhere. But it's Taco Tuesday. Get pumped."

"I bet it's the same tacos we ate on Friday," Jams said under his breath.

"Possible," Lumberjack Beard said with a jovial shrug. "Go on, B. We're waiting."

"My hand wasn't up," Brandon said.

"Come on. It's the prodigy litmus test," he said, his lips appearing in a smile from the depths of bushy brown beard. He held up his phone, the timer displayed on the screen. "Ready when you are."

Brandon let out a puff of a sigh that sent a strand of hair flying up off his forehead like an elephant's trunk. Wedging his tongue into his bottom lip, he spun the Rubik's Cube dexterously between his fingers.

I tried to imagine how I would describe Brandon to my friends when I got home. Already, it was easy to describe the rest of the team. Leigh was unpredictable and funny. Kate was uptight in that maybe churchy, maybe never spoke to real humans before kind of way. Perla thought she was better than the rest of us. Galen thought no one noticed that he also thought Perla was better than the rest of us. And in the last forty-eight hours, Jams and Hunter had become our golden couple. No one batted an eye as they held hands and shared not-so-secret looks.

But Brandon was at once grudging and giddy. He was the loner boy hiding behind his too-long hair and his typewriter while also being the first person to catch my eye and smile from across rooms or study tables. He wore plain clothes like a uniform and almost never raised his voice above a murmur. He tried so hard to be indistinct that it brought all of him into sharper focus. Watching him with the Rubik's Cube made me think of the way he flipped pencils when he was sitting across from me in the sci-fi section.

And then there was Brandon, I'd tell my friends as we sat on the bleachers, recreating that scene in *Grease* with the split screen. *He looked like his name was John, and he went to a school for geniuses—I know, I had no idea that was a real thing either. And he had the most nimble fingers I've ever seen.*

And all of my friends would start screaming with laughter like I'd said something accidentally filthy, and I'd use it as a chance to slip back into the memory of this moment, when he twisted the Rubik's Cube smoothly into the algorithm I had memorized—front, front, up, left, right inverted. And, just as fluidly, he backtracked the same steps in the same order, setting the cube exactly as jumbled as he'd found it. No one else seemed to have noticed.

No one but Lumberjack Beard, who stopped the timer, his dark eyes going stormy.

"Sorry," Brandon said. "I guess someone else should have a try."

"It sucks that guy on Ben's team won the Rubik's event," Brandon said as we settled into the sci-fi section after the monstrosity that was Taco Tuesday. He slid his binder toward me. "I know you and Leigh studied really hard for it. You made good time."

"We did." I heard the Lawrence clip in my voice.

Brandon didn't notice. "That Onobanjo kid lasted a long time during amoeba tag, too. I caught him right before the end. Cool name, though. Nigerian, maybe? I'm almost positive that there's a university in Nigeria called Onobanjo . . . No. It's *Onabanjo*. With an *A*. Very close." He huffed a laugh. "More useless information that will not help me win a scholarship."

I snapped a knot in my hair, looking up at the Arrakis poster next to Magrathea. The desert planet looked remarkably like Mars, terra-cotta pot red-brown. "But you don't want to win."

I had meant to phrase it as a question, but the realization had been brewing inside of me for hours. As we went from class to class, as we sat through meals, as his shoe clicked against mine before he stepped off the elevator onto his floor to get his binder. I couldn't say anything in front of the rest of the team, in case I was wrong.

Which I wasn't. I could tell from the way his head sank lower instead of popping up in defense.

"You know how to solve a Rubik's Cube," I said. It was a silly accusation, and I felt childish saying it with so much weight, but my skin was too tight—had been too tight for hours now.

"Yeah," he said. "Of course I do."

"Of course," I repeated, chewing at the skin on my lower lip. My mouth was Arrakis-level dry. "There's the elitist asshole."

His head did pop up then. Confusion and hurt clouded his face. "You're mad?"

"Why wouldn't you let people know that you're good at something?" I thought I'd feel better for asking, but I didn't. The questions inflated inside of me, filling my veins to bursting. "Why botch something so stupid? That counselor, your friend, Lumberjack Beard—"

"His name is Ben."

"Right. Whatever. Ben knew that you were faking it. So why bother?"

He scratched at the soft white skin inside his wrist with the side of his thumbnail, but said nothing.

I picked up my binder and slammed it back onto the table with a shotgun-loud bang. "We've been studying together for days now. Why? Are you pitying me? Are you doing me a favor bestowing all your genius boy knowledge on me?"

He goggled at me. "No! Why would you think that? Because I didn't solve a Rubik's Cube?"

"Because you *pretended* not to solve it," I corrected. "Because you're so smart that you can coast here while the rest of us struggle."

"I'm struggling too!" he said, and it was the loudest I'd ever heard him speak. "You've watched me do it. I can't tell you anything about the baroque period! It falls out of my brain every single time."

"But you can tell me that Onabanjo is a university in Nigeria," I said, burying my hands in my hair. I gripped hard at the roots to keep my focus. "Are you going to pack up and go home? Like that girl yesterday? Are you going to quit? You live in town. It wouldn't be hard for you to go."

His jaw dropped. "Do you want me to leave?"

"No," I said, talking too fast to have time to be embarrassed by how firm my answer was. "It would just be easy if you wanted to."

"It really wouldn't be," he said. "Not everyone's parents would let them walk away from a camp that they already paid the tuition for."

I stabbed a finger in the air at him. "So you have thought about it!"

He let out a quiet growl that, under other circumstances, might have been adorable. "I don't know what you want from me, Ever. No, it wasn't my idea to come here. But I'm here and I'm studying and I really don't understand why we're fighting right now. I'm sorry I didn't solve the Rubik's Cube. Next time, I will make sure that the whole world knows that I can solve one in about twenty seconds, which is four times slower than the record. Okay?"

I shoved my chair back, ire continuing to spark inside my chest. I heard Brandon's chair fall to the floor and the soles of his Chucks squeaking behind me as I slipped between the redwood bookcases into A–D. On autopilot, I bent to the lowest shelf and plucked the hardcover copy of *Survivor* that I had discovered on the first day of classes. The scrap of "This Blessed House" that I had torn off for a bookmark was sticking out of the top. As I straightened, I found Brandon standing beside me. I pressed the book to his chest.

"This is an out-of-print Octavia Butler novel," I explained. "She thought it was too *Star Trek*-colonial-cliché to stay in print, even though it's part of a series, and I have waited years to read it."

Without waiting for him to reply, I walked farther down the aisle, scanning the stickered spines. I grabbed another hardcover and handed it back to him. "That's a limited edition of Cory Doctorow's *Little Brother*. It's illustrated and has maps of the San Francisco Mission District. It was never available to buy in the U.S."

From another shelf I grabbed Ernest Cline's *Armada* and added this to the growing pile. "And this is *Armada*, which was a total letdown, and I want to write papers about why."

He almost smiled. "Ever . . ."

"If I don't get a scholarship here, I don't know what I'll have that's all mine. When we go home, Isaiah will be the smart one again. He'll always be the smart one. But here, I get to be more than just the girl who runs fast. I get to be capable. And I want to hold on to that in a way that no one can take away from me." I paused to wet my lips. My pulse was fluttering like a wasp in a jar. "Do you ever miss things before they're over?"

He looked at me over the small stack of books balanced on his wrists. "Sometimes. Christmas morning. Good songs. Funfetti cake. You know, the kind with the sprinkles mixed into the batter?"

I nodded. Beth made excellent Funfetti waffles from scratch on Ethan's and my birthdays. "I already miss it here. I miss this room and the books you're holding and the quad and the garbage trees in Mudders Meadow. I want to find the rest of the tree houses and figure out what Fort Farm is used for and why one of the counselors is living out there. I have to know that I can come back here someday. I can't afford to skip a footnote or a section of the binder or—"

"Or pretend like you can't do a Rubik's Cube," he finished for me.

I plucked *Armada* out of his hands and stuck it back onto the shelf. "I don't want you to study with me because you feel sorry for me."

"I already told you that I'm not. Why would I feel sorry for you, Ever? I understand that you have a lot riding on this scholarship, but, honestly, so does everyone else. Putting your future on the line is a big deal, no matter what. Other than that, you're a six-foot-tall hot genius who can do parkour. Which part am I supposed to pity?"

I opened my mouth to correct him—for real, I'm only five ten—when my brain caught the rest of that sentence.

I'm a what now?

"I'm here because my friends conspired against me. Someone sent the brochure to my parents and they shipped me off. They didn't ask if I wanted to be here or if this was even a school I'd be interested in going to. But I'm a screwup, so I don't get a vote anymore," he said, his face flush with newfound steam. He shook out his hair and started to pace the aisle, shoving *Survivor* and *Little Brother* back into their places. "Also, if you want to go here so badly, then why don't you let me take all of the dives? If I won that Rubik's challenge, then you wouldn't have. Now I want you to win the scholarship. How is that supposed to help anything?"

I caught his wrist as he tried to pace by me. His arm was hot under my palm. I set my other hand against the back of his neck. His hair bristled against my fingertips.

The kiss had seemed like my idea a moment ago, but somehow his mouth met mine when I was halfway to where he had been. Our lips bumped, awkward and mismatched. My stomach plummeted to the floor, then buoyed, as Brandon slipped his arm from my grasp and wrapped it around my waist, gripping me tight as we readjusted our bodies in the narrow space between the bookcases. I combed my fingers through his hair, leveraging him closer—closer lips, closer tongues, closer hands and legs and bodies. It was a kiss that couldn't be portioned out in sips. We took in heavy, gasping chugs of each other that only got thirstier.

When I came up for air, I found my hands fisted in the fabric of his shirt. I left them there as our chests rose and fell, hammering heartbeats pressed together. Our panting breaths turned the air around us humid. Brandon's gaze was sharp with surprise, but his thumb was sweeping arcs on the small of my back. The inside of my head was thrumming, past runner's high and into stolen sips of champagne on New Year's giddy.

"You are one of the things I already miss." I stole another urgent kiss from his stung lips. "So I want you to win, too."

"I will memorize baroque composers for you. Not just three examples. All of them. Once I figure out how to go back to studying after this. I don't want to stop the *this* part." He gave me a jittery grin and squeezed my waist. "I wasn't studying with you so that this would happen. I never thought that this would happen, that you would want—I mean, you know I'm a nerd, right?"

"You're a nerd?" I pushed the hair away from his forehead. "We are standing in the science fiction section of the most selective liberal arts college on the West Coast. If there was gelato nearby, this would literally be my heaven."

"Get gelato. Noted," he said, inching close enough that the syllables brushed against my lips. "I really like you, Ever."

I could feel my heartbeat from the top of my head to the soles of my feet.

"Ever is a nickname. My real name is Elliot," I murmured.

He smiled. "I really like you, Elliot."

I wound my arms around his neck, pulling his face down to mine again. My eyelids closed. My tongue licked at his lower lip, requesting permission.

The lights flashed like lightning as a familiar screech lacerated through the former silence. Brandon and I stumbled apart, staring up at the ceiling at the fire alarm.

"Do you think it's real this time?" I asked.

"Does it matter?"

It didn't. We grabbed our binders and ran.

24

Goose bumps raised on my arms and legs as Brandon and I hustled into the cool evening air. The sky was sapphire streaked with orange clouds, the setting sun hidden somewhere behind the administrative buildings, where windows burned white in time with the alarm.

"This is probably a bad time to ask," Brandon said, power walking beside me. "But if the school doesn't burn down, do you want to maybe go out? Like actually out? Off campus out?"

I looked at him, worried that my tongue had dislodged some of his IQ. "We're stuck here."

He tripped over a seam in the pavement. "Only technically."

"Eventually we're going to have to talk about how cryptic all of you Messina Academy people are."

"The Mess," he corrected, and then gave an agitated shake of his hair. "That's not the point. If I could get us safely off campus, would you want to go?"

"Safely as in 'not getting caught and disqualified from the Melee'? Remember before we made out, when we were talking about how much I *have* to get that scholarship?"

He snorted. "Remember how all of my friends are counselors and it hasn't been useful for anything? It might be useful for this one thing. I thought of it when you said gelato. There's a gelato place downtown, across the street from this movie theater that shows old movies and serves food. I could get us there with limited blackmail."

I hitched my binder higher against my chest. "You thought of all of that while we were making out?"

"Not all of it. Just the gelato part. I was going to get off campus anyway because the theater does an *Independence Day* limited run during Fourth of July week that I don't want to miss. And you love science fiction and I love Irish nachos—"

Our binders knocked together as I stopped short and turned to him. "*Independence Day*? The nineteen ninety-six Will Smith movie? My dad and I have watched it together every Fourth of July of my life. I've seen it more than I've seen real fireworks. I thought I was going to have to stream it in my dorm this year."

"Is that a yes?"

I kissed him quickly and scooped up his hand, pulling him down the path. The closer we got to the residence hall, the stronger the alarm got. The sound made my molars buzz.

"'I know how to run without you holding my hand,'" Brandon quoted loudly.

I grinned at him over my shoulder. "If you start quoting *Star Wars* at me, we're never going to get anywhere."

"When you catch my references, I really don't care if we get anywhere. Did you say yes to going out with me?"

"If the school isn't on fire and you can outline exactly how effective your blackmail is and you actually learn the names of three baroque composers, then yeah. I'm in."

"You had to throw the composers in there."

"You promised!" I laughed. "And I didn't include any rules about the typewriter, so . . ."

We rounded the corner, the quad coming into view in short bursts of light from the surrounding buildings. I dropped Brandon's hand as I saw the somber crowd standing in front of the dining hall. No one seemed to be in team formation, just scared clumps. There were people visibly crying together, but no one seemed to have taken charge of consoling them.

"What the hell?" I whispered.

"This way," Brandon said, and took a turn for the grass that separated our residence hall from the dining hall. A cluster of counselors stood at the edge of the green, keeping watch over the campers. In the pulsating light, I recognized some of the Messina counselors.

"I thought we only had the alarm disconnected from the fire department for amoeba tag," Lumberjack Beard said.

"We did," Cornell said. He ran his hands over his scalp. The noise seemed to be getting to him, too.

"Well, then someone had better go start a fucking fire," Meg snapped.

The Perfect Nerd Girl rubbed her arms and bounced a little for warmth. "I'll be so glad when this year's experiment ends. The swearing is wearing on my nerves."

"Don't start with me, Beatrice Lea," Meg said. "You guys are so close to getting us all fired—"

"Ever! B!" Cornell said, noticing Brandon and me getting closer to them. I was sure he wasn't actually over the moon to see us, but our names worked as a verbal blanket on the grease fire that was Meg's rage.

She rushed forward and, for a second, I thought she might hug me, until she reached out and pried my binder out of my arms.

"Um," I said, holding back the urge to snatch the binder back from her. It wouldn't have been difficult. My hands were twice the size of hers. She was lucky not to be living inside of my pocket.

The Perfect Nerd Girl held her hand out to Brandon. "I need your binder, too, B."

He glowered at her, but surrendered the binder. "Why?"

The Perfect Nerd Girl didn't look up from riffling through the pages. "It's full of typewritten notes. It checks out."

"We could have Mary-Anne confirm it, but the handwriting here all seems to match the name on the front," Meg said, reading through my notes.

"Can you guys cut the forensics for a second and tell us what's happening?" Brandon said.

Cornell blew out a long, puttering sigh. "Did you guys bring your binders to dinner?"

"Yeah," I said.

"And you didn't return to the residence hall?" Cornell asked.

"We went straight to the library from the dining hall. We've done the same thing for the last four days," Brandon said, yanking his binder back from the redhead. He frowned at me. "Is this what you meant by all of us being cryptic?"

"Yes," I said. "This. Like all the time."

"Binders left in the residence hall between open study and the end of dinner have gone missing," Lumberjack Beard said. "All of them."

I looked back at the campers standing together outside of the dining hall. Their shell-shocked, stricken faces suddenly coming into too-crisp focus. They all looked like Fallon, realizing that all of her notes were gone. Except it wasn't only notes. Without the binders, there was no way for anyone to study, and there were only six days until the first skirmish.

"The rest of the counselors are doing a search of the rooms to see if they can track anything down," Cornell said.

Lumberjack Beard reached out, pulling the Perfect Nerd Girl to him. He crossed his arms around her waist and rested his chin against her temple. No one else seemed surprised to see them publicly snuggling, so I checked my face for placidity.

"No one would be stupid enough to hide forty stolen binders under their bed," he growled. "Or did you all forget what it was like to be surrounded by evil geniuses? One of these rug rats probably buried all those binders in Mudders Meadow for the thrill of it."

The Perfect Nerd Girl patted his hand. "Then that's where we'll search next."

"We're so fucking fired," Meg muttered.

"Why don't you guys leave your binders with us?" Cornell said to me and Brandon. "It's not a great time to flaunt them around."

Brandon chewed on the inside of his cheek, but surrendered his binder to Cornell. Meg waved me away, since she was already holding mine. I knew a dismissal when I saw one. I led Brandon toward the dining hall, scanning through the crowd for any of our friends.

"There," Brandon said, pointing at the stairs.

A jolt of cold shock flooded across my chest as I spotted Leigh sitting on the stairs, her arm around a sobbing Perla. Hunter and Jams sat nearby, motionless and pale.

"I thought Avital was such a moron for leaving," Perla sobbed into Leigh's shoulder. "We made it through the UCLA camp together a couple of years ago. And she and Samira did the Columbia immersion program last summer. Columbia! But this was too much for her. She was right. This is cruel."

Leigh stroked Perla's hair. I noticed that her face was blotchy red, too. "It's too far."

Perla hacked a wet cough, her body trembling. "They won't be happy until we all drop out."

"You guys don't think the counselors set this up?" Brandon asked, aghast under his hair.

Leigh glared up at him, tears dripping down her cheeks. "Why not? They set everything else up."

Hunter swung his head. "If we can't study, we'll all get trounced in the Melee. There won't be anyone left to win."

I considered pointing out that our team had at least two binders left and that we could share the study materials, but I thought of Cornell's warning about flaunting that and stopped.

"It's just paper. It's not irreplaceable. They'll print out new pages for us," Brandon said. "It won't take long."

"Blank paper," Jams said heavily. "All of our notes are gone."

Leigh wiped her nose on the back of her wrist. "And any essays that weren't written on a computer."

"Where are Galen and Kate?" I asked.

"Kate wanted to freak out in private," Leigh said. "She went to hide in the bathroom."

"And Galen?" Brandon asked.

"He went to check on something in our room," Hunter said, eyeing Perla nervously before mouthing, *The list.*

Balls. The Cheeseman list. We'd all memorized its contents, but the original copy was living in Hunter and Galen's room. And if the counselors found it, we'd be royally screwed.

The fire alarm cut out abruptly, leaving the quad in expansive silence broken only by the sniffling and whimpering of campers.

There was an amplified metallic click and then the tinny distortion of a bullhorn-magnified voice saying, "All students, please return to the lobby of the residence hall."

Wendell Cheeseman had arrived.

It was vaguely humiliating to be asked to sit while all of the counselors and Wendell got to stand. I was pretty sure that when real college kids got in trouble, no one told them to sit crisscross applesauce. But that was most likely the point that Cheeseman was trying to get across. We weren't grownups. We were a group of seventeen-year-olds—plus Isaiah—and we were in the deepest of shit.

Kate and Galen joined the rest of our team as we settled onto the scratchy carpet of the lobby. I felt some of the tension go out of my shoulders when Galen gave us a discreet nod, indicating that the list was safe. Kate refused to look at anyone. She kept her eyes trained on the floor, her narrow face ashen.

The overly jocular, finger-guns-pointing Wendell Cheeseman was gone. His gap-toothed smile was missing, replaced by a furious thin line. His button-down shirt was rumpled and missing a tie, as though he'd dressed in a hurry. He wasn't even sweating. I would have put twenty dollars down on him being a pod person, if I thought anyone was in a betting mood.

He ditched the bullhorn. He stood in front of the crowd of sitting campers, his arms folded tight across his chest. He let the line out on his silence. I was familiar with this tactic because my father also used quiet as a weapon, letting it weigh everyone down until they were ready to confess anything just to hear sounds again.

It didn't work here. Unless Cheeseman's intention was to highlight how many people were still crying.

"What happened here this evening is not a joke," he began, which seemed too on the nose, considering all of the sniffling and wheezing. "I understand that you all have had an exciting first week of camp. The events of the counselors' endowment may be fun and games, but this is not."

So he did know about the Cheeseman trials, even if he didn't know that they were his namesake. It did shatter some of the illusion, knowing that the games were authorized by the governing authorities. They had probably even had to clear their events with the college before putting us through them.

"This evening, a person—or persons—broke into multiple dormitories and removed the study materials found there. At present count, thirty-two binders are missing." Cheeseman paused, letting this sink in. With Avital gone, there were forty-seven of us left at Onward. So, fifteen people—myself and Brandon included—had binders left. I wondered how many had also taken their binders to dinner. It wasn't uncommon to see people reading and eating in the dining hall.

"At this time," Cheeseman continued, still rooted to the carpet, "it is unclear if anything else was taken. Later, you will be excused to make an itemized list of anything else missing from your room."

I closed my eyes, momentarily inventorying my room. My laptop and cell phone were on my bed. There was cash in the front pocket of my backpack. My train ticket for my journey home was tucked into one of the N. K. Jemisin books on my desk. My debit card, with my real name embossed on it, was hidden in a pair of socks in my suitcase, in case of emergency. If any of it was missing, I would be completely helpless.

It was getting hard to breathe.

"Do you think my typewriter is okay?" Brandon whispered in my ear.

I swallowed thickly and saw his wobbly smile. It was strange to have someone consistently noticing when I started to get under water. It was the kind of surprise sweetness you could get used to if you weren't careful.

I wrapped one of his shoelaces around my finger, the same way he did when he was thinking. It was comfortable closeness, but not Lumberjack Beard–Perfect Nerd Girl loud about it. His pinky brushed mine in a way that made me think maybe he didn't mind the quiet route.

"At this point, there are two courses of action we could take," Cheeseman said, drawing my attention regretfully back up front. "The first and the easiest is that the person or persons responsible for this come forward. The binders will be redistributed and we will continue with the camp as it has been run for the last twenty years.

"The second option is that the camp goes into lockdown. Instead of the collegiate-level freedoms you have been given in the last week, you will answer solely to your counselors, who, in turn"—he glared at the line of standing college kids—"will answer to me. Study materials will be shared, one binder per team, so that everyone will be equally disadvantaged by this heinous and invasive act. You will not go to the bathroom without permission and a written pass. Use of the campus facilities outside of the dining hall will be prohibited. Lights-out will be pushed up to nine p.m." He shook out his wrist and theatrically held it in front of his face. I couldn't help but wonder if he'd ever been part of Eugene's community theater scene. He would have made an excellent Dr. Chasuble in *Earnest*. "Which would start in seven minutes."

Heads turned, everyone searching the lobby for the one person who would stand up and put a stop to this. I saw Isaiah mean-mugging near the back of the room. Leigh was ripping at her fingernails with her teeth. Onobanjo, the possibly-Nigerian Rubik's Cube whiz, was whipping his head frantically, conducting a seated one-man investigation of the room. Next to the girl with the petal-pink hijab, Perla had started to cry again, her shark eyes getting puffier.

But no one spoke.

Wendell Cheeseman's head lowered an inch, just enough to close the lid on the conversation.

"Counselors," he said, disappointment making his voice rumble. "Please collect your teams and escort them to their rooms. Lights out in three minutes."

"Oh God," Perla sobbed unabashedly. "I hate this place."

As we filed toward the counselors, to be sorted by floor, I caught Brandon's elbow. "What were you saying about being able to get us off campus?"

"Give me two days," he whispered back. "It just got a little more difficult."

25

S ocks, check," Leigh murmured to herself as she sifted through the pile she'd amassed on her bed. "Face wash, check. Beanie, check . . ." She gasped. "The burglar stole like four of my fancy tampons!"

"That was me," I said, flipping through the pages of N. K. Jemisin's *The Hundred Thousand Kingdoms* until my train ticket came into view. Safe and sound. Thank God.

"Oh, that's fine, then. Only top quality for my bestie. No cheapo cardboard," Leigh said, raining feminine hygiene products back into her battered blue backpack.

"Aww," I said, setting the book back on my desk and smiling over my shoulder at her. "That's true friendship."

It felt nice to smile. The atmosphere at camp had completely curdled from the second we'd been left to our new lights-out the night before.

Breakfast had been about as cheerful as the buffet line at a wake. Each table in the dining hall now had a piece of paper taped to either end, with a team number on it. Hari had forcibly removed Perla from Team Three, sitting her down between himself and Meg at our new spot near the beverages.

Perla's sullen demeanor paled in comparison to the counselors'. It hadn't escaped anyone's notice that they were also being punished. Their table in front of the picture window had been abandoned. There were no Starbucks cups in hand. Meg was makeupless and unsmiling in wrinkled UCLA sweatpants. After we'd bused our table, they'd marched us back to the residence hall and given us fifteen minutes to inventory our rooms for stolen property. Meg hadn't even flourished the blank paper when she'd handed them out. It was unnerving.

Leigh sloughed the rest of the pile into her backpack. The springs whined as she bounced down onto her mattress. "Anything missing on your side of the room?"

"A bottle of hand sanitizer and a bag of trail mix. Both from my backpack." Strangely, both had been in the same pocket as my money, but all of that remained. And I'd checked my debit card's hiding place after Leigh had gone to sleep the night before. I wasn't sure if our burglar had been extremely inept or simply snackish and germaphobic.

"They got my binder, my notebook, and," her lip curled in disgust, "all of my pens. Who steals a woman's pens? I ask you. They weren't even good quality."

I sat down on my bed, kicking closed my suitcase. It was comically large, sitting across from Leigh's single bag. "It has to be someone trying to wipe out the competition. Why else would they take all of the binders? I don't think the counselors did it. Their misery feels too real and it wasn't on the Cheeseman list."

"It could be a prank." Leigh shrugged, drawing her legs under herself. "Or a secret high-stakes bet. Or ghosts. I have it on pretty good authority that the school is haunted."

She waggled her eyebrows at me and I kicked the air between us. "Shut up."

I couldn't stop myself from pulling up the memory of last night in the sci-fi section in vivid, photographic detail. Zoom in on a thumb brushing against the stripe of skin under the hem of my shirt, the taste of Brandon's hot exhale.

God. I was made of pins and needles. There couldn't be a worse day to be forbidden from taking a run.

"What is that face?" Leigh asked.

I reached up, touching my cheek. "What face?"

"Ever." She tipped her head at me. "Come on."

I groaned. "Don't start that again."

"Then tell me about your face!" She laughed, flinging her pillow at me. It flew in a black and white blur and landed at my hip.

I picked it up and hugged it, half hiding behind the zebra stripes. I hadn't expected to feel so embarrassed. It wasn't like I'd never kissed a boy and told my friends about it after. My friends back home would never let me get away with keeping that kind of secret. They would want all the gory details so they could do a director's commentary over it. *He said what? Now you know he's a virgin.*

And so on.

"Something happened yesterday," I said.

She braced her hands against the edge of her bed frame and leaned forward, her slanted front teeth biting down on her lower lip.

"I might have kissed a ghost," I squeaked. "And by 'might have,' I mean 'Whoa oh my God that definitely happened.'"

She let out a squeal that bordered on banshee-like. "I knew it!"

I threw her pillow back at her as footsteps slammed to our door, which flew open without a knock. Meg gripped the door frame, ready to throw herself at whatever horror was waiting for her.

"What happened?" she gasped.

"Sorry," Leigh said in a strangled voice. "The burglars stole my tampons."

Meg let out a long sigh that was more weary than relieved. "Oh. Put it on the list. You guys only have a couple more minutes before I have to walk you to your first class."

"Will do," I said, quickly grabbing the single sheet of paper we'd been given. I waved to Meg with it as she closed the door again.

Leigh smothered a fit of giggles in her pillow.

I threw the paper back at my desk, not caring as it floated to the floor. "Now when they find the burglars they're going to be like 'Hey, why did you steal all of that girl's tampons?'"

"Good!" Leigh snickered. "I hope they have to buy me a new box. That's what they get for putting my entire future in jeopardy." She propped her chin on the pillow and forced herself to stop grinning. I could see the tic of more giggles lurking in her jaw. "Please go on. You were telling me about the haunting of your underpants?"

"Oh my God," I said with a shocked laugh that echoed off of our cement walls. "No, I one thousand percent was not. We kissed. Well, we kissed a lot, but it was strictly first base. Not even a hint of stealing second."

But that might have been the fire alarm's fault. Not that I was going to posit that theory to my dear roommate, who was busy joyfully bouncing on her bed again.

"Save your sports metaphors for someone who gets them," she said. "I have been on this hype from day one."

"Which was nine days ago."

"Nine days of being hell of right. You guys had the stink of high school sweethearts all over you. Just like Jams and Hunter. And I was right about them too! I should work at a carnival or something." She stared off into space, possibly imagining her booth at the carnival of her dreams. She blinked at me a second later. "So, what now?"

"What now is we're in lockdown," I said, leaping off my bed and grabbing the list of stolen items off the floor. "We were talking about trying to get off campus, before we found out that camp is kind of, you know, ruined."

"Getting off campus is a great idea!" she exclaimed.

"I don't know if that's actually true." I shook the paper at her. "Burglaries. Lockdown. Entire future slipping through my fingertips."

"You're only seventeen once. You're young, you're hot, you're away from home, and you're sucking face with a ghost. Live your life! We can't study after hours anymore. What do you have to lose?"

"If anyone catches us, we'll be sent home and we will both lose the chance to go to this school."

And my parents would kill me twice. Once for running away from home and once for getting caught sneaking around with boys.

Leigh's mouth flattened into unbridled annoyance. It was the way the Lieutenant looked at Isaiah's diet and my hair. "Ever Lawrence, is there a nice boy with too much hair and the wrong name waiting for you in Sacramento?"

The only thing waiting for me in Sacramento was a swamp-ass August, a car with half a gallon of gas in it, and the name I had to share with my dad. There might be parties or hangouts with stolen kisses from nobodies, but there wasn't a somebody. There wasn't a typewriter-wielding, esoteric-fact-spewing, pencil-twirling, just-enough-tongue-using ghost in Chuck Taylors anywhere but here. Balls.

I threw my hands up. "No. There's not."

She clapped her hands like a giddy child and hopped to her feet again. She sang an off-key jingle to herself. "I am the rightest girl in right town. The mayor of right town is Leigh!" She skipped over to my phone and pressed a button to see the time. "I can buy you like seven minutes if you're okay with me telling stories about your bowels to Meg and Trixie."

"Wait, what?"

She dropped to the floor and gave a shave-and-a-haircut knock against the carpet. It took a moment for the two answering knocks to sound under my bed.

She glanced up at me, eyebrows high on her forehead. "Seven minutes, starting now."

I was out of breath by the time I made it to the upstairs lounge. As I groped in the darkness for the door handle, I was struck by a cold flash of panic that it would be locked and I'd be stuck on a forbidden floor, in the pitch black, with nowhere to go. But the handle eased under my fingertips and I slid inside the pumpkin.

As my eyes adjusted to the dim, uneven light coming through the small windows, my pulse was deafening in my ears. I flexed my bare feet against the pumpkin's thin, knobbly carpet, glad that I'd thought to kick off my shoes and socks before slipping into the stairwell. The floor below me was full of competitors, none of whom would bat an eye before reporting any sign of rule breaking, especially today.

Sneaking around was practically begging to be dragged off campus and thrown back into the furious and heartsick arms of my family. All over a dude. Some white boy with shaggy hair who I'd known for barely over a week, who I'd once mistaken for a figment of my own imagination.

The absence of old friends one can endure with equanimity, I recited to myself in an imagined British accent. *But even a momentary separation from anyone to whom one has just been introduced is almost unbearable.*

I'd never believed it before, although I'd heard half a dozen different actors playing Cecily say it with varying degrees of ingenue swooning. My homesickness was a rock in my shoe, about the same size as the pang of hurt when I thought about how long it'd be until my mom's next visit to California, or the thought of Ethan finishing growing up without me in the house.

But here I was, punchy with want for someone I hardly knew. And compared to the pebbles of the rest of my worries, it was like a boulder that kept knocking me sideways.

It was entirely stupid, but even if I'd had the password to stop it, I probably wouldn't have typed it in. Because, as Brandon's meringue-light voice entered the room through a crack in the door, I felt like all of the electricity in my body could have powered the entire coast.

"Ever?"

"I'm here," I whispered back.

The door opened fully and he slipped inside, careful to muffle the sound of the latch. He was in the white T-shirt and jeans combination he had been wearing on the first day of camp. He took three long strides and stopped short an arm's length away from me.

"Is everything okay?" he asked. He shook his head so that his hair brushed over the bridge of his nose. "Stupid question. Is everything okay other than, um, everything? Nope. Sorry. Let me try that again . . ."

"I'm okay." I took a hesitant step forward, suddenly afraid that he might run away like a startled deer if I moved too quick. "Is anything missing from your room? Is your typewriter safe?"

"It's safe. Who else would want it?" He rubbed a hand over the back of his neck. The friction made a quiet shushing sound. "But Jams's binder is gone. And most of my socks. I had a pair for every day of camp." He shrugged, his arms flopping by his sides. "I didn't want to pay to do laundry fifteen minutes away from home. What about you guys? Anything missing?"

"Nothing vital. Other than Leigh's binder."

Silence filled the room like a flood, pushing against the squash-orange walls and lodging deep inside of my throat.

"I can't stay long," he said, shifting his weight from one Chuck to the other. "Cornell's going to do an inspection soon."

"Right," I said, shoving the word out of my suddenly dry mouth. "Same here. With Meg."

I'd felt like there was too much to say before, and now I was legitimately struggling to find a single word that wasn't the most awkward. It didn't help that I was pretty sure that each of Brandon's fidgets and flinches was making my heart crank the emergency brake.

Maybe he didn't want to be sneaking around with me. Maybe he was trying to flinch his way to the door and down the stairs and away from me forever. Or until our first class, which was in something like three minutes.

"Brandon?"

His throat constricted as he gave an audible swallow. "Yeah?"

"I didn't imagine last night, did I? I was kind of picturing a different reaction to having a time crunch in this empty room."

He moved in a blur. High-tops scuffed my toes. An arm around my waist. A hand cupping my jaw. A kiss seared against my lips, which I caught up to only in time for it to be over.

"Sorry," he breathed. "I didn't want to assume—"

I buried my fingers in his hair and rubbed my nose against his cheek. "I didn't want to attack your face when you walked in. I mean, I did want to, but I didn't want to freak you out."

"I know we ate breakfast next to each other—"

"You put jam on waffles. Who does that?"

"I wasn't sure if you'd changed your mind—"

"Nope. I am so all about this."

I caught his lower lip and used it to tug him back until we collided with the wall, a crush of mouths and heartbeats. Kisses rained down against my neck, accompanied by a brush of eyelashes on skin that made me shiver.

"I can get us off campus for Friday night. There's no Cheeseman trial then, so we won't miss anything here," he said, each word a puff of hot air against the thin skin under my ear. "We'll need Jams and Leigh to help cover for us."

"What do we tell them?"

His head popped up so that we were nose to nose. If I'd wanted to, I could have counted his eyelashes. "That we're going on a date?"

"Oh. That's like really official, isn't it?"

He gave me that wide-open smile that I adored. "I was told that it's best not to leave these things ambiguous."

I ran my thumb across the apple of his cheek. "You were told?"

His laugh hiccupped our chests together. "You thought that I was naturally cool enough to know how to ask you out? I'm a nerd, Ever. A certified and well-documented nerd. I had a rolling backpack until last year." He reached up, gently twining my hair around his fingers. "So yeah, I asked for advice as to how not to immediately screw this up. I can't even kiss you without permission."

"You shouldn't kiss anyone without permission. That's called assault."

"You know what I mean."

I did know. What if it all disappeared? What if he changed his mind? What if the wanting went one-sided? I was pretty sure my ribs would cave in on my organs and I'd shrivel up like a sex-starved raisin.

"I want you to kiss me, Brandon. But we have to go back downstairs."

"Ten more seconds," he said.

His hands braced against my shoulder blades. I locked my arms around his neck and closed my eyes. It was just a hug, underscored by an almost unconscious sway.

But it was the first time all day I had no urge to run.

26

I watched the envelope pass from Meg to Brandon. It was about the size of his palm, cheerfully coral, with a nondescript stamp in the top corner. I only had a chance to read "B. Calistero c/o Camp Onward" before it disappeared into the pocket of his jeans. He caught my eye and grinned as Meg started shooing us to clear our lunches so she could walk us to our next class.

At least, we were supposed to think we were going to our next class. I knew from our pinched schedule that the campus run was today. If the Cheeseman events were still allowed. Which I prayed they were, because I hadn't been allowed out of sight of a counselor in days, much less allowed to get actual exercise. Leigh kept trying to get me to do yoga with her, but it was too much standing still. I had way too much energy to burn. I'd tried jogging the length of our floor, but Perla's shouts for quiet had drawn Meg out of her room and had sent me back to sit on my mattress. I really regretted not stealing the Octavia Butler book out of the Lauritz before we'd been denied access to it. I suddenly had free time.

While everyone else started collecting plates and silverware, Brandon and I volunteered to stay behind to wipe down the table with one of the sudsy rags that had started being left out in big red buckets at the end of every meal. I got the feeling that Lumberjack Beard was taking the lockdown particularly personally. Three days in, our food wasn't even imaginatively bad anymore. Lunch had been last night's meatloaf set out with bread for sandwiches. Add in our new "clean your own table" mandate and some rumblings about teams being told to wash dishes, and all signs pointed to one grumpy, gangly Lumberjack.

Brandon wrung out a rag and handed it to me and then got one for himself. We stood on either side of the table, wiping down the wood in tight circles. Uneven streaks made Meg twitchy. Then again, few things didn't make Meg twitchy these days. She kept glaring at the Perfect Nerd Girl and snapping at Hari.

"Did you get fan mail?" I asked Brandon, keeping my voice quiet so as not to draw attention from the surrounding tables.

He made a confused face before jumping with recognition and pulling the envelope out of his pocket. He tore it in one long swipe and shook out an index card. He smiled. "Good. Our ride is secure."

He passed me the card. The handwriting was inhumanly neat, nearly its own font of round corners and ruler straight lines.

Meet me at the corner of College and Hillview at 8 pm on the dot. Stick to the shadows. If you get caught, I don't know you. Hang in there, kid. –HKL

I handed it back across the table and continued buffing ketchup out of the wood grain. "That looks like a ransom note. Are you sure you aren't being kidnapped?"

He folded the card with three creases and slipped it back into his pocket. "Well, we are. Technically. Only in the strictest legal parameters."

Under the strictest legal parameters, I had kidnapped myself the second I'd crossed the state line into Oregon, but I really didn't want to think about that right now. "If we get caught—"

"We won't," he interrupted. "I've already talked to Jams. He and Hunter will cover me. Leigh will make sure that no one comes looking for you, right?"

"Yeah." Leigh had been too delighted when I'd unfolded the plan for Brandon and I to leave campus on Friday night. In return, she wanted a box of Raisinets from the movie theater and a full recitation of the menu of gelato flavors, since I wouldn't be able to transport a waffle cone for her.

I hadn't told her that this was my first real date. I was afraid that she'd start joy-screaming again and the whole plan would completely unravel.

"Back to the trenches," I said as I wiped up the last shred of lettuce. "I'll take the towels back to the bucket."

He pushed in the bench and met me at the head of the table. Instead of handing me his towel, he gave mine a tug, pulling me an inch forward. He placed a kiss on my cheek and a towel in my hand.

Beaming, I dropped the towels off and dashed down the dining hall stairs. My fellow campers were clumped together in the quad sans counselors. Bryn Mawr stood alone under the oak tree on the green, her hands on her hips as she spoke in a carrying voice.

"Today's event is a three-mile run around the interior of campus, following the directions given to you by the counselors along the way. Each counselor will hold a different color straw, which you will collect as proof of your route. The first person with every kind of straw across the finish line," she pointed at a line of bright blue painter's tape stretched across the pavement in front of the residence hall, "wins. Obviously."

"Why are we bothering with this crap?" Perla asked loudly, as I joined my team at the edge of the grass. "They should be looking for my binder, not making us run a footrace."

"Why do you care?" Kate asked. "Do you even want to go here?"

Perla looked stricken. "Here? In the middle of nowhere? Are you kidding?"

"I'm going to regret asking," Jams said, rubbing his forehead.

"But then why do you want to win the Melee? Winning means going to this school."

"No," Perla said sharply. "Winning means being the best."

Kate made a sputtering whinny of disbelief.

"I'm glad we still have the Cheeseman events," Hunter blurted. "If none of us can study, at least we might win for the extracurricular stuff."

"But should anyone else even bother to enter this one?" Leigh asked. She covered her mouth with her hand and fake whispered, "Ever does this for fun."

"Because only one person can be good at running?" Perla asked, tilting her face so that her nose was literally in the air.

"Yes," Kate said in a sarcastic flat line. "That's obviously what Leigh meant. How astute of you for picking up on that deep subtext."

Perla gave a disgusted sigh and, without any counselors to stop her, stormed off.

"After the break-ins, she called her parents and begged to go home," Kate said, watching as Perla joined her friend at Team Three. "They said no, but I'm holding out hope that they'll change their minds. Her snoring is so much worse when she's been crying."

"Team Six lost someone this morning," Jams said. "One of their guys quit. I heard Hari and Cornell talking about how his parents came to pick him up after breakfast. They didn't think the camp was safe if people could break into the rooms."

"The same thing happened with one of the girls on the floor above us," Kate said. "Team Four or Five? Someone was talking about it when I was in the shower this morning. I guess this girl's parents came to get her because they were pissed that Professor Cheeseman didn't call everyone's parents to let them know what was going on here."

Leigh sniffed. "The burglars didn't bust down the doors. Either they had a master key or they had a lock pick."

The hair on my arms stood on end. How had the burglars gotten into all of the rooms? Leigh and I were pretty consistent about locking up behind us. But if anyone got locked out, the counselors must have master keys to let them back in.

So, had someone gotten ahold of one of the master keys, or had someone with a master key abused their power?

"Perla has a point, though," Galen said. He barreled ahead as the rest of us scoffed. "Why haven't they found the binders yet?"

"When would they have time to look?" Hunter asked. "They're stuck babysitting us."

"And it's not like all of the binders have to be together," Brandon said. "If it were me, I would have taken the pages out and dumped a little in different garbage cans, so that none of them would be overly full. No one would notice if there was some garbage in every can on campus . . ." He made a face and smoothed his hair over his eyes. "That was too specific, wasn't it?"

I patted his arm. "Hopefully, you're too smart to have just blurted out your entire evil plan."

He smiled. "More like I'm too lazy to have an evil plan."

"That does make sense, though," Hunter said, combing his hands through his hair so that all of his muscles flexed against his shirt. "I don't think we're going to see the binders again, guys. No one here would be stupid enough to hide them where they could be found."

"Even if they did, how would we even redistribute them?" Kate asked. "It would take so much time, and you couldn't guarantee that they'd end up with their original owners."

"And anyone who still needs to read full pages out of the binders is going to get crushed next week," Leigh said. "At this point, we should be working mostly off of flash cards."

"All right!" Bryn Mawr called. "If you're running, line up behind the blue line!"

Hunter flicked his eyebrows at me. "Or trying to beat Ever in this race so we have a shot at getting the Cheeseman scholarship."

Leigh raised her arms over her head. "Release the beast mode!"

"Beast Mode, Beast Mode, Beast Mode," Galen, Hunter, and

Jams chanted. Kate and Leigh joined in, pumping their fists over their heads.

"We need a chanting intervention," I said, but my voice was drowned out.

Brandon leaned over and swept a kiss against my cheek. "Good luck, Beast Mode."

I won, riding high on a wave of hormones and spite.

I really hated that nickname.

27

I touched each of the pockets of my shorts with quivering fingers. Debit card. Cell phone. Dorm key. Tube of organic beeswax lip balm that Leigh had fished out of her backpack and thrust at me, insisting that it was better than the plain ChapStick I normally wore.

I was going on a date. I was running away while running away. I was about three seconds from freaking the hell out, because I really couldn't gauge my own ratio of excited to scared.

The last two days had been unbearably long, but dinner tonight had taken the cake. I'd picked at a bland helping of spaghetti, running through the plan that Brandon and I had made in snippets, when the counselors weren't paying attention to us.

Sneak out of the residence hall separately, after dinner but before lights out.

Meet behind one of the closed residence halls.

Catch our ride at the Rayevich College sign on the corner of College and Hillview.

Attempt not to get caught, but especially not by any of the Rayevich counselors, since Brandon had no blackmail on them.

I was curious what he had on the Messina counselors. My money was on pictures of the Perfect Nerd Girl's real hair color or Lumberjack Beard's chin.

"You have my number in case you need me?" Leigh asked, hugging her pillow to her chest.

"Yes," I said. I had dutifully inputted her number into my contacts that morning. It felt like a friendship upgrade. I could imagine sending her texts once I got home, of ridiculous, non-genius-camp things that happened, and she'd probably send selfies of her inquisitive face and links to her current favorite mindfulness meditations.

Was it weird that I didn't have Brandon's phone number? Maybe it wasn't weird now, but it would be next week when we left. How did you ask for someone's phone number after you had already gone on a date with them?

"Are you going to be warm enough in shorts?" Leigh asked.

I tugged at the frayed hem of my cutoffs. "I only have shorts. That's why I'm wearing a sweatshirt."

I wanted to be more annoyed with her for fussing over me, but it was nice to be able to release some of the pressure that had been building inside of my head. Every time Leigh asked me to double-check for my debit card or the time or which side of the sign Brandon and I were supposed to wait on, it made tonight feel real and exciting, instead of just being a list of things that could get me thrown out of Oregon.

I had never really fantasized about my first date, but if I'd been pressed to picture it, it probably wouldn't have taken place mid-Bunbury. I would have imagined Beth worrying over my clothes and getting overly emotional before I reminded her that it wasn't that big of a deal. My mom would have demanded that I text her selfies so she could check my hair—which, as per always, she would recommend that I get braided. My dad would have handed me twenty bucks so that I could pay for myself, because boys "got ideas" when they started spending money to spend time with you.

None of my parents would have approved of my cutoff shorts.

"It's seven forty," Leigh said, reading from her phone. "Time to go."

She got to her feet and wrapped her arms around my middle, giving me a brief, oddly strong hug. "Have fun, Ever. For real."

"For real?" I echoed with a laugh. "I will."

Getting out of the residence hall and across the quad was the most dangerous part of this mission. As I trotted down the stairs and out of the lobby, I mentally ran through the series of excuses I had planned, in the event that I bumped into any wandering counselors: *My phone is in the dining hall. I need to puke and the bathrooms are full. One of my contacts fell out!*

The night air hit me in a blast as I slipped through the glass doors and into the quad. I quickly pulled my hood over my hair. There weren't a ton of other black girls at camp, and I was definitely the one with the biggest hair. I didn't need anyone peeking out of their windows and ID'ing me. The sun was in the process of very slowly setting, but the streetlamps were on, spilling orangey pools of light at intervals. I skirted around them, clinging to the more shadowy parts of the concrete.

The closed residence hall was a dark block erupting out of the grass. With one last look across the quad, I ran around the building. There was a long hedge, another streetlamp, and Brandon, biting the pad of his thumb. He was in the same clothes he'd worn all day, but his hair was freshly combed, making it tidier and spilled-molasses glossy.

His smile was immediate and beautiful as he threw his arms around my waist and caught my lips in a kiss that went on long enough that I started to wonder why we were even bothering to leave campus. We could totally make a fort behind this hedge and live in it until the first Melee skirmish.

What an impetuous boy he is, my brain quoted dazedly. *I like his hair so much.*

"We gotta go," he said. "She'll leave us behind if we're late."

He clasped my hand and together we sprinted off the grass and up the sidewalk, into the parking lot. We had to squeeze between two Toyotas to make it to the scrubby pine trees that separated the lot from the winding front drive. Pine needles pricked my legs and clung to my sweater as we wove between trees. Up ahead I could see the massive posts on the back of the low, wooden Rayevich College sign, and the glint of a silver car.

I slid to a stop. "Wait."

He dug his heels into the dirt, spinning around to look behind us. "What? Did you see someone?"

"No, I forgot something. Name three baroque composers."

He turned back to me, his eyes wild. "*What?*"

"You promised, Brandon," I reminded him. "Three composers or I can't get in the car."

"Bach. Handel." He grabbed two fistfuls of his hair and made a low groan. "Monteverdi?"

I shrugged and pulled one of his hands out of his hand. "No idea. Sounds right."

"Oh my God." He gaped at me. "That was evil."

I kissed his cheek, just under one of his wide eyes. "You need to study more."

"You need to run."

The headlights on the silver car turned on as we rounded the giant sign. There was a *shunk* of car locks. Brandon dove for the handle of the back door and held it open for me.

I slid in, peeling back the hood from my head and feeling more than a little awkward as I clipped the seat belt. Brandon closed the door behind himself and said, "Hey, Harper. Thanks for the pickup."

The driver turned to face us, flipping back a sheet of icy blond hair. A pair of rose gold glasses rested on top of her pert freckled nose. She peered over the top of them. "Hey, B. Are you going to introduce us?" Her eyes flicked back at me, unreadably blue.

"Harper, this is Ever. Ever, this is Harper. We went to the Mess together."

I swallowed, my eyes caught on the corner of the back window, where the NPR logo and a dark green Dartmouth sticker were side by side.

If I am occasionally a little over-dressed, I make up for it by being always immensely over-educated, sneered Oscar Wilde.

With a jolt, I realized that I'd been in this car before.

"Holy shit," I blurted, catching the blond girl off guard. "Are you Cornell's girlfriend?"

One of her sandy eyebrows twitched. "Please don't define me by my partner. I'm Harper Leonard."

"Sorry. Hi. It's nice to meet you," I said.

"Likewise." She took another glance at us in the rearview mirror before putting the car in gear and making a U-turn up the drive.

I took Brandon's hand and tried to resist the urge to watch the Rayevich sign fade behind us.

"How's camp?" Harper asked.

"Oh, you know," Brandon said. "Genius kids stirring up shit and the administration overreacting by punishing all of us."

She laughed, a surprisingly twinkly sound, like a tiny set of bells was trapped in her throat. "They never learn. You trap that much IQ in one place and someone is bound to go rogue. Cornell said that the dean in charge was kind of a sitting duck."

"Associate dean," Brandon corrected. "Yeah, he's pretty ineffectual. Doesn't show up much."

"But you aren't the one who decided to go on a study material rampage?" she asked.

Brandon scoffed. "Nope. I was actually having a good time before someone broke into all of the dorms."

"I bet you were." She looked directly into the rearview mirror, her eyes smiling and inquisitive. "Do the others know that you're going on a date?"

"*Ixnay*, Harper," he hissed.

"The others?" I echoed, momentarily unable to imagine anything except a long line of genius school girls in matching uniforms—all private school kids have uniforms, right?

"Our friends," Harper said, guiding the car smoothly around a corner. Long stretches of brown field and power lines whipped past us. I'd nearly forgotten how remote the college was. "B, doesn't everyone think it's suspicious that you're friends with literally half of the counselors at camp?"

"No one knows," Brandon said.

"I know," I said. "And I have wondered . . ."

"Well, a few months ago," Harper started, seemingly delighted to elaborate, "we all got an email from the principal at the Mess, asking for candidates for the Onward counselor positions. They ask all of the alumni of a certain age every year, and normally we all say no because we're busy and don't live here. But then Brandon told us that his parents had enrolled him this summer. And then Meg didn't get the internship she wanted and I agreed to do inventory for the comic book store and Trixie and Ben were looking to get a new apartment at the end of summer anyway—"

"Trixie and Lumberjack Beard live together?" I asked Brandon. "Like *together* together?"

"You couldn't tell?" he laughed. "They are terrible at hiding it."

"They've been together for almost three years now," Harper said. "They started dating a month or so after me and Cornell. The time line is kind of wobbly. It was an odd period in our lives."

"Huh," I said, counting back the years in my head. "So, is there something in the water at the Mess?"

Brandon frowned. "No. It's Eugene. We don't even have fluoride in the water."

"You know two different couples who went to college together and stayed together."

"Trixie and Ben go to different colleges," he said with a shrug. "They live in the middle."

"It's okay, Ever," Harper said. "If we ever forgot how abnormal we are, we have Meg to remind us. She likes to quote the statistical probability of relationships that start in high school . . ." She trailed off and made a soft clicking sound with her tongue. "Which is not a great first date conversation. How about some music?"

Coffeehouse acoustic guitar and throaty female singers played us on and off the freeway and into Eugene proper. There were people wandering in and out of restaurants and packs of cyclists cruising through the streets. It looked sort of like midtown Sacramento, which put me at ease. We turned a corner and I was startled to see the Amtrak station.

"Are you shipping me home?" I asked Brandon quietly.

He tightened his grip on my hand. "Not a chance."

Harper pulled to the side of the street, next to a warehouse, and opened the glove compartment. She passed back another coral envelope, identical to the one our escape plan index card had come in.

"Two tickets to the nine o'clock showing of the Roland Emmerich classic." I thought I detected a hint of air quotes in her voice. "I will pick you up in front of the Minor at midnight."

"Thanks, Harper," Brandon said. "I owe you big-time."

She waved him off. "Just don't tell Cornell until after camp is over. I can't promise that he wouldn't report you. He gets so sanctimonious about rule breaking."

We got out of the car and stood on the sidewalk, fingers locked together.

"Eugene, Ever," Brandon said, inclining his head to the street. "Ever, Eugene."

"Would it be embarrassed if I called it Skinner's Mudhole?" I asked.

"I think it's only Skinner's Mudhole to its family," he laughed. "I should have asked if you wanted to see the touristy Eugene. We're like ten blocks up from downtown. And U of O is in the other direction. And you probably haven't seen Hendricks Park or had a Voodoo doughnut or seen the duck statues—"

"Hey." I squeezed his hand. "You nervous?"

He made a face at me. "You think?"

"Me too," I said. "So, point us toward gelato."

"That I can do."

We started to walk up the street and I paused. "Wait."

"Do I need to name more composers?"

"No." I touched his jaw and brought my lips to his for a brief, almost chaste kiss. "That helps with the nerves."

"It helps with some nerves and aggravates others," he murmured.

"Why didn't we just find a tree house to make out in?"

"Was that an option?"

"It's an option now."

He squeezed his eyes shut. "Let's go get gelato before I chase down Harper's car and make her take us back."

28

The patio outside Jilly's Gelato was small, only three round tables with wide blue umbrellas and a single string of white paper lanterns strung overhead, but we had it to ourselves. I hadn't realized how quiet things were on campus. I was on sensory overload with the indistinct voices floating down the street from the crowded sushi restaurant and brewery up the block and a steady stream of cars coming and going. It was strange to see the world spinning while my whole brain had been wrapped around camp for two weeks.

The cold iron of my chair bit into the backs of my thighs as I twisted to look up at the tall brick building beside us. "What is with this town and brick?"

"No clue. The libraries are brick, too. It's a real mason's paradise here," he said. I could smell dark chocolate and peanut butter on his breath as he huffed a laugh. "Wow. Is that the least interesting thing I've ever said?"

"In seventeen years, you don't think you've said anything worse than 'mason's paradise'?" I leaned toward him, my elbows braced against the table—manners be damned. "You never got super interested in World War Two or Pokémon or rare coins? I bet you know how much a Buffalo nickel is worth."

"Pokémon, yes. Coins, no." He stabbed his spoon back into the large paper cup in front of him, hiding his eyes from me under his hair. "Fine. I've been more boring. But I don't want to be boring tonight. Not with you."

I stuck my spoon between my teeth and clapped my hands together. "Dance, monkey, dance."

He stuck his arms out at angles, bobbing side to side in the worst robot dance I had ever seen. He looked like a broken marionette with his hair flopping around his forehead. I choked and covered my face with both hands as I laughed until I wheezed.

He took a victorious bite of gelato. "You asked for it."

"I did," I said, wiping at the corners of my eyes. "So, is this what you would be doing if you weren't at camp for the month? Hanging out at Jilly's, going to see *Independence Day*—a great movie, no matter how much your friend Harper sneers at it?"

"Don't mind her. I once heard her say that *Goonies* would have been better without Chunk," he said.

"So she's a stone-cold monster?"

"She has very pretentious taste." He pulled a napkin out of his pocket and dabbed at the corners of his mouth, checking for chocolate stains. "If I weren't at camp, I would have tried to see *Independence Day*, but my parents would have probably vetoed it. I have a nine-thirty curfew."

"Seriously?" I asked. I had an eleven o'clock curfew on weekends, but even then I got a lot of wiggle room in exchange for babysitting Ethan and volunteering at the theater. "You have to be home early so that you can get in all that genius school homework?"

"You're joking, but that's real. My parents were always really dedicated to making sure my sisters and I were exposed to as much culture as possible. We all learned piano and French with tutors, like we were in a Victorian novel. But then I tested into the Messina and it got—I don't know, 'worse' sounds really entitled—but, yeah, it got worse." He rubbed his thumb over the lump of his wrist bone. "That's why I'm at camp, actually. I didn't get my grades up last year, so I'm sort of grounded. At Rayevich."

"Your parents shipped you off to win a college scholarship because they didn't like your grades?"

"Well, first they took my phone," he said, drumming his fingers against the open weave of the metal tabletop. "And my laptop."

"Oh!" I said, the last piece of the puzzle finally locking together. I bumped our knees together. "That's why you have the type-writer."

"I had to type my homework, so I started using it for spite. It was my grandpa's and it was around and it was loud. But my parents adjusted to the noise and I got used to using it. And then they signed me up for camp. Messina students don't have to test in, since we have the same entrance exam."

I couldn't imagine my parents shipping me off if my grades slipped, even if it was just across town.

"I'm sorry," I said.

"Don't be." He smiled at me sheepishly. "If I hadn't flunked Economics of Globalization, I wouldn't be here with you."

"And what good is global econ?" I asked, pushing through the flutter that had started up in my chest again. I blew a raspberry. "Financial structures. Pishposh."

"Enough of my crap," he said with a huff. "What about you? What would you be doing if you were in Sacramento right now?"

"Right now? I would probably be lacing up my shoes and getting ready for my run." I pulled out my phone and opened my weather app. "Yeah. It's eighty degrees now. I'd want to wait until later, but my stepmom gets nervous when I go out too late."

"How long have you been a runner?" he asked.

"I've always liked running," I said. "When I was a kid and we had to run the mile in PE, I was the person who was like 'Hooray!' while everyone else complained. But then my cousin got back from BMT . . ."

His eyes scrunched before he guessed, "Bone marrow transplant?"

"Basic military training," I corrected, bracing as the truth started to seep out. " We're an air force family. And my oldest cousin, Sid, came back and kept talking about all the different stuff you had to be able to do to survive boot camp. Run a mile and a half in less than twelve minutes. Do forty-five push-ups and fifty sit-ups." I thought of Sid writing down the list of requirements on a piece of Aunt Bobbie's fancy stationery and how I'd hidden it under my mattress for years. "I didn't find out until way later that those were the guys' requirements. Sid didn't want me to slack just because I was a girl. Anyway, I always kept those numbers in the back of my head. I made sure that I could do them. I never really thought, *I'm doing this for BMT.* I wanted to know I could do it, so that if I decided to enlist, I'd be ready."

"Would you want to enlist?" he asked, digging back into his gelato. "If you've been training for it your whole life, why run away to Rayevich?"

I twirled my plastic spoon in my mouth. The salted caramel gelato felt like cool heaven against the roof of my mouth. "*Want* isn't the right word. I was born in a hospital on base and went home in a USAF onesie. It's literally never not been on the table." I couldn't ignore the skin-crawling feeling of stepping back hard into my own problems. Ever Lawrence would never have spent her first date talking about the air force. But I also wasn't going to let Ever take my first date from me.

"And it's not easy," I said slowly, each word melting a little bit of the gelato on my tongue. "Making a choice that you know people will hate. My dad and stepmom have never been subtle about the fact that they don't want me to enlist. They want me to stay closer to home, to do something with less risk, less moving. My dad kind of never forgave my mom for having to live on different bases when they were married, especially since she settled in Colorado right after they divorced. She teaches engineering at the Air Force Academy."

He paused, midchew. "So she's pretty invested in you joining up?"

My brain replayed a dozen conversations with my mom, all at the same time, her voice flat with expectation—the ongoing countdown of how long I had left in Sacramento, the weighty comments about Colorado weather. Even the way she shook her head when she saw me, as though she could picture the regulation haircut waiting for me in the future.

But she'd never tried to talk me into following Sid's footsteps and becoming a pilot. Unlike Grandmother Lawrence, she'd never poked the soft spots of my stomach, pointing out everywhere BMT would firm up. To my mom, the future was an unspecified better place.

"I think she wants us to live near each other," I said. "I think she'd be pissed if I enlisted but didn't go to the academy. And I love her, but we haven't lived together since I was in kindergarten. College isn't the time to play perfect daughter. I think she'd be disappointed if I tried."

The wrought iron chair legs screeched against the pavement as Brandon scooted closer to me, his eyes shiny with concern. "Who could be disappointed by you?"

"My mom's never really had to deal with the fact that I'm as much Beth's daughter as I am hers. I have this whole other family that she's never even met. And it's not just that they're white—they're Minnesotans. They're Midwest white. It's like the direct opposite of my mom's family. And that's part of me now, too."

"So what? She doesn't get to complain if she's the one who left."

"But she left for the air force. That's the trick. She didn't leave because she didn't want to be my mom. She left because she had to. So she gets to have her cake and eat it too. She gets to expect me to do things because she's my mom, while also not knowing what my day-to-day life looks like. I don't know if I'm . . ." My tongue seized on the word *Lawrence*; I remembered almost too late that it was the name Brandon thought was mine. "Enough of her daughter to be air force. To uphold the legacy." I shrugged. "I don't know if it's better to be another name in my family history or to not exist in it at all."

"I think my parents expect me to start a legacy," he said with a frown. "My sisters didn't care about academia enough. They were fine going to community college. And then I tested into the Messina and suddenly my parents had the chance to have a kid on the track to Ivy League . . ." He reached over and stole a spoonful of my gelato. He smiled dreamily as he tasted it. "But I just want to do math for a living. It's what I'm best at."

My spoon froze halfway to his cup. "Really?"

"I told you that I was the student counsel treasurer, didn't I? The administrators picked me because I had the highest math scores of the freshman class."

"Brag." I laughed. "So why does it matter where you go to school? Are they doing more math at Harvard than they do at state schools?"

"I guess not. But then my parents throw out words like *underachiever* and *potential*—"

"And it feels like you're not running fast enough to catch up with your destiny," I finished for him. I thought of Isaiah warning me to talk like a civilian, and Beth burying my USAF Academy packet in the recycle bin. My stomach clenched.

"Yes," he said with a sigh. "Exactly."

"So why did you tell Meg and Hari that you didn't know what you wanted to major in?" I asked, dipping into his cup. I'd never been giddy about sharing before, but this felt oddly personal. An invitation to disregard germs and personal space.

"There's no math in the Melee," he said. "It wouldn't instill a lot of confidence in the team if they knew that the thing I'm actually best at won't help them move forward in the skirmishes. Advanced math doesn't work well in a lightning-round scenario. Too many long equations. The Melee rounds would be endless. Or *more* endless, I guess." His leg stretched out, his ankle resting against mine. "The other night, when you said that you wanted something that was just yours, I thought about statistics. That's mine. The probability of things, of life. It's like religion condensed down into percentages. If you put in everything you know, you get the most likely outcome. It sucks that it's so boring to other people. There's nothing sexy about math."

"I don't know," I said. "Try saying all of that again, but in French."

His cheeks went strawberry milkshake pink. "L'autre soir, quand tu as dit que tu vouliez quelque chose qui était à toi—"

I cut him off in a searing, gelato flavored, heart pounding, possibly not cool to do in front of a dining establishment kiss. Deep in the recesses of my Gabaroche genes, there must have been a latent hunger that could only be awakened by French. Who knew?

I heard a sound in the back of my throat that I didn't consciously conjure, somewhere between a sigh of satiated hunger and a moan of pornographic proportions. I considered being humiliated by this, pulling back to explain that I definitely hadn't meant to make loud yummy sounds into his mouth. But Brandon's hands went into my hair and he gave a gentle growl in response, which maybe later I would find silly—once goose bumps weren't raised on my skin and my brain wasn't mentally trying to punch me in the face for not staying on campus and rolling around in the pumpkin. Rolling around sounded kind of perfect, and I really doubted that Jilly's Gelato would allow for anything even vaguely horizontal. Even a severe right angle would probably be grounds to shoo us away.

"Fudge?"

Brandon yanked away from me so hard that I almost lost a filling from the force of the decompression.

"Crumbs?" he squawked.

There was a girl standing alone on the curb, her hands hidden in the pockets of a denim jacket. She couldn't have been much older than the counselors at camp. Her face was angular, and her thick black hair was shaved close to her scalp on one side and flopped into her eye on the other.

"What the shit, Fudge?" she asked.

My hand curled into a fist and I looked over at Brandon, unsure if I'd just been thrown the strangest racial slur of my life.

"She means me." His shoulders went concave with a sigh. He raised a hand at the girl. "Hey, Crumbs."

She raised an eyebrow at him. Of all things, it was her eyebrows I finally recognized. Those black calligraphy strokes as wide as my thumb. She was a shorter, slighter, more feminine version of Brandon.

"You have a sister named Crumbs?" I asked under my breath.

"I have a sister named Jen who makes everyone call her Crumbs," he whispered back.

"And she calls you Fudge—why?"

"Did you ever read *Tales of a Fourth Grade Nothing*?" he asked. When I nodded, he said, "My oldest sister thought I looked like Fudge when I was a baby. I didn't eat a turtle—"

"It was a tadpole," Crumbs interrupted. "And it was going to be Abby's best friend. She cried for days."

Brandon scrunched his face toward his sister. "What are you doing down here?"

"I'm catching my baby brother running away from smarty school." Where Brandon's voice was woolly, hers rode the line toward raspy. It was like ice cubes rubbing together. "And sucking face with a very pretty girl."

He brushed his hair back into his eyes with the heels of his hands and spoke rapid, furious French at her. I sat on my hands to keep still as she threw a stream of French back at him. It was fascinating, but from Brandon's deepening frown and his sister's lifting chin, I got the feeling that the conversation wasn't going well. I took a bite of gelato as Brandon threw himself to his feet and switched back to English.

"You can't make me go with you," he snarled.

"Um, go where?" I asked.

"Anywhere," Brandon huffed.

Crumbs looked at him with blasé pity. I knew that look. It was how I looked at Isaiah when he said something particularly stupid, or when Ethan threatened to tattle on me.

"I can call Dad," she said. "And he can cart you back to Raye-vich. Or I can take you back and you can say, 'Thank you, Crumbs. I love you so much more than Abby and Darcy.'"

"We have a ride," he said. He cut his eyes at me and then back to Crumbs. His tone disintegrated into ragged sincerity. "S'il vous plaît ne pas."

She ignored him, swooping forward with her arm outstretched to me. "Sorry, pretty girl. Any chance you have a younger brother?"

I awkwardly shook her hand. Her hand was smaller than mine, but her grip was viselike. "I do, actually."

"Then you'll understand that I have to stuff mine into my car and drive him back to genius camp before he gets into even deeper shit than he's already in. Are you a smarty-smart-pants too?"

I nodded. There was no point in lying. I wasn't going to let Brandon get dragged back to camp and go to the movies by myself.

"Great," Crumbs said. She jerked her head toward Brandon's abandoned cup of peanut butter cup gelato. "Hand me that ice cream and we'll be off."

The back of Crumbs's car was much more cramped than Harper and Cornell's Prius and smelled faintly of cigarettes and fake cotton air freshener. The fabric on the roof was peeling in places, undoubtedly leaving bits of fluff in my hair. The radio was turned down low, letting in a distant rattle of drumbeats.

"I'm so sorry," Brandon said in a choked whisper, passing my phone back to me after borrowing it to text Harper that we wouldn't be needing a ride back. He stuffed a list of phone numbers back into his wallet. "This is truly fucking humiliating."

"It's okay," I whispered back. "I know like three different kinds of self-defense. If I didn't want to go with you, I could have taken her down. It seemed like shitty etiquette to roundhouse your big sister."

He almost smiled. "Not this sister."

"You can passive aggressively whisper all you want," Crumbs

said, tapping her fingers on the steering wheel. "I'm so not going to be responsible for you flunking out of another super expensive institution. It's getting embarrassing how much money Mom and Dad are spending on your education. Have I mentioned that I have two jobs?"

"And yet you were ready to go drinking on a Friday night," Brandon shot back. "Yeah, you must be swamped with work."

I wet my lips to ease the jolt of shock that raced up my back. "Flunked out?"

"He was expelled," Crumbs said over her shoulder.

Mortification drained the color out of Brandon's skin. "I wasn't invited back. They gave my spot on the roster to another applicant."

"Because he flunked out," Crumbs sang out, the lights of passing headlights bouncing off her teeth in the rearview.

He swallowed hard and turned away from me, pressing his forehead against the window. "This is a new low."

I reached over and set my hand on his knee. "Hey. I've been meaning to ask you something." I waited for him to look at me before I asked, "How familiar with *The Importance of Being Earnest* are you?"

"Moderate to very." He frowned. "Why?"

"Ask me when we get back to campus."

Maybe by then I'd have the courage to say it out loud.

29

We waited for ten minutes after Crumbs dropped us off before sneaking back through the trees to the front of the school, where we were less likely to encounter any wandering counselors. Brandon was really patient as I explained my Oscar Wilde–inspired decision to leave home, take the train over state lines, and spend three weeks living under a false identity. He even waited until I stopped talking before he totally freaked the hell out.

"Shit. Shit. Shit," he chanted, slamming the back of his head against the Rayevich sign. "Ever, this is really serious. Are you even eligible for the scholarship if you're here under a pseudonym?"

"It's not technically a pseudonym," I said, drawing my knees up to my chest. Sitting on pine needles wasn't super comfortable. "It's a nickname and one of my last names. I used my real social security number."

His hands started to flap and fist at intervals. I wished I had a pencil for him to twirl. "But what if someone finds out? What if you get sent home? Or what if your brother gets sent home and then they find out about you?"

"Oh." I bit my bottom lip, tasting the honey-scented beeswax of my new lip balm. "Isaiah isn't really my brother. He's my cousin. And he's fifteen. No. Wait. Yesterday was his birthday. He's sixteen. He's also a giant sack of crap who will drag me down with him if he gets caught up here. He told Cornell that we're twins so that they'd let him compete under age." That felt like a lot of bad news to drop in one go, so I added, "I do have a real little brother. Ethan. He's nine. I miss him a lot more than I thought I would."

He rubbed his eyes and stared at me blearily. "I don't know how to process all of this. Why are you telling me this now?"

"Because when I freaked out about you faking a Rubik's Cube and then vomited basically all of my hopes and fears on you, you didn't even tell me that you've been lying about the school you go to."

"I didn't lie," he said. "I haven't gone to any other school yet."

I snorted. "Oh my God. That is such a weak technicality. You flunked out of the Messina, Brandon." He flinched. "It's okay, but I don't understand why you wouldn't just tell me. I feel like an idiot for grilling you for details about it. Wouldn't it have been easier to tell me the truth?"

"Is this really the best time for you to define the morality of lying?" he asked flatly.

It stung, but I pushed ahead. "If you breathed a word of what I told you tonight to any of your friends or any of the other campers, I would be on the next flight home. If my parents didn't decide to show up and drag me back by the ear. It's not the same thing as you letting me believe that you go to a school you don't."

His head dropped into his hands. "It's not something I'm proud of. It's embarrassing. Almost as embarrassing as having my sister ruin our date." He half-smiled, but it evaporated when he saw my face. "I did fine for the first two years. I stayed pretty high in the class ranking. That's the big selling point of the Mess: the monthly class rankings go public so that you and your parents can keep track of your progress."

I shuddered. I had no idea where I would have fallen in my class and I didn't need to know. "No offense, but that sounds like a night-mare hellscape."

"It is. I thought I'd get numb to it. Everyone else seemed to. Sure, sometimes there was crying or fights or people getting pulled into the school psychologist's office, but mostly people dealt with it. I dealt with it until last year. And then I just . . . I don't know. Started suffocating. There was no way to give one hundred percent in all of my classes at the same time. I really tried. I even liked what I was studying. But all of a sudden I was getting Cs in everything. And then less. And then I was getting hauled into a meeting with my par-ents and the principal and the school psychologist about how I would do better in a less vigorous environment. I didn't even under-stand that they were throwing me out until my mom started crying." He swept away a piece of pine tree shrapnel from the canvas of his shoe and watched as it joined the brush and dirt on the ground. "I didn't realize how much of my family's vision of me was as this con-summate prodigy, the alpha and the omega of all things academic."

"Is it your family's vision of you or your vision of you?"

"Both?" His fingers twined around one of his shoelaces. "When people always tell you that you're smart, you get used to it. It be-comes the thing you *are*, you know?"

"I don't, really," I said. He looked up at me with annoyed disbe-lief and I shrugged. "Isaiah is the family prodigy. His family moved off base so he could go through a gifted program. He skipped the eighth grade. It was a big deal."

"Why?" he asked. "No one learns anything in the eighth grade."

I smiled at him. "I know that and you know that, but the Law-rences were blown away. Anyway, Isaiah's real sister—Sidney—is the air force poster child, so she's always been the real favorite in the family. Top of her BMT class. Lieutenant by twenty-four. I'm . . . I don't know. The one being raised uppity. I think my aunts and uncles see me as bougie. My dad is kind of a shithead about money. He's not shy about letting people know that he has it, which on my mom's side is really verboten. And my stepmom is about ten years younger than him, and white, so there's plenty for people to talk about."

"But that doesn't have anything to do with who you are."

"Yeah, well. What does you being good in school have to do with who you are?" I scooted over to rest my leg against his. "It doesn't cover the fact that you're funny and sort of a grump and use your hair like an invisibility cloak. Or that your voice gets really soft when you speak French."

"It's a quiet language," he muttered. "Elliot Lawrence Gabaroche."

He gave my last name a throaty flourish that made all of my tendons go limp. I put my hand on his jaw, drawing his face closer to mine.

"Should I even call you Ever?" he asked, his nose inching toward mine. "I can call you Elliot. Or Ellie?"

"Ellie is what my family calls me, so no. But you can call me Elliot or Ever. You're one of the only people who calls me Ever. I made it up for the Onward application."

"It suits you," he breathed.

I curled a piece of his hair around my index finger. "I really enjoyed our date."

He wrinkled his nose at me. "We didn't even get to go to the movies."

"We can stream it. We can sneak out again and use the Wi-Fi in the pumpkin. If you don't mind hanging out with an impostor."

"I don't care what name you're using."

"And I don't care what school you're enrolled in."

The fauna underneath us crunched as our lips came together. His kiss was inquisitive, as hesitant as it had been the first time in the sci-fi section. I pushed back against him with certainty. My feelings hadn't changed. I was as sure as ever that I wanted to be here, to be with him, even if he wasn't going to graduate from some fancy prep school.

He curved his body toward me, his hands gripping the sides of my sweatshirt. I strained to be closer to him, my legs lifted off the ground like one of Leigh's complex yoga positions. My heel caught a pinecone and I slipped. I threw out an elbow to keep from bashing my head into the signpost. My funny bone clipped Brandon's jaw. We both made unnatural, pained sounds as I landed hard back on my side of the dirt.

"I'm so sorry," I said, scrambling to my knees to check his face for signs of injury. His skin was blistering hot, but seemingly un-scathed. "Nature sabotaged me. What a mood killer."

"It's okay. I'm a seventeen-year-old guy," he said, peering up at me as my fingers touched his face. "There isn't much that kills my mood."

"You're kind of a pervy nerd, you know that?" I said. His face fell into panicked lines before I laughed. "Chill. I'm into it. Be less scared of me, please."

"Be less amazing, then. I don't deserve to be anywhere near you."

"We need to work on your self-esteem." I planted a swift kiss on his lips and hopped to my feet. "We weren't planning on being back until midnight. Let's go somewhere else. Somewhere with no pine-cones or stabby needles. Also maybe not directly next to the front entrance?"

"Earlier, you said something about a tree house?"

We stayed as far away from the main path into the arboretum as possible. We stole kisses between buildings and across the unlit stretches of grass. The sky sparkled with stars like spilled glitter. The air was cool and clover scented.

With every step, I felt buoyant. I hadn't understood how burdened I'd been with my secrets. Saying them out loud made me feel like a new person. Or like myself, outside of the cage of living up to being either Ever or Elliot. Even if it was just for tonight.

"It was so nice of the counselors to track down a tree house for us," I said, pulling Brandon by the arm as we approached the fork in the road in the middle of the tree canopy in the arboretum. "I still haven't seen another one on campus."

He wrapped his arms around my waist, walking backwards in a clumsy hug. "We could go looking, if you want."

"There are a lot of trees to examine."

"I'm up for it if you are."

"I'm sorry," I said, rubbing my nose against the curve of his cheekbone. "I didn't quite catch that. Once again in French, please?"

"Je serais . . ." He stopped abruptly at a rustle around the corner. Voices and footsteps coming toward us. He gestured to the dark cluster of trees behind me. "Hide!"

I crossed my arms. "I so don't need your altruism."

"This isn't some misguided sense of chivalry," he hissed. "I don't want you to get sent home. If I get kicked out, I can take Crumbs' car back here to see you! You can't drive back from Sacramento."

"Oh," I said. "That is sweet."

"Elliot!" he stressed.

It was halfway between the trunks of two knobby trees when the clatter of sneakers on pavement got louder. Hunter and Jams rounded the corner, both wild-eyed and whispering to each other in apparent distress. They both halted when they saw Brandon.

"Oh, thank shit," Hunter said, clutching his heart.

"Ever?" Jams said. "Why aren't you guys seeing that naff movie?"

I had no idea what *naff* meant, but it didn't sound complimentary. I climbed back onto the sidewalk as casually as I could, even though Hunter and Jams could tell that I had been attempting to hide.

"We got, um, sidetracked," I said. "Decided not to go."

"My sister caught us," Brandon elaborated. "And dragged us back here under threat of tattling."

"Oof," Hunter said with an exaggerated wince. "Tough luck."

"What are you guys doing?" I asked.

"We were taking advantage of the Team One date night," Jams said, folding his fingers into Hunter's. "But now we're going to look for a counselor."

"Why?" Brandon asked.

"We found something," Hunter said.

"The binders?" I guessed, unable to hold back a spark of hope.

"One binder," Jams said, uncomfortably. "But also like a metric fuck ton of stolen stuff."

"Metric," Hunter chuckled.

"What kind of stolen stuff?" I asked.

"Food, mostly," Hunter said. "A computer or two. A bunch of liquor. I think someone's been living in the tree house."

Jams nodded. "On a positive note, I think I found your socks, Brandon. Yay?"

30

Brandon and I ran toward Fort Farm while Hunter and Jams waited for us at the tree house. It was nice to run, but even more so to have Brandon keep stride with me.

The tree canopy disappeared behind us, revealing the twinkly night sky again. And, in the distance, the single fort draped in rippling blue sheets surrounded by bare wooden structures.

Brandon led the way through the clover and wildflower field, his shoulders rigid as we approached the occupied fort. There was clearly something rustling behind the sheet. A soft laugh made Brandon's shoulders go rigid before he reached out and knocked on the fort's frame.

I stood to the side as the sheet whipped open. The Perfect Nerd Girl's head popped out like the gatekeeper in *The Wizard of Oz*. I nearly expected her to ask, *Who rang that bell?* Instead, her eyes narrowed.

"B?"

"Hey, Trix," Brandon said, raising his hand in an awkward wave. He raised his voice slightly. "Hey, Ben."

"Hey, Bran," said Lumberjack Beard from inside the fort.

Trixie's head stretched forward. She looked from Brandon to me and back again. "What are you guys doing out?"

"Come on, Trix," said Lumberjack Beard, still out of sight. "We're really not in a place to lecture."

She glared over her shoulder. "I am."

Brandon cleared his throat. "Can you guys, um, put some pants on so we can talk?"

The sheet closed with a *fwump* of air. I tucked my hands into my back pockets and gazed out at the field, ignoring the thumps and curses coming from behind the wall of cotton.

"It was an art installation," Brandon blurted.

I glanced at him over my shoulder. "Excuse me?"

"Fort Farm." He coughed. "It was originally an art installation representing deforestation. Or suburban anonymity? Something like that. But the students like having an outdoor space to study, so they petitioned to keep them."

"And apparently they're big enough to have sex in." I snorted. "Who wouldn't want to keep them around?"

"Yeah, we can hear you," Lumberjack Beard said.

"I was in no way trying to lower my voice," I said back.

Brandon wheezed a laugh into his elbow.

"I told you that you could find me here in the event of an emergency, Brandon," Lumberjack Beard said. "So, where's the fire? We dismantled the alarm again—"

"Hunter and Jams found a bunch of stuff hidden in the tree house," Brandon interrupted. "Including a binder."

The sheet flew open again and Lumberjack Beard unfurled himself from the depths of the fort like an expandable water toy. He looked down at us. "Who?"

Trixie scrambled out behind him, tugging the hem of her shirt around a pair of fleece pajama pants that seemed too baggy to be hers. "Team One's Hulkling and Wiccan," she said.

"God, I loved *Young Avengers*," Lumberjack Beard said, stretching his arms over his head. "Why hasn't that come back?"

Trixie whacked him in the side. "Ben, focus."

He grunted. "Oh. Right. Nice kids."

"Let's go see this contraband," Trixie said, crunching through the field. "And also maybe talk about why Meg's team is wandering around after lights-out."

"Again," Ben said, skipping to keep up with her, "I'm not sure we have the moral high ground here."

"You really don't," Brandon said.

"Also, I'm pretty sure that Harper bet the two of you that you couldn't last three weeks living in the dorms," I said to the back of Trixie's orange hair as we all stepped onto the sidewalk. "And living in a field doesn't count . . ."

Ben threw his head back and laughed. "Cold-blooded but so accurate."

Trixie shot me a look, her steely irises particularly spectral in the starlight. "I'm not going to ask how and why you know about that stupid bet."

"I'd guess Harper has succeeded in developing her telepathic gift," Ben said. "Or she made Brandon spy on us again."

"Surprisingly, no," Brandon said.

"Again?" I echoed.

"Don't worry about it," Ben and Trixie said in unison.

Brandon rolled his eyes and took my hand. "It's not as bad as it sounds. I'm only moderately traumatized."

"Did we or did we not get jobs here just to keep you company for the summer?" Trixie asked him with a sniff.

"Did you or did you not send the brochure to my parents?" he snapped.

"*We* didn't," Ben said, scuffing his heel on the pavement. "Meg did."

"Hey, my one true love?" Trixie said, glaring up at her boyfriend. "Shut up."

"I knew it was Meg," Brandon grumbled. "It's always Meg."

Trixie threw her hands up. "You were really scared about not having the grades to get into a good school—"

Brandon cut her off with a shake of his head. "It doesn't matter. Let's deal with this fresh pile of crap."

"It's been years since we went crime solving," Ben said, a jaunty spring in his step. He wrapped his arm around Trixie's shoulders and kissed the top of her head. "I feel like we should be wearing uniforms."

"I feel like we could be wearing nothing," she said, severely underestimating how carrying her whisper was.

"Are they always like this?" I asked Brandon. "I only ever see them separately."

"No," he said lightly. "Usually they're bickering and feeling each other up."

"Shut up, B," Trixie said, in a hum that made me think of Meg.

"He's not wrong," Ben said.

"I didn't say he was wrong," Trixie said. "I told him to shut up. You should do likewise."

Ben's teeth appeared in a grin that split his beard. "Make me, gorgeous."

"How do you guys get anything done?" I asked, mostly to remind them that Brandon and I were there. "Don't you go to these exalted schools where you'd have to, you know, focus?"

"Uh, yeah," Ben said, raising his eyebrows at me. "Why do you think we don't go to the same school? Can't be trusted within a mile of each other."

Trixie let out a long, put-upon sigh. I almost felt bad for her, until I remembered that she and Ben were going to get to go back to Fort Farm and I was going to get shuffled back to my dorm, having to go back to communicating with Brandon through knocks on the floor.

Life was entirely unfair.

When we made it back to the right half of the fork in the road, Hunter and Jams were sitting on the ground under the tree house. Jams's head was resting on Hunter's shoulder as they murmured to one another. At the sound of our approach, they started to scramble apart, but Ben waved them off.

"Don't mind us, gents. We're all here unofficially." He planted his hands on his hips and tipped his head back, examining the underside of the tree house. "How'd you guys get up there?"

"We climbed?" Jams said.

"Damn. I was hoping for a ladder or something. All right." He leaped up, his long arms grabbing the lowest branch. He walked up the trunk. The exposed skin above the line of his beard purpled with effort as he swung his legs up and onto the floor of the tree house.

Trixie walked to the base of the tree. "You okay?"

"Peachy," he called back. "I landed on a bag of marshmallows. Hey, these are from my kitchen!"

"It's his kitchen now?" Brandon asked.

Trixie shrugged. "He really likes to cook."

"It's a shame he sucks at it," Jams whispered.

"Yes," she said warily. "It really is."

"Jesus!" Ben called down. "Look at all this booze. This summer could have been a lot more fun if we'd known this was up here."

"Ben!" Trixie snapped.

"Right." His head appeared over the edge of the tree house. "Stay high on life, kids."

"Did you guys leave the binder up there?" I asked Hunter and Jams.

"We left everything up there," Hunter said.

"We didn't even put fingerprints on anything," Jams said. "I'm not going home because someone wanted to live in a tree."

"The tree houses are for living in," Trixie said, one eye on the bottom of the tree house. "That's what the Rayevich counselors said when we were setting up the climbing challenge. Students make them to live in when the weather's nice. They go around town, loading up pallets from Walmart and Fred Meyer to string up in the trees. And when they get caught and have to dismantle them, they take them out to the river to have bonfires. It's a whole ritual thing."

"Incoming!" Ben called.

We all jumped back as a binder came flapping down from the sky

234 ★ LILY ANDERSON

and smashed into the ground. Ben followed it with significantly less grace as Trixie retrieved the binder. She cradled it in her arms.

"I need light," she said.

Hunter dug into his pocket and pulled out a jumble of keys. He turned on a tiny flashlight and aimed it at the binder's pages as Trixie started frantically flipping them.

"That's the only binder up there," Ben said, dusting himself off. "But it's a pretty sweet study cave."

"It was empty when we did the climbing challenge," Jams said.

"Which made it perfect when someone needed to ditch all the stuff they stole out of the dorms," Hunter said.

"Someone who wanted to keep studying while no one else could," I said.

"Studying while also getting absolutely frakking blotto," Ben said. "I can't stress how many bottles of booze are up there."

"There are no notes," Trixie muttered. She looked around at us, her pupils tiny in the light of the flashlight. "It's totally clean."

Brandon craned his neck to see. "Really? What the hell? That's unnerving."

"You think?" Ben said. "What kind of maniac doesn't take notes? Not even a highlight?"

Trixie swung her head. "Not even an underline."

"You genius school kids are creeped out by the wrong things," I said. I pointed over our heads. "There's a tree house full of stolen shit here?"

"Of course," Trixie said, closing the binder. "We'll need to go get the other counselors so we can clear it out and inventory what we have here."

Ben pointed an accusing finger around at us. "Which means you runaways better scarper back to your dorms and tuck yourselves in. And tomorrow we will pretend that we never spoke to each other."

"Any chance we can get one of those bottles?" Hunter asked. "It's gonna be a stressful week with the Melee—"

Trixie threw him a terrifying look. "Goodnight, campers."

Jams, Hunter, Brandon, and I didn't wait to be told a second time. The four of us started back up the path through the arboretum.

"Do you want to take the long way back to the residence hall?" Hunter asked Jams.

Jams beamed at him. "Obviously."

"Good night, you two," Hunter said with a chuckle, as he and Jams took the fork toward Fort Farm.

I wrapped my arms around Brandon's bicep and kissed his cheek. "Not what I was expecting from my first date."

"Me either." He frowned up at the tree canopy. "I can't even walk you to your door."

"You can walk me to the door of my floor."

"Or," he said, drawing the word out until it had a dozen *R*s on the end, "I could walk you to the door of the top floor and then to the door of the upstairs lounge?"

"Huh," I said, pretending to think about it while my heart started boxing my ribs. "You know, I heard somewhere that all of the counselors are going to be out soon to clear out a tree house that someone might be living in."

"What a perfect time to watch *Independence Day* and make out."

"Um, hello? It's always a perfect time to watch *Independence Day* and make out."

"God. Please don't ever go back to California."

"I'm sorry, what was that?" I blinked at him innocently, cupping my ear. "I couldn't quite . . ."

"S'il vous plaît ne pas aller à la Californie."

31

Lack of sleep scraped at the backs of my eyelids and memories of the night before filled my muscles with cicada buzzing. It had been after three when Brandon and I had sneaked back down from the pumpkin, our eyes bleary from the harsh glow of the laptop screen and lips aching from use. It wasn't until after lunch, when Bryn Mawr clapped her hands together and told us to line up in the quad, that I remembered that we were heading into a double Cheeseman event today.

I hadn't even thought to stretch. Whatever was coming our way was going to hurt.

Jams and Hunter exchanged a blushing glance as the counselors marched all of us into the arboretum, taking the right fork out of the tree canopy. The sky over the ash tree was so blue that it hurt to look at it directly. Other than the trampled grass around the trunk, there was no sign that all of the counselors had ransacked the tree house the night before. I couldn't tell from the path if all of the stolen goods had been cleared out from under the blue tarp roof.

"Why hasn't anyone mentioned it?" I asked Brandon softly as we passed by. "I expected an announcement at breakfast or lunch, but nothing?"

He smothered a yawn in his elbow. His hair was frizzy and matted over his eyes. "No one wants to hear that everything except the binders was found. Especially not when the first skirmish is the day after tomorrow."

"Don't remind me," I said, squinting into the fierce daylight. "I don't think I'm ever going to feel truly prepared."

"No one does," he said. "That's why they can't even hint at getting the binders back. Everyone wants to keep studying, to have some semblance of readiness. Anything else would be spit on."

"Yeah?" I asked with a smile. "You don't want your socks back?"

He sighed heavily. "I do miss my socks. I borrowed a pair from Jams today. They aren't the same."

"I will bore the pants off of you talking about properly cushioned socks," I said.

"Really? I'm listening."

Laughing, I popped a kiss onto his lips. Behind us, I heard the snapping of fingers. We turned to see Meg, tiny and furious, sweeping her hands at us.

"Eyes on the road, please, little rabbits," she chirped. "I'm not explaining any pregnancies to parents, thank you very much."

Leigh cackle-snorted.

Brandon's shoulders rounded up to his ears and his eyes squeezed momentarily shut. "I have three older sisters, and yet no one has ever embarrassed me more than Meg."

I giggled and poked him in the side. "I think she'd take that as high praise."

Ahead, the paved path stopped and a dirt trail appeared, cutting a serpentine curve between pine trees so narrow that we had to squeeze two by two to keep from running into the trees. Galen looked elated when Perla fell into step with him ahead of me and Brandon.

"I'm understanding why they'd call this the Mud Trail," Galen said with a strange forced laugh. "Most of the year, this must be soup."

"Don't you want to study archaeology?" Perla asked, more confused than sneering. "You'll have to be less of a wuss about dirt to go digging for artifacts."

"Perla," Kate said with a frown, "you do know that not all archaeologists are Indiana Jones, right?"

"Really, my interest is in cartography," Galen started.

Perla cut him off, rolling her eyes and pointing as the line veered off the trail. "No time for maps, Doctor Jones!"

Bryn Mawr was shooing everyone into the trees. Our part of the line followed, sidestepping branches and crunching across the cracked, dry ground. The landscape tipped up and then slanted down. The trees thinned out, possibly to a clearing, but ahead there was only the unnatural crawl of dense, blue-tinged white fog.

"I take back every time I made fun of you for thinking the school was haunted," Leigh said, appearing at my elbow.

The air had an unmistakable, cold cloy. It was a smell that stuck in your nostrils and swelled in your lungs like chewing and swallowing a pair of tights. I knew it from too many of Beth's plays to count. *Hamlet, Macbeth,* even *Oklahoma!* all cranked up the fog machine and let the billowing white stink clouds fill the stage like a crappy TV dream sequence.

"Welcome to a double event," said Bryn Mawr, standing in front of the wall of fog. "Today's challenge is to crawl through the swamp on Dagobah." The word seemed to physically pain her. I didn't believe for a second that she had any idea what Dagobah was or which Jedi master had lived there. "Once on the other side, you will fight to the 'death.'" She threw up finger quotes in case anyone was worried. "In a lightsaber duel. A ribbon will be awarded to the person with the fastest time through the swamp and to the person who defeats the most opponents in the duel. But you may not compete in one without the other. It would be an unfair advantage. Those who do not wish to compete will be led to the other side of the swamp by their counselors. If you'd like a chance to win one of these two ribbons, make a single file line in front of me."

"No way," Galen said with a shudder. "That fog is going to give me an asthma attack from here. I'm not crawling through it."

"I'm not crawling for shit," Perla said.

"Wonder of wonders," Jams said. "Perla doesn't want to play."

"Don't pick at each other," Meg chided. "Come on. We'll go to the other side and watch all the excitement."

She led Perla and Galen through the trees, following the long line of other campers who were opting out.

"I thought the lightsaber duel would be more of a draw," Hunter said, as the rest of us trudged to Bryn Mawr's queue.

"I doubt they're real lightsabers," Kate said.

"You'd better hope so," Leigh said. "Otherwise, we're gonna have a lot of hasty amputations to explain."

"The heat of the lightsaber does cauterize the wounds on impact," Brandon said. "So at least there wouldn't be any infections or complications."

Jams laughed. "I'd call decapitations bloody complicated."

"But the cauterizing would *stop* the bleeding," Kate said. Her face fell. "Oh. Sorry. Slang."

A whistle blew on the other side of the fog and Bryn Mawr tapped the first two people in line—Meuy and another of the girls on our hall—to go into the fog. It was only a few minutes before the whistle blew again and the next person was sent down. It was disconcerting not to be able to see what was going on through the fog. Only the shouts and groans of the crowd reacting came back to us.

I snapped at a tangle in my hair as the line moved forward, only to stall for another stretch. When Brandon kissed me for luck and slunk into the fog, I tried to think of a quote from *Earnest* to distract myself and came up short, so instead I started mentally reciting the Litany Against Fear from *Dune* on a loop to steady my heartbeat.

I must not fear. Fear is the mind killer.

The line moved again.

Fear is the little-death that brings total obliteration.

I stepped past Bryn Mawr into the fog.

I will face my fear. I will permit it to pass over and through me.

My eyes adjusted as I walked into the wall of fog, enough to see that the sides of the clearing had been walled off with the same kind of blue tarps that formed the roof of the tree house full of contraband. At knee level there was a series of hula hoops half-buried in the soil, forming a long, worming trail. In front of them was a blond girl with a surgical mask over her mouth and a stopwatch in her hand. It took a moment for me to recognize her as Ben's cocaptain, Faulkner.

"We'll pay for your laundry," she said, her voice muffled through the surgical mask. "I'll time you once you're down."

There was no point in mulling it over. I dropped to the ground. The dirt scraped at the skin on my elbows and knees as I crawled under the first hoop, dragging my legs behind me. I could almost hear Sid's voice in my ear, telling me to go faster, to wear my Lawrence on the outside. Getting gassed was a BMT staple—facing tear gas with riot gear on and then peeling back the mask to report to the superior officer.

You'll watch grown-ass men sob and puke, Sid had told me. *But you'll be smart and you'll listen when they tell you that having milk with your breakfast ups your chances of vomiting. You'll let your eyes cry and not make a sound.*

This wasn't tear gas. This was stank-ass CO_2. I could handle dry ice. I could handle anything. Fear was the goddamn mind killer.

I got to the end of the hula hoops and ran to the edge of the field, past the double fog machines churning out clouds and into crisp, fresh air. The spectators were sitting farther ahead, interspersed with the pine trees. Directly in front of me were Cornell, Ben, and a girl with purple streaks in her hair, who I vaguely recognized from the dining hall. She was holding a fake, blue foam sword that was slightly longer than her arm.

Cornell clapped at me like an enthusiastic coach. "You made great time, Ever!"

Ben handed me a red foam sword. There was blue and red dust

in his beard. "The foam is covered in chalk that will track any shots made. Faces and bathing suit areas are out of bounds. First to make contact wins the round."

The sword was unevenly balanced in my hands. It had a short, almost useless guard at the top of the hilt. I would have been better off with an actual plastic lightsaber. Still, I'd helped Beth learn enough stage combat over the years to be vaguely competent with a fake blade. I gave it a practice roll around my wrist.

Show-offy? Yes. But I could taste blue ribbon and I wanted everyone else to know it.

Cornell blew a whistle and Purple Hair stepped to me, her sword raised. She swiped hard at a diagonal, wanting the clink of swords together, like we were playing Peter Pan versus Captain Hook. I went low. A red chalk dust appeared in a neat line across her shin. Cornell's whistle blew again.

Waiting for the next person to come down the hula hoop crawl, I bounced on the balls of my feet to keep alert. Ben reapplied chalk to both swords.

I hesitated when Leigh came scurrying into the clearing. I didn't love the idea of attacking my own roommate. But she beamed at me as she took the blue sword and said, "When are you ever going to get to attack someone with a sword again?"

I caught her across the stomach within the first three strikes, because she leaped toward me when she should have retreated.

Kate let out a battle cry before she threw herself at me with the sword held high over her head, leaving her entire torso open.

There was a tall Korean boy whose elbow I clipped while he tried to spin away.

A light-skinned girl with pressed, glossy black hair, who tripped and fell into my foam blade.

The girl who won the *Breakfast Club* challenge, who didn't even take the lightsaber from Ben because she had a mouth full of dirt from crawling through the fog.

Sweat was stinging my eyes and dripping at the nape of my neck.

My shoulders were starting to ache. My mouth was painfully parched, the remnants of dry ice taint, and pine dust seared into the inside of my cheeks. I looked out into the crowd as I waited for the next competitor and spotted my team waving and cheering. Meg was beside herself, hopping up and down with Leigh.

Ben and Cornell gasped in unison. I turned back in time to see Isaiah lurching out of the fog, his shoulders hunched so hard that Grandmother Lawrence would have stuck a yardstick in his shirt to straighten him out.

Ben whistled, handing me back the red sword. "Twins are an important part of the *Star Wars* universe."

I gripped the hilt until my knuckles cracked. "I'm aware."

Cornell elbowed Ben. "We should have hooked up the speakers out here. Can you imagine 'Duel of the Fates' dropping in here?"

Ben's eyes glazed with joy. "Chills, dude. Chills."

At least now I knew whose bright idea this challenge was.

Isaiah sized me up as the fanboys tore themselves away long enough to hand him a sword and explain the rules. I could feel him taking an inventory of my sweat-drenched forehead, the scrape on my knee leaking blood.

His smile unrolled slowly.

Cornell's whistle blew. Ben hummed something atonal and staccato under his breath. I heard someone shout "Beast Mode!" And then, shockingly, someone else called "Zay!"

Bolstered by the recognition, Isaiah flew at me, and for a moment I was transported to the backyard of Aunt Bobbie and Uncle Marcus's house on base at Travis. Isaiah and I were little, and we had both received lightsabers that year, although I couldn't remember which of us had actually asked for one. Bobbie and my mom didn't think that one lightsaber would be fun. Then one kid would be attacked and the other would be the attacker. Two lightsabers was basically a party!

Except it wasn't. Two lightsabers meant there was a winner and a loser. The only way to end a lightsaber fight was to end it past the point of bouncing back. You couldn't just win. You had to salt the earth behind you, because otherwise someone was going to think it was a good idea to attack while you were coming out of the bathroom or when you were taking a sip of juice. Isaiah liked to strike the second both of your hands were full. He always aimed for the neck, like a tiny psychopath.

It was no different now. I watched as the blue foam sword soared toward me, and I jumped backwards, spinning to catch his back. Our blades connected, sending a poof of chalk dust into the air.

"Why don't you let me win this one, Sis?" he asked, the smile wearing thin in his eyes. "You've already got two."

I spat in the dirt, rinsing some of the chalk residue off of my tongue. "Why don't you actually win? Instead of wanting someone to give you a prize just for showing up."

He swung all of his weight to the side, like he was going to hit a home run with my rib cage. I parried and hacked toward his face. He blocked.

"Why does it always have to be so personal with you?" he asked, his arms shaking as he held his sword in a bunt over his head. He shoved hard, throwing me backwards. "Nothing can ever just be fun. You have to be such a bitch. I've never done anything to you."

I rasped a laugh that I couldn't feel. "Everything I've ever done has been compared to you. Everything I'll ever do will be compared to you."

The blue sword swung low and Isaiah panted, the dust undoubtedly starting to clog his weak lungs. "You think I have any choice but to follow what you do?"

"Then don't!" I snarled, making a hasty jab for his middle and missing. "Make up your own mind!"

"And what should I decide?" He whipped the dreads out of his face and swung his sword in a figure eight between us. "Go to college and get disowned? Enlist and hate the rest of my life? It's a lose-lose and you know it."

"No one's going to disown you. You're the baby and you're the brain. If anyone is supposed to go to college, it's you."

"Yeah?" Swipe, block. Swipe, block. Spin away. "Then why is Sid telling me what to eat? Why are you pointing out when I can't run fast enough to pass the BMT standard? My whole life is supposed to fit into this box just because yours does."

"My life does not fit into any box. Why the hell would I be here if it did?"

"Because you want more. Not something. *More.* You'd be perfectly happy if you got shipped off tomorrow. And I'd probably die. If you really cared about going here, you wouldn't be here skanking around. God, if the family knew that you were making out all over campus with some dude, they couldn't hold you up as the paragon—"

Rage lifted my leg up in a blur. The heel of my shoe connected with his solar plexus, folding him in half. With a wheeze, he collapsed to the ground and slid on his back, his face scrunched in agony.

The whistle blew.

I stood over Isaiah, feeling nothing but a black hole of anger spreading out of my chest and over my extremities. "If you want to live your own life, here's your first lesson. Stop whining and make a choice. Stop letting other people make your choices for you. And do not ever fucking threaten me again." I looked over my shoulder at Cornell and Ben. "You guys didn't say 'no kicking,' right?"

"An oversight," Cornell said.

I wiped the sweat out of my eyes. "Too late now."

After a day of letting my anger cool, I was slightly less proud of the third blue ribbon taped above my bed. Annihilating Isaiah in amoeba tag had silenced anyone questioning my loyalty to my team and labeled me a straight-up cutthroat.

But it turned out that kicking your own twin in the stomach to win a lightsaber duel was less beast mode and more . . . unhinged.

Since he was the only other person who knew that I wasn't actually a twin, Brandon was more understanding than most, seeking me out while everyone else kept their distance. As we walked back to the residence hall so I could shower and brush the chalk off my teeth, he had asked what Isaiah had said to provoke the attack.

"I don't want to be the thing he holds over your head forever," he had murmured, after I gave him a rundown of the smack talk.

"If it weren't you, he'd find something else," I'd said. "The point is that he shouldn't be trying to extort me at all anymore. We agreed at the beginning of camp that if one of us got caught, we'd both go down. I thought we had a truce."

"Maybe he wanted to make sure you didn't change your mind. Since you, uh, hate him."

"I don't hate him," I'd said instinctively. Grandmother Lawrence would never let hatred stand in our family. "I just wish I didn't ever have to deal with him ever again. I would be fine if we could live in complete ignorance of each other's lives."

My wish was more or less granted in the days that followed. Isaiah didn't look at my side of the dining hall or stand too close to me in line. His team was always there to buffer us, to encircle him in a human shield.

Which was great about fifty percent of the time. Maybe seventy percent.

The rest of the time, the quiet stares and muttered comments stripped everything out of my head except for a single razor-edged line of *Earnest*: *You seem to me to be perfectly heartless.*

32

My eyes opened the morning of the first Melee skirmish to the same cement walls and the same view of Leigh tangled up in her zebra print sheets. The bathroom was silent when I went in to shower. I put on my lucky Angry Robot shirt and shambled to the dining hall with the rest of the pre-Melee zombies.

Meg, on the other hand, was on red alert. It was entirely possible that she had found a stash of coffee somewhere and decided to drink all of it in one go. She had sent Brandon and Jams back to the buffet line twice to add more protein to their breakfasts. She squinted at all of our faces, searching for signs of sleepiness or fear. When I set my most recent Crap You Don't Know list on the table next to my toast, she snatched it up before the creases even considered smoothing.

"No studying," she said, folding the paper down into a palm-sized square and tucking it under her plate. "You'll psych yourself out. You already know it. If you tell yourself you don't, it'll all fall out of your brain."

"That's not a thing that happens," Galen said, shooting a panicked look around the table. "Is it?"

248 ★ LILY ANDERSON

"No, Galen," Kate said. "Knowledge can't fall out of your head. Unless it's stuck in your gray matter at the time."

"You'll be fine," Hari said. Both of his elbows were on the table. He speared a piece of honeydew from his plate and bit it in half. "And if you aren't, we'll all go home early."

"No, we won't. Everyone is going to be great," Meg said, her already sharp voice spiking into new realms of squeakiness—Minnie Mouse on helium. "Just remember to keep your answers short. If the proctors need more information from you, they will ask for it. Rambling is more likely to lead you to a wrong answer. Keep it short and sweet."

"And correct," Hari drawled.

"And profanity free," Meg added, with a glance at Perla, who glared in return.

"Best get it out of the way now," Jams said, grudgingly shoveling a heap of fluffy yellow scrambled eggs into his mouth. "Piss. Bollocks. Assclown."

"Shit sandwich," Leigh added.

"Ew. We're eating," Kate whined.

I only half listened as everyone started throwing in their favorite curses. A glint of something shiny outside of the front window caught my attention. It took a moment for me to realize it was the sun refracting off Wendell Cheeseman's head. He was standing with Trixie and Ben. Trixie had an R2-D2 resting against her leg. Only after I saw the large canvas duffel slung over Ben's shoulder did I realize that the R2 must be Trixie's luggage. Because of course she would have a droid suitcase.

Except why would they have their suitcases out now?

"Balls," I blurted out.

"I already said 'bollocks,'" Jams said, exasperated.

I nudged Brandon in the side and jerked my head toward the window. He set his fork down with a clatter and shoved the hair out of his eyes. "Meg, what's going on out there?"

Meg didn't turn around. "Don't worry about it."

His mouth flattened into a scowl. "Meg."

She gave him the same pitying look that Crumbs had. That *Don't mess with me, kid* look. Being the youngest had to suck. Everyone was ready to cut you down just for asking questions.

"Focus on the Melee, B," she said. "You've got forty-five minutes before the first skirmish. We can talk afterward."

I looked over at the Team Four table, where Faulkner sat alone with her team. I examined a piece of my toast, which was actually browned and crisp on both sides this morning. And Jams's scrambled eggs weren't dripping between the tines of his fork. Hari had a fruit salad on his plate.

Since when did we have fruit salad?

"Who made breakfast?" I asked.

Meg threw up her hands. "Guys, let it go. They'll be fine."

"Why do they have to *be* fine?" I asked. "Why aren't they fine now?"

"They got caught out of bounds," Hari said, impassively eating another piece of melon. "The rules apply to everyone."

"Huh?" Hunter asked. "Who got caught?"

"Trixie and Ben are going home early," Meg said, the words leaden. "They weren't upholding the rules."

"They were found in Fort Farm this morning," Hari said.

"Who found them?" Galen asked.

Hari blinked at him. "Excuse me?"

Galen's eyebrows went up indignantly. "No one is supposed to be out before breakfast, so who found them in Fort Farm?"

Hari scowled. "Does it matter?"

"It doesn't," Meg said.

"It does if the person doing the snitching wasn't punished when they also had to be breaking the rules," Jams said.

"There are so many flaws in that logic," Kate said.

"Let it go," Meg said, in her own version of the Lawrence clip, every word like the snip of scissors. "They will be fine. They will crash at one of their parents' places until they're ready to go back to California. Now can we please focus on today's skirmish—"

"Did they steal the binders?" Hunter asked.

"What?" Meg cried. Her cheeks turned an offended pink. "No. Why would they steal the binders?"

Jams sat back, crossing his arms. "Why do they have to go home when the person who stole the binders is presumably still here?"

"Because the person who stole the binders had more sense than to have sex in a field," Hari said to his plate.

"Hari!" Meg snapped.

"Sorry," Hari said, totally forgetting to sound apologetic. "It's too stupid to be believed. Especially for two *geniuses*. If you Messina people acted half as smart as everyone says you are—"

"Good riddance," Perla said pertly. "Breakfast is edible for once, and we're going up against Trixie's team today. Now they'll be butt-hurt that their counselor is gone and we can beat them while they're weak." She looked around at the nine unsmiling faces surrounding her and huffed. "Jesus. There's no winning with you people, is there? Silver lining? Hello?"

We were led past the super modern glass walls of the theater building and around the corner to a squat brick building that I'd passed dozens of times without truly knowing what it was.

The hallways were plain and narrow, with a vague dusty smell that made me think that there had been carpeting until recently and the sweet mustiness of freshly cut wood that had to mean that there was a scene shop behind one of the closed doors.

Hari pulled open a heavy door and propped it open. On the other side was a smallish black box theater—black walls with rubbery black floors and bulky unfiltered Fresnel lights strapped across the ceiling, casting a yellowy wash over the furniture. Two long tables sat across from one short one, all of them empty except for adjustable microphones.

I thought about my mom's assumption that I was spending the summer working at the theater. I hadn't expected that to be partially true.

Team Two filtered into the room, and I realized instantly that Perla was right. Every team member looked shell-shocked at the loss of one of their counselors. But there was no time to pity them.

Cheeseman was striding into the room, buttoned up in a lumpy blue suit and chatting somberly with a Latina woman about my height, who wore a heavy necklace like plated armor across her chest. She was probably my mom's age, with lines spiderwebbing out from the corners of her eyes and plum-colored lips. A shorter man with a silver goatee and matching slicked-back hair brought up the rear.

The three of them sat down at the small table facing us. Meg, Hari, and the single counselor from Team Two all rushed away to have a seat at the back of the room. Out of the corner of my eye, I could see Brandon disappearing under his hair.

"Good morning, campers," Cheeseman said into his microphone. His voice was uncomfortably loud in the speakers. "Welcome to the first round of the Tarrasch Melee. Before we get started, my fellow proctors will introduce themselves."

"My name is Dr. Celeste Benita," said the woman, her face breaking into a smile. "Serving as a proctor for the Tarrasch Melee each year has been my honor for the last seven years."

Cheeseman turned to face her, although his mouth stayed aimed at the microphone. "The last seven years that you've been the dean of students at Rayevich?"

"Of course," Dr. Benita said with a sparkling laugh. "I suppose I forgot to mention that, didn't I?"

My stomach dropped. Jesus. None of the counselors had mentioned that one of the "proctors" would be the actual dean of the freaking college. Didn't she have more important things to do than run a trivia contest?

"As some of you may know," said the short man at the end of the table, "my name is Dr. Stuart Mendoza. I helped to cofound Camp Onward when I was a professor here, and I have proctored the

Melee every year since. I have the great fortune of being the principal of the Messina Academy for the Gifted."

I couldn't stop myself from looking down the table at Brandon. His skin was jaundiced under the harsh stage lights.

Great. One of our proctors had kicked him out of school. No pressure.

All three proctors set tablets down and swiped them open. The speakers echoed with a teeth-rattling buzzing sound that made my heart squeeze to a stop. One of the girls on Team Two yelped into her microphone.

"Sorry," Cheeseman said, sheepishly. "That's the sound of the buzzer. The volume's up a little high."

Dr. Benita smiled. "Let's get started, shall we?"

I had assumed—or maybe hoped—that the first skirmish would be more of a breeze, considering Team Two's emotional disadvantage at having lost a cocaptain that morning, but the following two hours were a backbreaking game of trivia tennis.

I remembered enough of the symbolism from the assigned reading to make it through six questions in a row about the literature section before the heat got passed over to Kate. Perla managed to keep from swearing at the proctors. I figured she had realized that they were, in fact, capable of destroying her entire future if she got snippy. No one cried until we were declared the winners, when one of the girls from Team Two finally broke down, her first sob echoing in her mic. None of her teammates moved to console her.

I expected to be forced to shake hands with the losing team, like it was a peewee sporting event, but instead Meg and Hari hustled us out of the building so fast that I was sure they thought that the proctors would take back our points if they heard us say anything that wasn't the answer to a question.

"After lunch, you'll have the rest of the afternoon off," Meg said, after we were safely out of the building and she and Hari had congratulated us. "Unfortunately, you're still not allowed to wander campus without supervision, but I did get permission from Professor Cheeseman for us to use the library again. Hari and I will split up. If you want to be in the quad, you can stay with him. Or, if you want to go to the library, you can come with me."

"And if we want to be left alone?" Perla asked.

"You can go to your room," Meg said in that sticky-sweet way that I was pretty sure meant she was picturing dismemberment.

Brandon took my hand. "Sci-fi section?"

33

hy does it feel like a thousand years since the last time we were here?" I asked, as we passed under the binary clock into the science fiction section. I hadn't been sure if Meg would actually let us go unsupervised, but she hadn't given it a second thought. Probably because all of the adults who could fire her were busy setting up for the day's second skirmish.

"It feels like a thousand years since breakfast," Brandon groaned. He cast a glance at the Magrathea table and shook his head. "Floor?"

"Floor," I concurred.

We stepped into the stacks and sat down next to each other, our backs against one of the redwood bookcases. Brandon's eyelids were heavy as he stared, unfocused, at the floor in front of us.

"Style largely depends on the way the chin is worn," I quoted, tapping lightly on his chin.

"You quote that play more than you think you do," he said with a smile.

"I doubt that." I combed my fingers through his hair, delighting in the closeness of it. "I think I quote it more than I want to, but not more than I think to."

"What a Wildean turn of phrase." He stroked his thumb against the soft skin behind my ear. "If you are not too long, I will wait here for you all my life."

A Gwendolen line. Maybe that was why it made the insides of my eyelids scratchy and my throat constrict, even as he lifted his face to mine and kissed me. It had been almost a full twenty-four hours since the last time we kissed, and twice as long since we'd been without an audience. It was a relief to sink into him, not worrying about being spied on or judged. Contentment swept away that flare-up of sadness and let an unfinished blueprint as to what might happen next take its place.

"Was it hard seeing your principal again?" I asked during a breather. I'd never made out with anyone for so long that I needed to take breaks to regain the strength in my lips and the oxygen to my brain. It was a good problem to have.

"Not as hard as I would have thought," he said. His eyebrows drew together into one long black line, visible under the bangs that I'd mussed. "It would have been nice to be warned, but the counselors probably didn't think we could handle the pressure."

"I don't know if they're wrong." I stretched my legs out until the muscles warmed from the tension. I'd been dreaming about running, for days, and waking up with my legs curled at painful angles underneath me. There was so much pressure—to stay, to win, to remember every single thing that was happening—and so few places to exert it.

"I can't believe we have three more rounds of that to go," he said. He set his head heavily on my shoulder, his eyelashes tickling the underside of my jaw. He set a nibbling kiss against the curve of my neck. "Four, if we're lucky."

"Let's not talk about it," I said, closing my eyes. "The Melee or the after or any of it. It's too depressing."

A chuckle bubbled out of his chest and another kiss, stamped between my neck and the collar of my shirt. "The entire future is too depressing to talk about?"

"Yes," I said definitively. "Other people moving into our dorms? Or the tree house getting torn down? Other people claiming the Magrathea table?"

He patted the carpet underneath us. "We aren't even using the Magrathea table. And the tree house is probably already torn down. It was full of alcohol."

"You know what I mean. Everything about this summer is going to disappear. I want to hold on to the you-and-me part while I can. It's bad enough we're on lockdown and can barely see each other while we have the time. We only have a few more days."

"Yeah, but that means in a few more days our brains won't be full of binder bullshit anymore. I can forget everything I barely know about classical music. And then we can . . ." He trailed off and lifted his head off of my shoulder. "Wait. You mean *we* only have a few more days? You and me?"

I stared back at him, shock ringing between my ears. Balls and bollocks. Was this what Leigh had meant on the first day, about IQ tests not measuring common sense? He couldn't possibly have not already thought of this. He was a genius. A genius who flunked out of genius school, maybe, but still. Certifiably smart.

"Ever," he said, not taking my silence as an answer. "If we don't win the scholarships, you're going to give up on us?"

"I told you flat out before the first time we kissed that you were one of the things I was going to miss about being here. You don't miss something you have."

"I thought that . . ." his hands flailed, indicating the two of us and the room around us, "*having* me would change that!"

"How?" I asked. "I can't keep you. You live in Oregon! Four hundred and eighty miles apart. One twelve-hour train ride. One very expensive three-hour flight!"

"I get it," he said flatly. "You ran away. You did your research."

I ignored this. "And even if we win the scholarships, college is a year away. You don't even know where you're going to finish your senior year yet. Things change. People change. And—"

His eyes were giant pudding cups of quivering hurt. "You want to end this."

I clasped my hands on either side of his face. "It's not about what I want, Brandon. It's what's going to happen. Some things are inevitable. Haven't you ever heard of a summer romance before?"

He shook off my hands, his hair flying around his forehead in wrathful tendrils. "Haven't you ever heard of long-distance?"

"I'm not even your girlfriend!" God, I didn't want him to think that I'd been staying up at night wondering why we weren't putting labels on this, so I barreled ahead. "Because we've only known each other for two weeks. Maybe in two more weeks we'd hate each other."

He looked scalded. "That's ridiculous. I really like you. And I thought the feeling was mutual."

"It was. It is! But it won't have time to grow into something else. You can't fall in love with someone you've known for two weeks. This isn't a Disney movie, and there's no white horse to ride into the sunset." I wished I'd never started talking. I wished that, instead of coming into the sci-fi section, I'd asked Hari for permission to run laps around the quad. I wished that Brandon and I were back in the pumpkin, watching *Independence Day* and breathing each other's CO2. Because I couldn't stop what came out of me next. "We aren't Ben and Trixie. They get to go home together, even though they can't stay here. Or Hunter and Jams—they can stay together if they want to because they live so close together. But when this is over, I don't know if I'll ever see you again. And not everyone gets a high school sweetheart. Most people don't! In all honesty, it's actually really weird that your friends all decided to stick it out."

He moved a single scoot away from me, but it felt like a gorge. "So, the second camp is over, we're nothing? We're strangers?"

My voice was tired and thin. "What else could we be?"

He scrubbed his hands over his face. "We could be two people who like each other, who care about each other. I want to know you. I want to know what happens when you go home. I want to know what you think about things and what you're reading and what you see."

I shook my head. "You want to be Facebook friends. That's what you're describing."

"No! Fuck. I don't even have a computer," he growled, digging his fingertips into the corners of his eyes. His Adam's apple bobbed. "You said your mom lives in Colorado. When was the last time you lived with her?"

I frowned. "When I was five?"

"And is she still your mom?"

"Yes," I said. "But that's not the same—"

"But it's similar enough for a chance." He reached out and scooped up my hands. He brushed his lips over my fingertips and I could feel him shaking. "Don't give up on me, Elliot. I won't give up on you, either. I want you! Just you!"

"I can't promise you that," I said, internally punching down every impulse to cry. Crying meant something was broken. Crying meant that I couldn't win. "I like you so much. More than I've ever liked anyone. I wouldn't be here with you if that weren't true. But you can't promise me that you'll be all mine forever, either. It's not realistic. So, why can't we have this?" I squeezed his hands, and I wasn't sure which of our pulses was hammering against my palm. "Just this. You and me."

"For the next five days."

I nodded.

He dropped my hands. They fell back into my lap, heavy and forgotten.

"That's not fair," he said in a harsh whisper. He looked away from me and through the books on the wall. "Every second we're together, I'm more invested in you. I want you to win the scholarship. I want you to get away with running away. And you're planning on forgetting everything about me."

"That's not what I said," I snapped.

"But it's true," he said. "You want to do the same thing as Perla: come in, get what's yours, and leave. Why did you even bother making friends with anyone? Why would you spend time alone with me?"

"Not everything has to last forever!" I said. Maybe I was shouting, but it was hard to tell over the sound of my rising panic.

"Not everything has to end immediately!" he shot back. "You're burning everything behind you as you go. Why even bother running away from home and spending time here? You're always looking to the end. What is the point of having a beginning or a middle?"

"I-I don't know," I said.

"Great. Cool. Good. Thanks for clearing that up." He got to his feet, his face hidden in the shadow of his hair. "Next time, maybe stick to the kick to the stomach. It's a cleaner finishing move."

I leaped to my feet as he started walking for the door. I ran to the end of the aisle and called after him, "Brandon!"

He paused under the archway, his face in profile under the binary clock. He looked up at the posters on the wall. "What's the difference of a couple of days, Elliot?"

The answer spread out inside of me, filling up my lungs and asphyxiating me in three syllables.

Everything.

34

Something is up with you," Leigh said, nipping at my heels like a yellow-haired Chihuahua, as we headed toward the dining hall for lunch after our second skirmish. The rest of the team was far behind us. "Is this about having to go up against Isaiah tomorrow?"

"No," I said, kicking a pinecone off of the path in front of us. It skittered and rolled toward the trees that blocked Mudders Meadow from view. "I've had weeks to deal with the fact that Isaiah and I are going to have to go up against each other. I'm ready for it."

Although, in all honesty, after the last two miserable days of hours and hours of skirmishes and rereading the books that had become mostly decorative on my desk, I didn't know if I cared about beating Isaiah anymore. Before, facing my cousin on the battleground of the Melee had felt like the culmination of all of my accomplishments and fears and risks tangled up into one three-hour-long proctored trivia challenge.

And now I wasn't sure.

Did I deserve to win because I'd run away first? Because I'd kicked him in the stomach to prove how much I wanted the scholarship?

Or were those the reasons that I shouldn't be here at all?

I didn't want to let my team down by taking a dive. We were currently leading the board in points.

The board itself had started out figurative. The counselors were kept up to date on the teams' points by the proctors, and that information was disseminated to us during dinner.

But then Bryn Mawr tracked down some lime-green poster board and started writing out the day's points, team by team, in oddly elaborate calligraphy. It was pinned up in the lobby of the residence hall, next to the elevator.

It made me think of Brandon's stories about the Messina publicly ranking its students. I couldn't begin to imagine how horrified I'd be if my personal points were listed, rather than those of our team as a whole. One of the best things about the Melee was that questions were thrown around so randomly that it was hard to get a sense of how many you, personally, had answered. I didn't need to know what percentage of our wins I was responsible for.

I didn't care.

"Okay," Leigh said, dragging the second syllable out into a needle point. She skipped in front of me, putting her tiny frame between me and my next step. "Then are you ready to tell me what happened with Brandon?"

I gripped my hands into fists, holding back the urge to pick her up by the shoulders and move her out of the way. It wasn't neighborly to put your hands on other people. Or so Beth always said when I threatened to practice my Muay Thai on Ethan.

"No," I said. "I'm not."

"Because something happened," she said, pretending not to have heard me. Or possibly actually having not heard me. It was hard to tell with her. She started skipping toward the dining hall again, leaving me to jog to keep up. "There's no point in denying it. You guys were holding hands like you were teddy bears with magnets sewn into your paws."

I couldn't help imagining a magnet being cut out of my palm.

Gross, yes, but not entirely inaccurate. It was a constant kick in the teeth to realize that all of my Brandon privileges had been revoked in the span of one conversation. No hand-holding. No secret smiles. No murmured comments during meals or team meetings. Like the Langoliers had come in and eaten all of the first two weeks of camp, leaving us with only the worst of it. I'd hurt him, too. Even more than I'd hurt Isaiah. At least Isaiah never had a reason to expect me to be anything but what I was.

And Brandon had liked Ever. She hadn't felt that much different than me for the first couple of weeks of camp, but it turned out that she was. Ever wasn't the kind of girl who kicked her brother in the stomach. She wasn't the kind of girl who pushed away the boy she liked.

But I was. Apparently. Because I had done all of that without even thinking about it.

"I'm not denying it," I said. "I'm just not talking about it. It doesn't need to be talked about."

Talking about it wouldn't fix it. It wouldn't fix me or undo what I'd done.

Leigh made a sound of disagreement, but let it drop. Together, we dashed up the dining hall stairs. Lunch was already in full swing for the teams that hadn't had skirmishes that morning. Chatter bounced off the wooden beams on the ceiling, filling the entire room with cheer. It had been like this all week. Once the final skirmish of the day was completed, everyone seemed so free.

I wondered if that was why the binders had been stolen from us. Having no opportunities to study after lunch meant that everyone's days opened up for hanging out or recreation or the occasional Cheeseman event.

Kate had come in second place in yesterday's extreme hokey pokey, which I had recused myself from because I was zero percent interested in sticking my Jordans ankle deep in a mud pit. Onobanjo had won *again*, tying us for the lead in the Cheeseman, with only two more events to go.

You're always looking to the end.

Brandon's voice was starting to slip in with Oscar Wilde's, both of them finding the perfect combination of words to make me feel like I'd been slugged in the face with the power loader suit from *Aliens.*

The buffet was filled with sandwich and salad makings. While Simone was a better cook than Ben had been, it was rare that our meals needed much actual cooking. There wasn't much to be done in the way of classing up the deli meats and iceberg lettuce selection.

"God, I would kill someone for a nonlettuce option," Leigh said, picking up a plate. She used a pair of plastic tongs to toss some turkey onto her plate. "Like spinach or kale or arugula."

I grudgingly reached for a dusty-looking slice of wheat bread. "What about a nonsandwich option? I can barely remember meals that weren't served between two wads of old bread."

She gave a gasp and faked a swoon. "Oh, to be close to the rest of the food pyramid. I wish I still had my binder just so I could dig through the bylaws and see what the rules about outside food are. I would pay like fifty bucks to have a different kind of grain option delivered. Barley or couscous or rice. Oh God, I miss rice. Do you think we could have food delivered without being disqualified?"

It was almost depressing that something so small could spark so much hope in my chest, but I would take any glimmer at this point. "Would restaurants come all the way out here?"

"All the way out to one of the five universities in town?" Leigh snored. "Uh, yeah. Delivery was basically invented to get food to the dorms."

The front door of the dining hall opened. Hari and Meg came in, with the rest of our team in tow. I ignored the way my organs tightened at the sight of Brandon, even when he was scowling and hiding under his hair. I abandoned my plate on the buffet table and turned my attention to the smaller of the two counselors.

"Meg," I blurted. "You have all of the camp rules memorized, right?"

She frowned at me. "Yes? It is my job, Ever."

"Right. So, is it against the rules to have food delivered to campus?"

Her mouth quirked to one side as she considered this. "In what quantity?"

"A pizza or two?" Leigh said. "Or fifty pounds of sushi rice?"

"You could do the first one," Hari said, drolly. "Not the second."

"You're such a spoilsport, Hari." Leigh pouted at him. "But pizza is always a morale boost. Sleepovers, Academic Decathlon tournaments, little league soccer. Everyone deserves a pizza of victory!"

Hunter pushed forward. "Pizza? Like real pizza? Not the gross crunchy thing that they've been putting out and calling a pizza?"

"I think it's matzo crackers with ketchup and cheese on it." Jams shuddered.

"I've had better pizza in a Lunchable," Galen said, joining the growing clump.

"Can we get a vegetarian pizza?" Kate asked, clambering toward us. "With real vegetables?"

"And name-brand sodas?" Galen asked.

Perla's eyebrows rose and she took a couple of steps toward the group. "I'd put in money for a real Coke."

"Bran," Hunter said, turning to Brandon, who was still hovering near the door. "You must know a good pizza place in town. We deserve a real victory dinner before we move on to the finals tomorrow morning!"

"Uh, sure," Brandon said, glancing up from the floor. "You'd have to look up their phone numbers, but there's plenty of decent pizza."

"If you guys are willing to chip in money for it," Meg said carefully, "I don't see a problem with it. We could set up a picnic outside during dinner, so it doesn't look like we're lording it over the other teams . . ."

Leigh punched her fist in the air. "Tonight we dine in hell!"

"I was thinking the quad," Meg said. "But I always appreciate your enthusiasm, Leigh."

"Why didn't we do this weeks ago?" Jams said, his eyes closed in delight as he stretched out on Meg's My Little Pony blanket, a plate heaped with pizza in front of him.

"And can we do it forever?" Galen asked, covering his mouth with the back of his hand.

"Crappy camp food is a time-honored tradition," Meg said, carefully selecting a slice from one of the three open boxes in the center of our haphazard circle of blankets.

Hunter laughed, displaying a lump of partially masticated mozzarella. "Yeah, constantly having the runs is an important part of your emotional development."

"Gross, Hunter," Kate squeaked. "I'm eating."

"We are all eating," Perla concurred darkly.

Leigh flopped down on her back, next to me, and stretched her legs out, feeding herself slices from above. "This pizza is so good that you could honestly talk about anything during it and it wouldn't deter me at all."

"Let's not test that theory," I said, popping a slice of bell pepper in my mouth.

Hari shook out a napkin and placed it over his lap before taking his first bite of the vegetarian pizza. "Goddamn I missed real food. Our dining hall actually makes really good food when it isn't being run by students. I can't wait for the chefs to come back from summer break. I'm never going to eat another frozen waffle in my life."

"Can we talk about tomorrow morning?" Kate asked delicately. "It is the second-to-last skirmish."

"It's the last skirmish for five teams," Brandon said. I had been trying so hard not to look at him, but his voice drew my attention across the circle, where he was sitting next to Meg. Only the tip of his nose and his top lip were visible between his hair and his bent knees. I wasn't sure he'd even had any pizza. Realizing people were listening to him, he added, "Hopefully not us."

"Not us," Meg said firmly.

Kate nodded. "Positive thinking."

Brandon rocked to the side in what might have been a shrug if he'd let go of his legs. "Logical thinking. Statistically, we're ahead by enough points that—"

"Never tell me the odds," I blurted.

Brandon's eyes flickered up to mine and, for the first time in days, held.

I hate this, I tried to tell him silently. *I don't think there's any way to fix it, but I wish I could. I wish I could stay here forever and not look ahead.*

I miss you. I miss you. I miss you.

"Sorry," I said dumbly, turning away first. "I didn't mean to interrupt."

"There's always time for *Star Wars* quotes," Meg said cheerfully.

"Ever," Brandon breathed. Or maybe I imagined it. When I looked up, he was uncurling himself to reach for pizza.

Wishful thinking, then. I returned to my dinner. I had put in most of my train snack money to help pay for it, after all.

Footsteps crunched against the grass. Cornell was coming from the residence hall with his head down and his hands in the back pockets of his jeans. He looked particularly gloomy for someone whose team was currently ranked in second place, behind us.

"Cornell!" Meg said, turning on her megawatt smile. "I'd offer you pizza but I don't want to share. Why aren't you at dinner?"

He winced half a smile at her in return. "I need to borrow Ever, if it's all right."

"Huh?" A long string of cheese fell across my chin. "Me?"

Cornell nodded, politely looking away as I scrubbed the cheese off my face. "Your brother needs to talk to you. Alone. He got a call from home and it doesn't seem like good news. He's pretty shaken up. Did you hear from your parents tonight?"

"No." I moved to pat my sweatshirt, but I knew it was empty. Not that it mattered. Isaiah and I didn't get the same emergency calls. "I don't have my phone on me."

"You can go on up to his room," Cornell said. "It's the last one on the left. Next to the lounge."

"Okay. Um. Thanks." I got to my feet and brushed blades of grass off my legs before jogging to the lobby.

I could feel my lips trembling as my adrenaline spiked. I pushed down thoughts of Uncle Marcus, deployed in God knows where, or Grandmother Lawrence, with her paper-thin skin and eternally high blood pressure. Or Sid, driving her car like it was a freaking fighter jet up and down the highway.

I took the stairs up to the first floor and elbowed open the door. With everyone at dinner in some fashion or another, the hall was quiet. The last door on the left was open. The chalkboard sign had been wiped away once, with fingerprints left behind. On top of the smear was written "Wy & Zay." It was almost adorable.

Inside, Isaiah's dorm was identical to my own. Same narrow beds and cheap desks and tall wardrobes. His roommate had clothes all over the floor, whereas Isaiah's side was tidy the way everyone in our family was tidy—compulsively and under threat of consequences.

Isaiah was sitting at his desk, facing the windows that overlooked the quad. With only his roommate's desk lamp on to illuminate the room, his shadow was gigantic on the wall. Seeing my reflection in the window, he turned around. His eyes were so red that he looked almost extraterrestrial, even more like the Predator than normal.

"What are you doing here?" he asked with a globby sniffle.

"Cornell came to get me," I said, leaning on the door until it closed. "Because I'm your sister for another couple of days. What's going on? Is Uncle Marcus okay?"

He flinched, his dreads snaking around his cheeks. "Oh, Dad's fine. He can't get out here in time."

I looked for a place to sit, but nowhere on Wy's side of the room was even remotely clean enough. I settled for standing at the head of Isaiah's bed, one hand on the bed frame. "In time to what? What's going on?"

"It's my mom," he said, with a snivel that was organic for once. Fat tears welled in his eyes and he wiped his nose on the back of his arm in one long swipe. "She knows. Sid's ex mailed my T-shirt to my house instead of here and my mom opened it."

My heart sped up. "Wait, so your mom knows you're here? Because of a T-shirt from leadership adventure camp?"

"There was a note in the package, wishing me luck on the Melee. That dumb asshole. I'm glad Sid cheated on him." He threw up his hands and didn't seem to notice that tears were leaking out of his eyes. "She's coming up here to get me. First thing tomorrow morning."

"Wait, that's it?" I gasped. "She's just going to pull you out of the Melee? You're so close to the end! You're in the semifinals! What if your team makes it to the end?"

He stood up, his shadow looming all the way up to the ceiling. "That's the point. We don't get to finish. We don't get to make this choice. We'll both be lucky if they don't ship us down to one of the military schools. There's one in Oakland. We wouldn't even have to move. It's only an hour away from home."

I shook my head. "The military schools are army. No Lawrence is getting shuffled off to be a goddamn ground pounder."

He stamped his foot against the carpet. His lower lip was quivering nonstop, but it wasn't an act. He couldn't stop crying. He had opened a valve and it was all coming out now. His bright red eyes narrowed with the effort of talking. "Do you think they care? We ran away, Elliot. We ran away and we lied and they know."

Panic started to spark underneath my skin, using my bones as a flint. "Why do you keep saying 'we' like this is on both of us?"

He put his head in his hands and let out a sob that racked his entire body. "I was so fucking close . . . I just wanted a fucking chance . . ."

I walked around the bed to stand in front of him. I thought about reaching out to touch him, to console him, but it wasn't what we did. I was sure he'd see it as an act of war and take a swing at me.

"What did you do, Isaiah?" I demanded. "What did you tell your mom?"

He sniveled and slurped and gulped down a breath before lifting his head to face me again.

"Mutually assured destruction," he said thickly. "You bitch."

35

Leigh was nursing a final slice of pizza when she stopped short in the doorway.

"Hey, Ever," she said in the same tone you would use on a rabid dog. Or on your deranged-looking five-foot-ten Muay Thai–trained roommate. "You wanna talk now?"

I looked up from ripping the sheets off my bed. My suitcase was open on the floor, most of my shoes already paired off inside. The glittery Firefly poster was laid across the top of my newly empty desk until I could track down a rubber band. I'd tried to talk myself into leaving it behind, but I couldn't bring myself to throw it out.

"I'm going home," I said. It was a relief to say it out loud. It had been playing on a loop in my head since I'd run out of Isaiah's room and checked my phone. Twenty-seven missed calls from all three of my parents. I hadn't managed to get through all of the voice mails, but the gist was that Beth had booked a flight for first thing in the morning and that repercussions the likes of which I had never imagined were about to fall down on me.

Aunt Bobbie had called Beth during her final dress rehearsal, so I had ruined not only my parents' night but also the integrity of

Woodland Opera House's umpteenth production of *The Importance of Being Earnest*. So that was one more mark in the Elliot's An Asshole column, alongside "Kicked her cousin in the stomach instead of discussing problems like a rational adult," "Broke a cute boy's heart," and "Was never nice enough to Perla and maybe that's why she's such a snob."

Oh. And the whole "Ran away, using Oscar Wilde as an excuse" thing.

"Is this about you and Isaiah not actually being related?" Leigh asked, edging into the room and closing the door.

I snapped around to face her and she shied closer to her wardrobe, eyebrows worn high and imperious on her forehead.

"What did you say?" I asked.

"Come on," she scoffed, waving her pizza in the air. "There is one thousand percent no way that you two are twins. Not even brother and sister. Are you ready to talk about it, because you look like you might have snapped and I have a lot of questions."

My fitted sheet finally detached from the farthest corner of the mattress and whizzed into my arms. I sat down, the wad of billowing cotton settling on my lap.

"You knew?" I asked.

"Are you serious?" She laughed, throwing herself down on her mattress. "From the second he showed up. You were shocked to see him on the first day. Like the-boogeyman-showed-up shocked. I mean, I let it go because it was your business, but now . . ." She gestured to my luggage. "It looks like shit's gone sideways?"

"The most sideways," I said.

"Can I help?"

"I don't know," I said. I rubbed my lips together. "Do you mind listening to a bunch of truth all at once?"

She grinned. "I've been waiting weeks for you to ask me that."

So I laid it all out for her. From the beginning, all the way until Isaiah pulled the trigger on our mutually assured destruction, with long, hyperventilating detours to explain how I'd told Brandon that we had no future together and that I hadn't returned a single phone call home since the night we'd watched *The Breakfast Club*.

"Hm," she said, when I'd run out of steam and she'd run out of pizza. "Okay."

"Okay?" I repeated. "Did you hear all of that crap I just spewed at you?"

She smiled in recognition. "Ever—"

"It's Elliot, actually," I interrupted. "My real name is Elliot."

"But my summer camp best friend's name is Ever. You chose it yourself, didn't you?"

I nodded.

"Then I am keeping it. I like it. It's a very romantic name," she said. She hopped up, dusting herself off. "All right. Let's go."

"Go where?"

She winked at me as she scurried for the door. "To my big secret."

I followed her out of the dorm, checking over my shoulder the entire way, prepared to see Meg or Harper jump out of the shadows.

"Calm down. You can't get sent home if you're already going home," Leigh laughed, as we entered the stairwell.

"*You* could!" I hissed at her back.

"Same difference," she said with a wave of her wrist.

I stopped protesting once we were out of the lobby and into the quad. The night was bracingly crisp and the stars were out in full effect. The crickets were louder than they had been when we'd been out for dinner, or maybe I was free to notice them now that basically everything had come crashing down around me. I felt like my whole body was made of raw, broken skin. Without the scab of secrets, everything was too free to sink in.

Leigh took a left, pointing us in the direction of the Lauritz and walking in surprisingly long strides on her short legs.

"So," I said. "You were going to tell me something?"

"No," she said in cheery singsong. "I was going to *show* you something."

"Is it a dead body?"

She goggled up at me, her mouth slack. "Why would I show you a dead body?"

"I don't know!" I huffed, skipping to keep up. "What else would you show me that you couldn't tell me about first?"

"Oh my God, so many things before dead body," she said. "A basket of puppies or a mossy log or a cloud that looks like a pony? All of those before dead body."

"There aren't any clouds out. It's nighttime."

"Okay, then maybe I wanted to show you the moon," she said.

I looked up, but it was impossible to find the moon beyond the shadowy rooftops and tree branches.

Leigh grabbed my arm and tugged. "I didn't want to show you the moon, Ever. You've seen the moon. And don't even guess that I'm a ghost, because I will be seriously pissed if you think I'm imaginary."

"Imaginary people don't have tiny sharp nails digging into my wrist," I said, wincing at the pain as she continued to pull me up the sidewalk. We took another left and entered the trees. "Are you taking me to Mudders Meadow?"

"Mudders Meadow is for freshmen and orgies," she sneered. "I can't believe they included that on the list of must-see places on campus. We are going *through* the meadow."

"I'm sorry," I said, ducking as branches started to lodge in my hair. "Did you just say 'orgies'?"

"Yes, Ever, my secret is that I'm a sex maniac," she said sarcastically. She gave my arm another tug. "You really make surprising you less fun than it could be."

"You make revealing surprises more cryptic than it needs to be."

"Touché."

We pressed on, cutting across the clearing that was Mudders Meadow and onward, deeper into the trees. Overhead, owls screeched.

Finally there was a glimpse of light. Ahead, the trees started to thin out, and I thought I could see something white on the ground.

Leigh pushed me to the right and we bumped into a knobby old oak tree.

"Up," she said.

"Up?" I echoed, but then I looked up and understood. A giant four-walled tree house loomed large over us. Not the rinky-dink kind that had been in the arboretum. This was more like one of the Fort Farm forts mounted in a tree, with two-by-fours holding it steady to the trunk.

"Will we both fit in it?" I asked.

"Sure," Leigh said. "I don't take up much room. Give me a second. I'll throw down the ladder."

And just like the afternoon of the climbing event, she hopped up the trunk and landed inside of the house. A metal ladder descended, the kind people use to escape the second story of a burning house. My parents had one in their closet.

I climbed awkwardly and landed on the wooden floor. Light erupted, and I threw an arm up against the glare. When my eyesight adjusted, I saw a camping lantern illuminating the inside of what Beth would call a "cozy studio" tree house. My hair brushed the ceiling, but otherwise the tree house was much roomier than it looked from below.

"I know," Leigh said airily. "It's bigger on the inside."

There was a single storage container on Leigh's side of the room, which she opened, leaving the lantern between us. She retrieved a single bottle with a pirate on the label and two plastic cups and set them next to the lantern. And then she pulled out a plain red leather wallet, which she handed to me.

I opened the wallet's flap and saw a small photo of Leigh. Her hair was black, not yellow, and was stick straight, so long that it disappeared out of frame. She also wore thick black glasses, the kind that people sometimes wore even without a prescription.

It took me a second to realize what I was looking at. On the top, in bold font, it read "Rayevich College: Class of 2019."

I looked up. Leigh twisted the top off of the pirate bottle and a

276 ★ LILY ANDERSON

strong alcoholic breeze filled the tree house. She poured some of the dark brown liquor into each of the cups and handed one to me.

"Surprise?" she said.

I took a long drink from the cup she'd handed me. It tasted like syrup that was also on fire. I couldn't tell if I hated it. I drank it again and my entire throat felt like it was pulsing red hot.

Leigh took her sips more carefully, watching me with nervous eyes.

"I shaved my head to get off the creamy-crack wagon," she said. "You know. The big chop?"

I couldn't tell if she really believed that her using relaxer was the biggest shock here.

"You *go* here?" I asked. The alcohol made my voice feel far away, so I said it again. "You. Go. Here. How?"

"I'm seventeen, just like you," she said, bouncing her head from side to side. "But I'm also about to go into my junior year. Of college. Here. The camp bylaws don't expressly say that preexisting students can't win the scholarship. There's no precedent for it, but it's not against the rules . . ."

"How?" I repeated, louder this time.

"Not all geniuses go to the Messina." Her forehead scrunched in distaste. "It's a very expensive holding pattern. I don't know who would blow all that money on *not* going to college."

"And the tree house?" I asked, very close to shouting now. "How how how?"

"That's what they're for," she said, giving a little snort into her cup. "Have you seen the prices for on-campus housing? It's ridiculous. There's a reason people fight for placement at this camp. That full ride is buku bucks. Anyway, if you want to live off campus, you have to have a car, because the buses don't run all the way out here all day. It's a nightmare. And I didn't have my driver's license when I started here because I was fifteen—"

I spluttered. "You're like a real genius."

"It's not like there's a difference between me being a genius and you being a genius."

"Except you go to college," I stressed. "And you live in a tree. A *tree*."

A handbag! shouted Oscar Wilde. Oh, God. Alcohol made the quoting louder. Or maybe it was the beginning of my real, live nervous breakdown.

"Most of the time, yeah." She shrugged. "When the weather is really bad, I can usually crash with friends in the residence hall. My parents only qualified for so much financial aid, so . . ." She stopped. "Are you like really freaked out right now or is the rum making your face do that?"

I touched my face. It did feel freaked out. My eyes were bugging and my mouth wouldn't close. My head was starting to spin. I set my cup down. "Did you take the binders?"

Her eyes went saucer round. "What? No. Of course not."

"There is no 'of course' when you tell me that you started college at fifteen and live in a tree."

"You lied about your name and having a twin and I didn't accuse you of stealing the binders. Plus, the binders getting taken was a blow to my summer, too, you know. I don't know shit about classical music. Who has a classical music section but no math? What kind of shit is that?" She scooted back until her back pressed against one of the tree house walls. "Fine. Yes, I took most of the water bottles from the dining hall, but that is it. I did not break into anyone's rooms. That's such an invasion of privacy."

"Sorry," I said. I rubbed my eyes until pinpricks of light floated behind my lids. "Why haven't any of the counselors recognized you? It's a small school, right?"

"Who said they haven't?" she asked. "I'm here under my real name. Simone from Team Five and I took medieval art history together last year. Not that we're super best friends or anything. It's hard to make friends when you're the baby everywhere you go. Camp has been really cool for having other smart kids around. I'll miss that when the semester starts back up." Her eyes stared past me. "Oh! Maybe that's why people go to the Messina. I never factor in the social component. Still. It seems like an expensive way to keep friends." My face must have still been rum-frozen, because Leigh reached over to pat my knee. "I'm really sorry about all of this. I don't have a way to keep your parents from stealing you back to California. I'll miss you when you go. I really liked having a bestie for a couple of weeks."

"I really liked being your bestie for a couple of weeks." My voice—too far away from my ears—was as tight as a hug good-bye. Without warning, my eyes burned with an entire ocean of tears. "I really don't want to go home. I'm not ready to be at the end."

"It's okay," she said softly. "You aren't."

I curled up on the floor, taking up almost all of it, like in *Alice in Wonderland*, when she became a giant and wore that cottage like a romper. Leigh petted my hair while I cried.

It was harder climbing down the ladder light-headed from rum and feelings. More feelings than rum, truth be told, since I'd let Leigh finish my cup when the tree house started to spin. She was kind enough not to judge me for being a lightweight.

It was funny. Being a lightweight but outweighing her by so much.

"Come here, swervy," she said, gently guiding me through the trees. "I thought the rum would take the edge off your shitty night. I didn't think about having to drag your Amazonian butt back across campus."

"You aren't dragging me," I said, pointedly striding ahead of her. I stopped short and looked around. All of the trees in front of me had forks and yarn wound through the branches. "But I might already be lost."

Her hands found my elbow again, pulling me away. "It's not your fault. Trees kind of all look the same."

"Racist."

"Arborist?"

"That one."

I started to laugh—or maybe cry again—when Leigh's hand

clamped over my mouth. My complaints were muffled against her palm. As I considered whether to bite her for freedom—a tactic Isaiah used on me dozens of times when we were little—I finally clued in to why we'd stopped walking. There were voices in Mudders Meadow.

"Dad said—" screeched one. A girl. A familiar girl.

"Dad said . . ." parroted another, this one crueler, colder. "You are being a child, Katie. No one else gets to use their security blankets. Are you saying that you aren't as smart as everyone else?"

"My team has missed the same question about the Murakami short story every single skirmish."

That was odd. Our team had missed the same question about "A Shinagawa Monkey" every round of the Melee so far.

A second too late, I froze down to my bones.

"It's Kate," Leigh breathed in my ear.

Our Kate? Kate with her narrow face and braying laugh. Why was Kate screaming in the meadow in the middle of the night?

"I want to know the answer before it costs us the semifinals," Kate continued, on the other side of the trash trees.

"Fine. I'll get you the stupid binder," said the other voice. "But this is it. You told Dad that you could handle the same pressures as everyone else. If you can't even memorize the binder, then how do you expect to survive your first term here?"

"It's not the same thing, Rowan!"

Rowan? I thought. I didn't know anyone named Rowan. I looked over at Leigh, who seemed as confused as I was.

Good. I was afraid it was the rum.

I squeezed my eyes shut. Okay. Some of it was the rum. Drinking looked like way more fun when the Shakespeare company got drunk at Beth's Christmas party. It mostly made my whole body feel like it was full of sand and sparklers.

"Meet me on my floor during breakfast," Rowan said. "You can look through the binder then. I need to get back before anyone notices that I'm gone."

"Yeah, me too," Kate said.

There was a peal of laughter. "Yeah, I'm sure your Salieri is desperate to know where you are."

Leigh and I crept forward as the girls' footsteps started to retreat, but both of them were wearing black hoodies pulled over their hair.

"Shit," Leigh hissed. "More siblings? What the hell is going on? Do you know anyone named Salieri? Since when does Kate have a sister here? Oh my God! She out-awkwarded me! I was so played!"

I clasped her shoulders, with awful, drunken awareness banging like a gong in my head. "It's a full-on Wildean farce."

36

A bottle of water was tucked into bed with me. There was a Post-it wrapped around the label that read, "For your first little baby hangover. Love, Leigh." My head did hurt a bit, but I wasn't sure if that was the alcohol dehydrating me or all of the crying I'd done last night.

I sat up foggily, unsure what had woken me. I had a vague memory of Leigh telling me she was going to breakfast, but I didn't know how long ago that was. I wasn't wearing any of my blankets.

Because all of my blankets were in my suitcase.

Because I was going home today.

This morning.

Now?

I looked over at my desk and saw my phone screen flashing with a text message from Beth.

You can ignore our phone calls all you want, Elliot. We will be at Rayevich at 10:00. Be packed and ready to come home. We have already spoken to Dean Cheeseman.

"Associate dean," I said to the phone. Not that it or Beth could hear me.

It was my last morning at Rayevich, and that was going to have to be okay. I had done the selfish thing. All of the selfish things, really. Running away, publicly humiliating and injuring Isaiah—twice—and almost, maybe, falling in love with a guy whose voice was like the coziest sweater. And then spent the night drinking and crying about it with my new college best friend. Who was already in college.

Today, I would own up to it. If it took military school or never driving again or only driving Ethan and his friends to and from Scandia Fun Center so that they could play mini golf while I sat in the car, that would have to be enough. It would be worth it, because I got what I wanted. I got two and a half weeks that were mine. That no one could take away from me.

Even if they could interrupt it. It was only two days early, and I'd gotten to keep my good underwear the whole time. Suck on that, BMT.

I chugged the bottle of water in full. I could feel it splashing into my stomach, creating tidal waves of rum-soaked acid. I padded down to the bathroom and washed my face and brushed the sour plaque off my teeth. I couldn't help myself from mentally saying good-bye to everything I passed. The broken soap dispenser next to my favorite sink with the water least likely to scald your hands. The lemon-yellow lounge in the hall. The chalkboard doors full of names I never bothered to learn.

And then I stopped.

I was accepting an ending again. I had gone to bed defeated and kind of drunk and possibly trying to convince Leigh that Kate's mysterious sibling had been trying to say "Salami yeti," not "Salieri."

I didn't know it was over. As long as I was on campus, I refused to jump to the end.

I went back to my empty dorm and got down on the floor. The thin carpet pinched against the lines of my hands as I pushed myself into a plank. I would live my last day at camp as Elliot Gabaroche. Starting with forty-five push-ups and fifty sit-ups.

I had left home looking for something that was all mine, something outside of my parents and their families. But that wasn't right.

According to the Onward entrance exam, I was a genius. And we needed geniuses in the service, same as anywhere else. Maybe more than anywhere else. You didn't want to hand a bunch of idiots military tech. Hiding my light under a bushel wouldn't help me or my country or my family—any of my families.

For as long as I had understood that college happened after high school, I'd known that my mother was waiting for me at the Air Force Academy. Not literally. She wouldn't be in the next room, ready to come in and chat when I couldn't sleep, or sit up sipping tea with me, the way Beth did sometimes. But we could experience more time together than we'd ever had before. Dinners. Weekends. Trips off base. Not just for a week or two at a time, like we did now over spring break, but for years.

Years when I was supposed to be spreading my wings.

That didn't scrub all of the military as a prospect. I didn't have to go to the Academy. Just like Brandon didn't have to go to an Ivy League school to do math. Being gifted didn't go away because you chose a different fork in the road. That was the beauty of taking your brain with you wherever you went.

You didn't have to be the first person to be good at something to own it. The air force wasn't my destiny, but I'd been running toward it and away from it for too long.

Maybe I'd enlist right out of high school, like my mom had done. Maybe I'd go to college first and enter as an officer, like my uncle Marcus. That wouldn't make it less mine. Just like sharing this summer with Isaiah wouldn't diminish my memories of camp.

I was ready to be comfortably in the middle of a story instead of running toward the end. I was done trying to outpace myself.

I got dressed and stacked my suitcase, laptop bag, and backpack on my bare mattress before descending the stairs to the first floor.

It wasn't like anyone could send me home. The freedom was empowering, like wearing an invisible mecha robot suit or one of the force fields that Isaiah always threw up when we used to play together. I was almost disappointed when I got to the end of the hall and didn't get caught. I knocked on the ampersand between the chalk *Wy & Zay.*

A rail-thin white kid with fluffy blond hair answered the door, his eyes wide as he said, "Uh-h-h . . ." with such sustained breath that I was actually impressed.

"You must be Wy," I said. When he didn't move, I gestured to myself. "I'm Isaiah's sister. I need to talk to him."

"Oh, right. I'll leave you guys alone," Wy said, jittering away from the door and clearing a path for me to step inside the dorm. Instead of closing the door behind him, he slipped through it. "See you at breakfast, Zay!"

Isaiah was sitting on his bed. He hadn't yet unmade it. The sheets were neatly tucked under the corners, ready for another night.

"Have you heard from Aunt Bobbie?" I asked.

He glared up at me. "Why?"

I put my hands up in surrender. "My folks are going to be here at ten. I was wondering if they caught the same flight."

"Must have," he muttered. "My mom will be here at ten, too."

"Good," I said. "I need you to stay with your team. Go to the skirmish. Start competing."

He squinted at me like I'd lost my mind. "What? No. Why?"

"Because I'm asking you to?"

"You're telling," he shot back.

I held my tongue and counted to ten. Then I tried it again with *Mississippi*s. There wasn't a world where he made it easy to be nice to him.

"Whoever they see first is going to take the brunt of this," I said.

"So?" He smashed his arms over his chest. The movement threw a wall of his cologne at me.

"So, that should be me," I said, wincing at the smell. I guess it would mask whatever was happening with all of Wy's dirty clothes. I squared my shoulders. "You were right, Isaiah. You need this more than me. You need the room to make this choice for you. Go compete. If you can beat my team, then I don't doubt that you'll get your placement here. You deserve a scholarship here."

He stared at me, possibly waiting for me to crack up and tell him it was all a joke. When I didn't, he sniffed. "Is this because you kicked me in the stomach?"

I scuffed my heel against the carpet. "Sort of. I don't mean to be a bitch to you. You're just . . ." I thought about Leigh saying how hard it was to make friends when you're always the youngest, and Crumbs ignoring Brandon's pleas in French. "You're the baby. It's not your fault that you're an annoying douche-canoe. You just make it so hard to be nice to you. We were doing okay before you tried to blackmail me during the lightsaber duel."

He hung his head, clasping his hands together. His thumbs rubbed together awkwardly. "I wouldn't have told anyone about your boyfriend."

I gritted my teeth. "The first chance you got, you told your mom I was here."

"Well, yeah." He rolled his eyes. "But she would have found that out when she got here, wouldn't she?"

"Make sure that you make it to the skirmish. Before I change my mind about trying to be nice to you."

He examined my face. "Are you going to enlist?"

I shrugged. "Someday."

"Because that's what Lawrences do?"

"I'm not a Lawrence."

"Are so. You've got two last names, don't you?"

He got to his feet. I was momentarily paralyzed with fear that he was going to hug me, but he straightened up tall and saluted me.

"Aim high, Ever."

I returned the salute. "Fly, fight, win, Zay."

As I opened the door to the stairwell, the pocket of my shorts buzzed. I froze, bracing for another rage-filled text from one of my parents, but was surprised to see Leigh's name pop up.

> Come to breakfast! I found Rowan! I am the greatest detective in the world!!! (Simone helped.)

I paused. I had some time before the plague of screaming adults was timed to hit campus. And I would get hungry while they were yelling at me. And maybe if I made it to the end of breakfast, I could say good-bye to Brandon. Or not say good-bye and just see him again. Depending on my current level of cowardice.

There wasn't much left on the breakfast buffet when I made it to the dining hall. I managed to get a single pancake and a couple of sausages before throwing myself down at the open spot at the end of the bench, next to Perla.

"Ever!" Meg said, barely concealing her shock. "I didn't think you were going to make it down today. I got a message from Professor Cheeseman last night—"

"I was hungry," I said simply, ignoring the confusion passing around the table.

"And just in time!" Leigh said, leaping off the bench and showing zero sign that she was feeling any of the rum we'd shared the night before. She threw her arms out wide. "May I have your attention, please?"

"Leigh," Hari said wearily. "Sit down."

"Stuff it, Bhardwaj," Leigh said, pirouetting to point a finger at him. She strode to the middle of the dining hall. "Pop quiz! Who is Salieri?"

There was a lot of confused muttering before one of the guys from the Team Five table called out, "He was Beethoven's nemesis!"

"Mozart, not Beethoven," corrected Fallon loudly from the Team Two table. "Get it together, Team Five."

"Hasn't anyone else seen *Amadeus*?" Jams wondered aloud.

"Nope," Hunter said. "I'll add it to the list of movies that we have to watch when we get home."

"Antonio Salieri was an eighteenth-century composer," Leigh continued, theatrically loud. "And yet he is best remembered for his rivalry with Wolfgang Amadeus Mozart. There's a whole section about it on his Wikipedia page. But unless you're like Jams and just have a passion for the Tony Award–winning play based on Mozart's and Salieri's lives, why the hell do any of us know this?"

"It's a question in the Melee," Simone said, warily looking at the camper on her team who had incorrectly answered the question to begin with.

"Yes!" Leigh said. "And isn't that strange? Who would consider classical music to be on par with English lit and psychology and science? Shouldn't we have, you know, a math section?"

For the first time, I let myself look at Brandon. His head had lifted at the mention of a math section, hesitantly interested. The skin under his eyes looked shadowy and unrested. I wondered if the stress of the Melee was keeping him up at night, staring at his ceiling and running through equations.

"According to an article the Eugene *Register-Guard* did about Camp Onward, there was a math section of the Melee until last year. And then it disappeared," Leigh said, wiggling her fingers mysteriously in the air. "When Wendell Cheeseman took over as the camp director. Which is weird. Why would a history professor care whether or not we know who Antonio Salieri is?"

She looked around, waiting for more of a reaction, but was met with mostly confusion. Except for Kate, who had started shredding her napkin.

"Last week," Leigh continued, undeterred by the silence, "someone with motive and means and a heart as cold as ice broke into every occupied dorm in the residence hall and stole all of the binders, most of the food, and some of my fanciest tampons."

Meg put her head in hands. "This is how I get fired."

"But who?" Leigh asked, waving a fist in the air. "Was it a camper who wanted to win at all costs? A counselor with a score to settle? An administrator with a filthy secret?"

Her hand froze in the air.

"The second one?" guessed Victor Onobanjo.

"All three!" Leigh cried. "Last night, a counselor and a camper were seen colluding in Mudders Meadow. Kate Brant and Faulkner."

That elicited gasps. Kate's hands flew to her mouth. "No!"

"Yes!" Leigh said triumphantly. She swung around to look at Faulkner, who was sitting, blank faced, with Team Four. "Faulkner, whose cocaptain was suddenly sent home from camp with no explanation. Faulkner, who happened to be put in charge of the classical music section of the binder. Faulkner, who has no first name!"

"Ben was sent home for abandoning his post," Cornell said. "He was sleeping in Fort Farm."

"With his girlfriend," Hari added.

"But if you all knew that," Leigh said, slightly miffed at being interrupted, "then why did Cheeseman show up and throw out two of the counselors days before the end of camp?"

"Can we go back to the part where Faulkner doesn't have a first name?" asked Meuy, adjusting her glasses.

Peter the MIT counselor shook his head. "Everyone has a first name."

"Yes, but Faulkner is a mononym. A single word to hide behind. But she was too clever by half. She had to sign her crime." Leigh had started to pace toward the Team Four table. "Isn't that right, Rowan Oak?"

Faulkner scowled at her in return. "It isn't a crime to change my name. Rowan Oak was the name of William Faulkner's estate. Which would you rather be called?"

Leigh tapped her chin, thoughtfully. "I don't know. Maybe I'd want to be called by my full name. Rowan. Oak. Cheeseman."

"Whoa," I said.

"Took the word right out of my mouth," Hari said, his jaw agape.

"But Rayevich is so exclusive that faculty members' families don't get special consideration for admission. They don't even get a discount on tuition! So, Rowan *Faulkner* was accepted to Rayevich College two years ago on a full scholarship as a winner of the Tarrasch Melee," Leigh said, her face wild. "And this year, a Kate Brant was also granted a position at camp. Of course, according to the Internet, Kate Brant of Coos County, Oregon, doesn't exist." Leigh narrowed her eyes at Kate. "But Katerina 'Katie' Cheeseman is well known as a piano prodigy. A homeschooled piano prodigy. And who would know more about classic music than someone who's been studying it since the age of two?"

"Whoa!" Galen shouted.

"Damn," Jams said.

"Ben and Trixie are going to be pissed they missed this," Meg said to Brandon, who nodded numbly.

"Admit it, Katie Cheeseman," Leigh said darkly. "You had your father and your sister break into the dorms and steal all of the binders. You weren't keeping up. You had the lowest percent-correct on the team. You wanted Perla gone because she has the highest IQ on our team!"

"No," Kate spat back, getting to her feet. "I wanted her gone because she snores and she's mean!"

Perla looked affronted. "I do not snore!"

"Yes," Meg groaned, "that's what we should take issue with here."

"Dr. Benita and Dr. Mendoza have already been informed as to the Cheeseman family's deception," Leigh said, dusting off her hands. "No Cheeseman will be allowed to remain in any part of the competition. Enjoy the rest of your breakfasts." She threw her crooked grin all around the room. "Except for Rowan and Katie, who should probably get the fuck out."

37

The dining hall emptied in stunned silence. I might not have believed Leigh's speech myself, but as we all stepped out into the quad, Wendell Cheeseman was spotted carrying polka-dot luggage out of the residence hall and disappearing toward the east parking lot.

"Now who will ring the buzzer at the skirmish?" Perla asked.

"That's your takeaway from this?" Galen asked. "We're down a teammate! Your roommate!"

Perla shrugged. "She did have the lowest percent-correct on the team. She was really only good for the classical music section and, considering it was made for her, she wasn't even that great at it. Should I mourn?"

I cleared my throat. "You guys are actually down two teammates."

The group turned to face me. Possibly in shock. Possibly blinded by the sun.

"Beast Mode?" Hunter said softly.

"It's a long story," I said. "But my ride is on its way."

Galen gaped at me. "But you're so close to winning the Cheese . . . the counselors' endowment! You just have to win one more event."

"It'll have to be someone else. Maybe someone that Faulkner didn't help cheat." I checked over my shoulder. The minutes were dwindling down to seconds. "Okay, quick hugs. No time to be sad. You guys need to go to your skirmish."

I hugged down the line of Meg, Hunter, Jams, and Galen. Hari shook my hand. Leigh squeezed me extra hard.

"That was some impressive detecting," I whispered in her ear. "I'm gonna miss you."

"Then come visit. It's only a twelve-hour train ride." She swatted my arm and breathed a laugh, although her eyes were wet. "Leave me your address. If I find any of your stolen stuff, I'll mail it back to you."

"Will do," I said.

I looked at Brandon and swallowed.

"Let's start walking to the theater," Meg announced. "Slowly. We have a new seating chart without Ever and Kate. We might need the extra time."

"Subtle, Margaret," Brandon snorted.

"You're welcome, rabbits," she whispered.

"Elliot Lawrence Gabaroche!"

My blood froze in my veins. There was no way. This couldn't be happening. I'd prepared for the worst, but this was the worst times a Bosch painting of the worst.

"Is that . . . ?" Brandon asked vaguely.

"Yeah," I said, unable to hold back the quiver of panic in my voice. "Those are my parents. All of them."

I'd known that this was a possibility from the second my train pulled out of the station the night I'd run away, but it was different seeing the fury of my family in person rather than in my imagination.

My mom wasn't in uniform, thank God, but she was a blazing fury. Six foot tall, solidly built, hair pressed and rolled away from her round face. The polar opposite of thin, pale Beth, who was keeping stride and was equally pissed. And my father and Aunt Bobbie bringing up the rear.

I supposed I should be thankful that they hadn't brought Grandmother Lawrence with them. The last thing I needed was Colonel Shirley Lawrence strutting around in her ancient dress blues, threatening to whup me and Isaiah for not waiting at attention when they got there.

I turned back to Brandon and grabbed his hand. "I don't want to leave you like this," I said as fast as I could. "I don't want to leave you at all. And I'm so sorry for how everything happened. Because I really do like you. More than I thought I could like someone and this is the absolute worst way to tell you that because if I kiss you in front of that angry mob we will both die. So please know that you made me believe in the Disney of it all and that I will never forget you and you'd better go win a scholarship and use it to major in math, you freaking sexy nerd."

"Ever," he said, his eyes wild and pleading. "Elliot. I can't—"

"You have to," I said, shoving him toward the retreating team. I turned toward my family again, aware that if I watched him leave I'd lose my confidence. I'd come this far. It was time to finish this.

Fear is the mind killer.

I stepped forward, keeping my face impassive, which was hard when a mob of adults was waiting to tear me apart.

"Where is your luggage?" Mom asked. "We are leaving right now."

"I cannot believe you did this to us," Beth said. "We were all in a panic. And you couldn't return a single phone call?"

"I swear to God, I will sue this school from one side of that river to the other," Dad said.

"Mom, Dad, Beth, Aunt Bobbie," I said, nodding to each of them in turn. "I need to talk to you about Isaiah."

"You don't get to dictate a single term—" Dad started, his voice like a grizzly's rumble.

"I'm not trying to get out of being in trouble," I interrupted. "I know I messed up—"

"You ran away," Beth said shrilly.

"I know," I said. "And I'm sorry. I won't try to explain to you why, because it probably doesn't matter."

"You're goddamn right," Mom said. "It doesn't matter. You scared the hell out of all of us. You lied and you played us against each other—"

"Yes," I said, swallowing hard. God, the force of their disappointment was enough to peel back a layer of my skin. I pictured my spine filling with steel to keep me standing upright when I so wanted to lie down and cry again. "But I need to talk to you about Isaiah."

"Where is he?" Aunt Bobbie asked, looking into the distance as though she could make him appear.

"He's about to win a scholarship to one of the best colleges in the country," I said. "And I think you should let him come here."

Aunt Bobbie tucked her chin back, looking at me like I'd lost all of my damn mind. She raised an imperious eyebrow at me. "Elliot, my son will be lucky if I let him cross the street when I get him back home, much less come back to the school he ran away to."

"Just think about why he came here," I said. "Please think about who Isaiah is. Picture him at BMT and then picture him here. He isn't Sid. Please don't make him outrun himself all the way into enlisting. It's not what's right for him."

"Elliot," Mom said. "That's enough."

I didn't take my eyes off of my aunt. I pointed the way my team had walked off. "And if you go watch the last round of the Melee, you can see how much he belongs here. He made friends here because he was with other genius kids. He belongs with people as smart as him. That's why you guys moved off base, isn't it? So that he could go to a good school and actually do something with his IQ instead of just talking about it? He's doing something with it now. Don't make him disappoint you because you wanted something from him he couldn't do." My throat convulsed. I balled my hands into fists. "We didn't come here to disappoint you. We came here even though we knew you'd be disappointed. Please see the difference."

38

I held *Starship Troopers* over my head, reading the yellow-ing pages while nursing a coconut water ice pop that Beth in-sisted on buying because they were low-sugar. They were also low-taste, but when it was over a hundred and ten degrees, the only thing to do was lie down on the floor of the kitchen and eat Popsicles, waiting for autumn or death. Whichever came first.

Upstairs, something bumped against a wall. A door slammed.

"Ethan!" I shouted. "What'd you break?"

A pause.

"Nothing!" he called.

A lie, for sure, but he was almost ten and there was a chance that he was finally mature enough to put whatever he'd broken back to-gether before I figured out what it was. And if not, we had hours be-fore Dad and Beth were home from work, and lots of superglue.

But not so much wood glue. Hm. That could be a problem. Espe-cially since I no longer had the right to drive my car. It was now parked at Beth's parents' house, waiting for me to prove that I was a responsible member of society again.

If Ethan broke a bone or I went into anaphylactic shock, our parents were willing to just pay the ambulance bill rather than let me have my car keys.

It had been a week since I'd flown home from Eugene. Thinking about my mom and Beth sitting together at our dining room table was still a little surreal. I had always assumed that they wouldn't be in the same room until I graduated from high school. Who knew all it took was one giant betrayal of trust to bring them together? After all of my privileges had been revoked—car, phone, computer, TV, friends—Mom and Beth had split a cocktail shaker of Dad's chocolate martinis and stayed up until the wee hours giggling together. I wasn't sure if I or Dad had been more unsettled by this.

Aunt Bobbie had stayed behind in Eugene to watch Isaiah compete in the last skirmish. She'd never turned down a chance to watch her son show off how much smarter he was than other people and she wasn't going to start now. When Team Three had advanced to the final round of the Melee, Bobbie had sprung for a hotel room and had stayed to watch Isaiah win his scholarship. She swore that none of the Lawrences could argue with free tuition to one of the top schools in the country, even if it meant that her baby wouldn't be joining up.

I wasn't sure if that logic would fly at the next family holiday, but I also got the impression that Bobbie and Mom had made some sort of pact to never tell Grandmother Lawrence about anything that had happened in Eugene. I was positive that it had taken a lot of blackmail to get Isaiah's scholarship locked down in spite of him being in violation of the age requirement.

Luckily, the dean of Rayevich and the principal from the Messina were terrified of news coming out about Cheeseman rigging prior Melees. It would bankrupt the camp to have to refund every student who'd come through for the last two years.

The doorbell rang.

"I got it!" Ethan screeched, his feet flying down the stairs so fast that there was a chance he was somersaulting.

"You'll be sorry if it's a kidnapper!" I called.

"You'll be sorry!" he called back. "You'll be grounded if I get kidnapped!"

"I'm already grounded!" I closed *Starship Troopers* and got to my feet. I took a moment to pluck the hem of my shorts back to a more ladylike position. "If you don't get kidnapped, remind me to teach you about double jeopardy."

I waddled out of the kitchen and through the living room and nearly dropped my Popsicle when I spotted the tall, slouching figure standing on the front porch. His hair was covering most of his face as he looked down at Ethan.

"She's not allowed to have friends over right now," Ethan was saying, barely containing his joy at being allowed to turn away a teenager. "She's grounded."

I swept forward and shoved Ethan back with one arm. "Go up to my room," I hissed at him, one eye on the vision on the porch. "Under my mattress there's a sock with fifty bucks in it. It's yours if you never, ever tell Dad and Beth that this happened."

Ethan considered this, his lips pursed into a duck's bill of thought. "Fifty bucks and your Greedo."

"Ugh. Go, booger," I said, shooing him away. I shouted at his back as he scurried back up the stairs, "But this never happened!"

"What never happened?" he called back.

I turned back. Brandon was still there. Standing on my porch. In a gray T-shirt and blue jeans and the same Chuck Taylors. Smiling. Real.

"Hi," he said.

"Hi." I wanted to reach out and touch him and didn't know how or where to start. "You're in California. How?"

He gestured behind him. "Wave to Ben and Trixie. Or don't. They don't care."

I peered over his shoulder and saw a small red SUV parked across the street from my house, covered in Spider-Man bumper stickers.

"They drove you to California?" I gaped.

He winced a shrug. "Crumbs felt bad for ruining my first date, so she told my parents that she was driving me up to Washington to visit our sisters. I don't know where she went, but Ben and Trixie were coming down here to find a new apartment, so I tagged along."

I laughed. "You're Bunburying."

"I learned from the best."

"I'm sorry," I blurted, moving out of the way of the doorway. "Come in. It's a million degrees out here."

He stepped up into the house, setting a black backpack at the foot of the stairs. I threw my Popsicle into the yard before I closed the door behind us.

I watched him taking in the meticulously organized throw pillows, the collection of pictures of Ethan and me as babies, the decorative candles that had never been lit.

"It's a little catalogy, I know," I said, perching on the edge of the long sofa. "Beth's a real estate agent and stages houses for a living, so it can be kind of sterile looking sometimes, but I swear we live here and we're normal and you can put your shoes on the couch."

He laughed. "I was raised to never put my shoes on the couch, but I'll take it under advisement."

He sat down next to me, his back pressed against a yellow throw pillow with a sea horse on it. I'd never questioned that pillow before, but now I couldn't help but wonder why it was here and what it said about me and my family that we owned it.

"This was supposed to be really romantic," Brandon blurted, sweeping his hair out of his eyes. "But I realize now that it's coming off like, uh, really fucking needy and stalkerish and probably the biggest mistake of my life? I'll just go kill Ben and Trix for not talking me out of it four hundred and eighty miles ago. They obviously don't know anything because they're high school sweethearts."

"What? No!" I moved closer to him, wrapping my arm around his neck and kissing him swiftly. "This is legit romantic."

"Whew," he said. "Because I was walking up to the door and realizing that this could be such an invasion of privacy. I got your address from Leigh, and before you left you said a lot of stuff that made me think that you wouldn't mind if I showed up here. But I've been wrong before. I've been wrong a lot, actually." He twirled a piece of my hair around his fingers, examining the curl. "I never should have left the sci-fi section that night. I don't need you to promise me anything. I want the chance to keep knowing you. That's all."

I picked up his free hand, which was roasting hot, even in the air-conditioned living room. But I couldn't set it down. What if he stopped being real? "I'm sorry I didn't understand that. I was so caught up in winning and being scared of what happened after I got back here, I forgot to, I don't know . . . hope? I'd love to keep knowing you. I don't want an ending. I just didn't think I could stop it from happening."

He leaned forward, his head tipped to one side, and planted a kiss on my cheek before getting to his feet.

"That took an unexpected turn," I said, watching him run to his backpack. He dragged it over to the couch and, from within its depths, pulled out a hardcover book with an ivory jacket and yellow lettering. He set it in my hands and I let out an involuntary gasp as I recognized the bar code in the top left corner. It was Rayevich College's copy of *Survivor* by Octavia Butler.

"What?" I squealed, unsure if I was thrilled or terrified to be holding this. "I can't steal this!"

He held up his hands, refusing to take the book back. "You aren't stealing it. First of all, I stole it. Well, I asked Meg to steal it. Second of all, you're borrowing it until next fall. There's nothing in the Melee rules that says we can't apply to Rayevich like normal people do."

"And if we don't get in?" I asked.

"Oh," he said as though maybe he hadn't considered this. "Then you're stealing it."

I hugged the book to my chest. "Thank you." I kissed him. "Thank you." I kissed him again. "Thank you."

"You're welcome," he said. He set his thumb between his teeth. "You know, I looked into it, and the military hires more math majors than almost any other industry in the country."

My heart beat so hard, I had to set the book down for fear of ruining the cover. "Oh yeah?"

He nodded. "Turns out statistics is really important to the armed forces. Who knew?"

"Are you saying that you could see yourself enlisting?"

"How many push-ups do I need to be able to do to make it through boot camp?"

"To make it through? Forty-five. To thrive? Seventy."

"Let's start with surviving," he said. He got down on the ground, raising and lowering himself with relative ease. "One, two, three—"

"I'm sorry," I interrupted. "That wasn't quite right. One more time, please?"

He pushed himself back down to the ground with a grunt. "Un. Deux. Trois."

I pulled him back to his feet and we both laughed until the laughter faded away and we were alone together again.

"If you hear so much as a floorboard creak . . ." I whispered.

"I've been a little brother for seventeen years," he assured me. "I know all the tricks."

We kissed like it was the end of the world, and then, after a break for a glass of ice water, like it was the beginning. And during the breaks, it was just us—two normal, eternally grounded teenagers who lived four hundred and eighty miles apart and occasionally stole time together.

After all, wasn't it Oscar Wilde who said that the very essence of romance is uncertainty?

CAN'T GET ENOUGH OF LILY ANDERSON?
DON'T MISS BEN AND TRIXIE'S STORY
IN THE COMPANION NOVEL,

the only thing worse than me is you

AVAILABLE NOW!

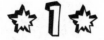

Ⓑen West spent summer vacation growing a handlebar mustache.

Seriously.

Hovering over his upper lip—possibly glued there—was a bushy monstrosity that shouted, *"Look out, senior class, I'm gonna tie some chicks to the train tracks and then go on safari with my good friend Teddy Roosevelt. Bully!"*

I blindly swatted at Harper with my comic book, trying to alert her to the fact that there was a mustachioed moron attempting to blend in with the other people entering campus.

"I know I should have made flash cards for the poems that Cline assigned," she said, elbowing me back hard, both acknowledging that she wasn't blind and that she hated when I interrupted her monologues about the summer reading list. "But I found Mrs. Bergman's sociolinguistics syllabus on the U of O website and I'm sure she'll use the same one here."

The mustache twitched an attempt at freedom, edging away from West's ferrety nose as he tried to shove past a group of nervous freshmen. It might have been looking at me and Harper, but its owner was doing everything possible to ignore us, the planter box we were sitting on, and anything else that might have been east of the wrought iron gate.

"So," Harper continued, louder than necessary considering we were sitting two inches apart, "I thought I'd get a head start. But now I'm afraid that we were supposed to memorize the poems for Cline. He never responded to my emails."

Pushing my comic aside, I braced my hands against the brick ledge. The mustache was daring me to say something. Harper could hear it, too, as evidenced by her staring up at the sun and muttering, "Or you could, you know, not do this."

"Hey, West," I called, ignoring the clucks of protest coming from my left. "I'm pretty sure your milk mustache curdled. Do you need a napkin?"

Ben West lurched to a stop, one foot inside of the gate. Even on the first day of school, he hadn't managed to find a clean uniform. His polo was a series of baggy wrinkles, half-tucked into a pair of dingy khakis. He turned his head. If the mustache had been able to give me the finger, it would have. Instead, it watched me with its curlicue fists raised on either side of West's thin mouth.

"Hey, Harper," he said. He cut his eyes at me and grumbled, "Trixie."

I leaned back, offering the slowest of slow claps. "Great job, West. You have correctly named us. I, however, may need to change your mantle. Do you prefer Yosemite Sam or Doc Holliday? I definitely think it should be cowboy related."

"Isn't it inhumane to make the freshmen walk past you?" he asked me, pushing the ratty brown hair out of his eyes. "Or is it some kind of ritual hazing?"

"Gotta scare them straight." I gestured to my blond associate. "Besides, I've got Harper to soften the blow. It's like good cop, bad cop."

"It is nothing like good cop, bad cop. We're waiting for Meg," Harper said, flushing under the smattering of freckles across her cheeks as she turned back to the parking lot, undoubtedly trying to escape to the special place in her head where pop quizzes—and student council vice presidents—lived. She removed her headband and then pushed it back in place until she once again looked like Sleeping Beauty in pink glasses and khakis. Whereas I continued to look like I'd slept on my ponytail.

Which I had because it is cruel to start school on a Wednesday.

"Is it heavy?" I asked Ben, waving at his mustache. "Like weight training for your face? Or are you trying to compensate for your narrow shoulders?"

He gave a halfhearted leer at my polo. "I could ask the same thing of your bra."

My arms flew automatically to cover my chest, but I seemed to be able to conjure only the consonants of the curses I wanted to hurl at him. In his usual show of bad form, West took this as some sort of victory.

"As you were," he said, jumping back into the line of uniforms on their way to the main building. He passed too close to Kenneth Pollack, who shoved him hard into the main gate, growling, "Watch it, nerd."

"School for geniuses, Kenneth," Harper called. "We're all nerds."

Kenneth flipped her off absentmindedly as West righted himself and darted past Mike Shepherd into the main building.

"Brute," Harper said under her breath.

I scuffed the planter box with the heels of my mandatory Mary Janes. "I'm off my game. My brain is still on summer vacation. I totally left myself open to that cheap trick."

"I was referring to Kenneth, not Ben." She frowned. "But, yes, you should have known better. Ben's been using that bra line since fourth grade."

As a rule, I refused to admit when Harper was right before eight in the morning. It would lead to a full day of her gloating. I hopped off the planter and scooped up my messenger bag, shoving my comic inside.

"Come on. I'm over waiting for Meg. She's undoubtedly choosing hair care over punctuality. Again."

Harper slid bonelessly to her feet, sighing with enough force to slump her shoulders as she followed me through the front gate and up the stairs. The sunlight refracted against her pale hair every time her neck swiveled to look behind us. Without my massive aviator sunglasses, I was sure I would have been blinded by the glare.

"What's with you?" I asked, kicking a stray pebble out of the way.

"What? Nothing." Her head snapped back to attention, knocking her glasses askew. She quickly straightened them with two trembling hands. "Nothing. I was just thinking that maybe senior year might be a good time for you to end your war with Ben. You'd have more time to study and read comics and . . ."

Unlike the tardy Meg, Harper was tall enough that I could look at her without craning my neck downward. It made it easier to level her with a droll stare. Sometimes, it's better to save one's wit and just let the stupidity of a thought do the talking.

She rolled her eyes and clucked again, breezing past me to open the door.

"Or not," she said, swinging the door open and letting me slip past her. "Year ten of *Watson v. West* starts now. But if one of you brings up the day he pushed you off the monkey bars, I am taking custody of Meg and we are going to sit with the yearbook staff during lunch."

"I accept those terms." I grinned. "Now help me think of historical figures with mustaches. Hitler and Stalin are entirely too obvious. I need to brainstorm before we get homework."